"It was your wife who Ulric killed," the old woman stated

Katz leaned closer. "Yes, but why? Was he trying to get to me? What had I done to him?"

"It was not anything you did. It was what your father did." The color in the woman's face was fading fast. "Your father killed my husband's first wife and child. So Gregor killed your father, and he poisoned Ulric's mind from the day the boy was old enough to comprehend such things."

A choking sound escaped the dying woman's lips. "He killed your wife, and he will kill you. But the killing must stop." The woman collapsed back onto the bed.

The closest thing to fear Mack Bolan had ever seen in Katz appeared in the older man's face. "Zhdanov wants the whole Katzenelenbogen family, Mack. He'll go after Sharon next."

I1040693

DON PENDLETON's
MACK BOLAN®
RETRIBUTION

A GOLD EAGLE BOOK FROM

WORLDWIDE®

TORONTO • NEW YORK • LONDON
AMSTERDAM • PARIS • SYDNEY • HAMBURG
STOCKHOLM • ATHENS • TOKYO • MILAN
MADRID • WARSAW • BUDAPEST • AUCKLAND

First edition December 1998

ISBN 0-373-61463-2

Special thanks and acknowledgment to
Jerry VanCook for his contribution to this work.

RETRIBUTION

Printed in U.S.A.

Revenge is a kind of wild justice…

> —Francis Bacon
> 1561-1626

If you prick us, do we not bleed? if you tickle us, do we not laugh? if you poison us, do we not die? and if you wrong us, shall we not revenge?

> —William Shakespeare
> *The Merchant of Venice,*
> III, i, 65

Reason disappears when family is under fire. A man has to protect his hearth and home, or he's no man at all.

> —Mack Bolan

PROLOGUE

Paris, France,
December 21, 1974,

The man on the phone had identified himself as a policeman, and informed Cynthia that her husband had been in an automobile accident near Versailles. That, of course, was bad enough. But when she considered who her husband was, and how he made his living, it made things worse. It was quite possible that the accident had not been an accident at all.

The woman slipped her arms into her coat, feeling the cold wind bite her neck as she hurried across the porch to the Saab parked in the driveway. Two houses down and across the street, she could see that the LeFlores had forgotten to turn off their Christmas-tree lights for the night. As she fumbled to insert her key into the car door, bright red and green light bulbs blinked merrily off and on along the edge of the roof.

It was as if the decorations were there to mock the anxiety Cynthia felt in her heart.

She mentally admonished herself to curb her imagination as her shaking fingers finally got the key into the lock. She slid behind the wheel and started the engine. The policeman had said her husband wasn't hurt badly—just a few scrapes and bruises, and they'd be keeping him overnight for observation.

Yes, but what if it was a lie? she wondered. What if the policeman just didn't want to tell her the truth over the phone? What if her husband was dead?

Possessing the imagination of a professional writer and being married to a professional soldier wasn't a combination that induced tranquillity. If her husband was fifteen minutes late, in her mind he had been in a car wreck. If another thirty minutes went by without him showing up, she watched an uncontrollable "mental movie" in which he got shot. The rational part of her mind always told her there was no proof. But no amount of forced rationality would comfort a writer's imagination at times like this. It was a lovable, yet damnable, two-sided coin that gave equal parts pain and pleasure.

Cynthia backed the Saab out of the driveway and threw it into gear. She passed the darkened lights of other Christmas decorations in other yards, her left hand on the steering wheel as her right pulled a tissue from her purse.

How many nights had she waited for this call to come? She guided the car mindlessly out of the residential area and onto the deserted late-night highway leading to Versailles. The answer was every night since she had married Yakov. At least every night that he hadn't been home with her. A cynical laugh escaped the woman's lips as she realized it would be far easier to count the evenings they had spent together over the years than to try to tabulate the nights when he hadn't been home.

Cynthia dabbed at her eyes with the tissue, then dropped it back into her purse as a road sign announcing Versailles 15 km appeared on the side of the road. Not that she would have had it any other way. She had married her French-Israeli husband because she loved him. The life of a professional soldier was part of him, and therefore part of what made her love him. Yes, she worried, because she knew what could happen to a man like him. But she couldn't change him. And wouldn't want to if she could.

Cynthia stared into the headlights as the Saab hurried along the dark road. Sinai tank action during the Six-Day War had cost Yakov his right arm. The same war had also cost them their only son. Then had come the years Yakov had spent as a Mossad operative, and then as a personal intelligence aide to Moshe Dayan. Each time he came home, it seemed he had a new knife wound or bullet hole, and Cynthia would cry silently because she feared that someday he wouldn't come home at all.

A drizzling rain began to fall on the Saab's windshield. Cynthia switched on the windshield wipers.

The moisture outside seemed to spawn more wetness in her eyes, and she reached into her purse for a fresh tissue. Another green-and-white sign flashing by told her she was now five kilometers from Versailles, and she focused on the road ahead, only vaguely registering the fact when a pair of bright headlights suddenly appeared in her rearview mirror. She thought of an expression her father had often used when she had been a young girl growing up, her writer's imagination troubling her even then.

"Don't borrow trouble, Cynthia. If it must come, it will come without any help from you."

Cynthia forced another smile as the car behind her pulled around her to pass. No, she wouldn't borrow trouble. The policeman who had called from the hospital in Versailles had said her husband's injuries were minor. Why would he lie? He had no reason to do so.

As the dark blue sedan drew even with Cynthia's Saab, another set of headlights appeared behind her. She frowned. Less than twenty yards to her rear, the car had to have approached with its lights off until now. She glanced to her side, expecting the sedan to be past her by now, and was surprised to see that it had slowed in the oncoming lane, keeping pace with the Saab. In the passenger's seat, less than five feet away, she could see a face wearing a black stocking cap.

Cynthia felt a sudden jolt, and her head snapped back on her neck. A scream of both surprise and fear escaped her lips as the car behind her accelerated again, ramming her rear bumper even harder this time. At the same time she heard the explosions of machine-gun fire, and turned to see that the man in the stocking cap had rolled down his window.

The barrel of an Uzi—she had been married to an Israeli soldier for too long not to recognize the weapon's distinctive shape—was pointed her way.

The vehicle behind the Saab slammed into her again. Instinctively Cynthia sped up. More rounds burst forth from the car to her side but, as far as she could tell, none struck the Saab. She wondered how the man in the stocking cap could miss at such close range, and wondered if he was missing the vehicle intentionally for some reason.

Cynthia screamed again as once more she was smashed from behind. She forced the accelerator down harder, increasing speed in the hopes of outdistancing her attackers.

The sedan next to her swerved suddenly toward her car, scraping her left front fender. Sparks flew through the night as metal squealed against metal. The Saab was forced to the edge of the road, and Cynthia fought the wheel, finally straightening it again. The sedan struck her again, and this time Cynthia caught a quick glimpse of a smiling face below the black stocking cap. She turned back to the front.

Too late, she saw the bridge.

Cynthia stomped the brake pedal, knowing even

as she did that the gesture was futile. The beams of the guardrail glistened for a microsecond in her headlights, then suddenly they were behind her. Strangely she felt no pain as a tornado of steel and glass seemed to carry the Saab off the bridge and into the dark night air.

But the fact that she felt no physical pain didn't mean Cynthia felt nothing as she sensed the airborne Saab begin to descend. Her last thoughts were emotional, as images of the son she had lost in the Six-Day War, and the husband and daughter she would never see again, flashed past her eyes.

CHAPTER ONE

The present

At rest in the water, the container ship *Jacqueline Marie* hardly looked any different than the other cargo vessels docked in the Marseilles harbor. But it was different.

Its cargo was *death*.

In the same vein, the big man dressed in khaki work pants, navy blue pea coat and black watch cap, ambling down the concrete walk toward the ship, looked very much like all the other half-drunk sailors reporting back to the ship after an afternoon's R&R in Marseilles. But if the *Jacqueline Marie* was different from the other ships, the big man was even more different than the men of the crew.

The other men were seamen and drug smugglers.

The big man was Mack Bolan, and he was known to the world as the Executioner.

Bolan tipped the wine bottle to his lips, took the final swig, then threw it against a wooden bench to the side of the walk. He swerved off the walk, steadying himself momentarily against the bench's backrest before collapsing to a seat. To anyone who might be watching, he appeared inebriated. But the eyes that swept up and down the docks were hardly those of a drunk. He had purchased the wine several blocks from the wharf, poured most of it out in an alley and ingested only enough to ensure that he'd wreak of the cheap grape vintage like the rest of the men returning from shore leave. Now the Executioner used the cover such intoxication afforded to survey the area, particularly the ship he was about to board.

The *Jacqueline Marie* was docked directly in front of where he sat, and as he watched, men dressed much like himself came and went across the loading bridge, carrying wooden cases of French champagne. Earlier that day Bolan had seen the container ship dock and watched the same men unload crates of Japanese electronic components. At least that was what the boxes had been marked as containing, and the Executioner had no reason to believe any different.

He *did* have reason to believe the champagne crates held more than what the words on the side admitted.

Several drunken men stumbled past Bolan's bench, moving down the walk and approaching the ship. A short bald man in a black wool turtleneck checked their identification cards, then waved them on board.

The Executioner watched two more seamen board. Mentally he checked the weaponry hidden under his coat. His trademark .44 Magnum Desert Eagle pistol was snug against his right hip in a close-fitting speed rig. A sound-suppressed 9 mm Beretta 93-R, capable of either single shots or 3-round bursts, rode under his left arm in shoulder leather. Bolan would be working clandestinely on board the ship and, if push came to shove, would rely on the near silent Beretta rather than the ear-shattering Eagle. And in case total silence was called for, the Executioner carried a third weapon—an Applegate-Fairbairn fighting knife. An updated and improved descendant of the Fairbairn-Sykes commando dagger of World War II fame, the A-F was as close to a perfect silent killing tool as had ever been designed. Carried grip down in a Kydex sheath under his right arm, the weapon was readily available to either hand.

Still playing the role of a tipsy sailor, Bolan started across the quay toward the ship, his mind reflecting on the whirlwind events of the past two days. Forty-eight hours earlier he had finally located Robert LeCharlemagne, the billion-dollar heroin kingpin he had come to France to eliminate. Following LeCharlemagne to the little principality of Monaco just east of Marseilles, he had watched the drug lord meet with Henri de Duve, a Belgian he would soon learn owned the *Jacqueline Marie*. The two conspirators had forgone the usual Monaco tourist traps such as the Monte Carlo casino, choosing instead the privacy they assumed a modest out-of-the-way café on a side street would provide. But a few hundred francs from the Executioner to their waiter had gotten an electronic transmitter planted under their table at the same time appetizers were served.

Bolan had listened to LeCharlemagne and Duve finalize their heroin-smuggling plans over a headset receiver from the alley behind the café. The entire crew of the *Jacqueline Marie* was aware of the plan, and each crewman would receive a specified percentage of the gross profit. Bolan had also learned that the heroin—several tons of it—would be loaded onto the ship in the champagne crates when the vessel pulled into port.

The Executioner reached the dock area and steadied his pace. He wanted to appear drunk like the other men boarding the ship but not so drunk that he drew special attention from the bald man in the black turtleneck. He stopped at the end of the boarding plank, making sure a strong whiff of wine-breath wafted toward the man along with the seaman's ID card he shoved into the outstretched hand.

Bolan waited, swaying slightly on his feet as he watched the bald man scrutinize the card. The ID had been made up hurriedly that afternoon, but by one of the best document forgers France had to offer. Bolan had no doubt it would pass scrutiny.

The man in the turtleneck nodded, handed the

card back and waved Bolan on board. "Sober up," he said in French. "We sail in an hour."

Bolan nodded and boarded the ship, unbuttoning his pea coat to allow access to his weapons as his eyes surveyed the main deck. The last of the champagne crates had been loaded into the brightly colored containers stacked one on top of the other, and he knew more would be below in the container hold. Moving swiftly inside the superstructure, the Executioner found the ladder and dropped down into the belly of the ship.

Other seamen came and went as Bolan moved along the narrow passageways beneath the main deck. All looked partially inebriated from their afternoon on shore as they hurried about their last-minute preparations for sailing. He passed the engine room, mentally noting its location so he could return as soon as he'd checked the cargo containers.

Turning a sharp corner, the Executioner saw several clipboards hanging from nails on the wall of an office. Ducking inside, he pulled one of the boards from its place and carried it in his hand for further cover as he moved on.

Two men holding 9 mm MAT 49 submachine guns stood in the hatch to the main container hold. Like the Executioner, both men wore a pea coat. The one guarding the left side of the entryway also sported a long brown goatee speckled with red and gray. His heavy eyebrows lowered slightly as the Executioner approached.

But it was the other man, a burly giant well over six feet with long blond tresses falling to his shoulders, who called out the challenge in French. "What do you need?"

Bolan tapped the clipboard and answered in the same language. "Inventory."

Both of the men frowned and looked at each other. "No one told us of this," the man with the goatee said, shaking his head.

The Executioner shrugged. "I can't help that," he said, and started to move between the two.

He needed to look inside at least one of the containers—double-check the ship's cargo—before he put the rest of his plan into effect. He had heard enough the day before to convince him that the *Jacqueline Marie* was part of the LeCharlemagne-Duve heroin operation. But the Executioner wasn't in the habit of taking chances with the lives of innocent seamen. He wanted to be more than convinced before he destroyed the cargo, the ship and the smugglers along with it.

The two men closed quarters, blocking Bolan's entrance. "We have orders that no one is to enter," the blonde snarled. "Now turn around and get back on top."

Bolan shook his head in disgust. "I have new orders," he said. "Written. Want to see them?"

Again the two men looked at each other. The man with the speckled goatee nodded.

The Executioner's right hand twisted under his

coat, his fingers closing around the handle of the Applegate-Fairbairn knife in a saber grip. The blade left its sheath with a soft clicking sound as steel slid across plastic. With his left hand, Bolan raised the clipboard up to block the view of the tall blond man. At the same time, he twisted slightly, thrusting the knife forward and into the heart of the man with the goatee. Pumping once up, once down, the Executioner withdrew the blade as quickly as it had gone in.

By now the blond giant had recovered from the surprise of having the clipboard thrust into his eyes. He swept it aside with a big hand, just in time to see the fighting knife coming toward his eyes. The tip of the blade penetrated the skin between his eyes and just above his nose and traveled on into the brain.

Both men fell to the deck in front of the hatch.

Bolan looked quickly over his shoulder to make sure none of the other crew members had chanced along. Satisfied that his actions had gone unnoticed, he tossed the clipboard into the container hold and dragged both men in after it. Ripping the pea coat from the big blonde, the Executioner returned to the passageway. The wounds to the men's chest and head, delivered as they had been, were mostly internal and had drawn a minimum amount of blood. What little stained the deck was easily absorbed by the coat.

Moving swiftly, Bolan entered the hold again.

The first container he came to held champagne cases. Using his knife to pry off one of the lids, he dug down through a layer of bottles spaced with sawdust and felt the cool plastic packages beneath. Withdrawing one of the packets, he saw the white powder inside.

The Executioner dropped the heroin back into the crate and closed the lid. He searched through the containers, now looking for room to hide the dead bodies rather than searching for heroin. The fourth container he opened proved empty, and he dragged the men over the side. He had barely slid the lid back in place when he heard footsteps outside the hold.

Bolan leaped behind one of the containers as he heard the steps halt outside the hold. He waited, his fighting knife held now in an ice-pick grip. A moment later he heard the footsteps enter. The man was quiet, trying not to be heard.

To the side of the container, Bolan could see the man's shadow as it moved across the hold. He was moving stealthily, which meant he knew something was wrong. In the hand of the shadow, the Executioner could see the outline of a small pistol. What appeared to be a sound suppressor—longer in length than the gun itself—was attached to the barrel.

Bolan watched the shadow near the corner of the crate. The muscles in his legs tightened, then relaxed again. He prepared to leap as soon as the skulking crewman rounded the corner. Finally the shadow became flesh as the man came into view.

The Executioner sprang forward, his left hand closing around the wrist that held the small pistol as his right raised the fighting blade high over his head. The man he jerked forward by the arm was of average height but more powerfully built. Gray hair stuck out on the sides from beneath the black Greek fisherman's cap that covered his head, and light blue eyes stared straight ahead at the Executioner.

The dagger point of the Applegate-Fairbairn knife had descended halfway to the man's throat when Bolan recognized Yakov Katzenelenbogen.

Bolan stopped the blade in midair, staring down at the shorter man. He didn't know whom he'd expected to round the corner of the storage container, but it wasn't the former leader of the counterterrorist commando team known as Phoenix Force.

Yakov Katzenelenbogen, now tactical adviser at Stony Man Farm—the top secret counterterrorist installation out of which Bolan sometimes worked—grinned up at the blade poised above his head. "Are you trying to say you don't like drop-in guests?" he whispered. He held up his right arm—a prosthetic replacement for the limb he had lost years before. "Don't make me give you the finger," he added wryly.

The Executioner smiled. What Katz was referring to wasn't any obscene gesture. Hidden within his prosthesis was a single-shot .22 Magnum pistol that fired through the false index finger.

Bolan lowered the knife and let go of his old friend's wrist, noting that the weapon in Katz's other hand was a sound suppressed .22-caliber Beretta, the favored weapon of Israel's renowned Mossad. It seemed a natural choice since Katz had been a Mossad operative before coming to Stony Man Farm and Phoenix Force. Tucked inside the Israeli's belt the Executioner could see the butt of a larger handgun, probably the Beretta 92 Katz favored.

"What are you doing here?" the Executioner whispered back.

"That will take a little explaining," the Israeli replied, glancing over his shoulder. "Do you think this is the time or place?"

Bolan shook his head. "You know what I'm here for?"

Katzenelenbogen nodded. "I called Stony Man to find you."

The Executioner nodded again. "Good. Then you know what I'm about to do. You can watch my back while I do it." He stepped around Katz and turned back toward the hatch. Katz followed.

They were halfway back across the hold when a trio of seamen armed with MAT subguns came barreling through the hatch. The men had evidently heard something as they had approached silently. But now, as Bolan and Katz instinctively moved apart the way they had done so many times when working together in years past, they made no effort to hide their movements or their weapons.

Bolan raised his fighting knife over his head, hearing the suppressed sputter of Katz's Beretta as he brought his arm forward and down, releasing the blade. The blade flipped end over end through the air, embedding itself up to the brass cross guard in the chest of a crewman wearing a khaki work shirt. The man opened his mouth as if to say "Oh!", but all that came out was blood.

The seaman to the man's right jerked spasmodically as a pair of .22 rounds drilled through his chest.

Drawing his own sound-suppressed weapon, Bolan fired two 9 mm rounds into the midsection of the third crew member. He staggered as the Executioner's hollowpoint rounds perforated his breastbone, then fell forward as a third round drilled through his face.

Suddenly the container hold was silent again.

Bolan retrieved his knife from the chest of the man it had killed and ripped off the khaki shirt. He also removed the shirts from the other two crewmen as Katz went in search of more empty space in which to hide the bodies. Together they tossed the corpses over the sides of a container, mopped the evidence off the floor and dropped the bloody rags in on top of the men.

The Executioner picked the clipboard off the floor where he'd thrown it. He glanced at his watch as he

led Katz out of the hold. If the man who had
checked his seaman's ID had been correct, they'd
be pulling out of port in twelve minutes. That didn't
give him much time.

Hurrying now, Bolan led the way back to the engine room. They passed several sailors on the way.
None gave them a second look. In the engine room
itself, they found only one crewman but he proved
more interested. Looking up and frowning as Bolan
and Katz stepped through the hatch, the man lifted
his T-shirt and clawed for the butt of a semiauto
pistol stuck in his jeans.

Bolan brought the clipboard around in an arc,
striking the man in the throat with the edge. A
hoarse choking sound escaped the man's lips.

Katz drew the .22 and jammed the sound suppressor into the man's ear. A moment later blood
and flesh blew out of the other ear. The man dropped
to the deck.

The Executioner glanced at his watch again. They
had less than five minutes before the ship set sail.
Turning to Katz, he whispered, "Find someplace to
hide him," then turned back toward the engines.

Bolan reached into the pocket of his pea coat,
then made the rounds, applying a small lump of C-
4 plastique and a detonating cap in several places.
Any one of them would lead back to the fuel storage
hold, but he would take no chances. Wiring each
device to a separate timer in case any of them failed,

he stepped back and viewed his work. All of the devices were hidden from casual view.

Katz had jammed the crewman's body into a corner under a series of pipes and was covering it with a tarp by the time Bolan turned back to him. He nodded that he was finished, and the two men hurried out of the engine room.

The ship's horn sounded as the Executioner mounted the ladder. By the time he and Katz reached top-side, the *Jacqueline Marie* had begun to back out of port.

Bolan turned back to his partner. "Only one way home."

Katz nodded.

The Executioner led the way along the containers stacked on deck, past the masthead light and the forecastle. Just past the anchor-windlass room, he looked both ways for curious eyes, took a deep breath and vaulted the rail.

The Executioner hit the surface as the ship continued to glide out of the harbor. A moment later he heard another soft splash and opened his eyes to see Yakov Katzenelenbogen descending through the water next to him.

Slowly Bolan swam back to the top. By the time the detonators blew the C-4, the C-4 ignited the fuel in the engines and in turn ran back through the lines to explode the entire fuel storage hold, the *Jacqueline Marie* would be too far from harbor to damage any of the other vessels. The only deaths would be those of the crew who had conspired to smuggle heroin and therefore forfeited any right to leniency.

As his head broke the surface, Bolan watched the ship come about in the distance and head toward the open sea. A moment later Katz's head appeared. The Israeli grinned as he opened his mouth for air.

Bolan couldn't keep the smile off his own face as he swam slowly back toward land. He didn't yet know why Yakov Katzenelenbogen had suddenly appeared out of nowhere, but he was about to find out, and it had to be something big to have brought the former Phoenix Force leader back into the field.

THE CAFÉ LE SORBONNE WAS, like its namesake, a place to get an education. But what one learned at the Le Sorbonne on the Marseilles wharf was an education of a different kind than that offered at the famed university.

Bolan led the way through the door into the dingy tavern. His first sight was of a dust-covered bar in front of a cracked mirror. Over the mirror hung a nude painting that showed a Rubenesque woman reclining on her side eating grapes.

Tables and chairs were scattered haphazardly throughout the room, most filled with people who looked as dismal as the bar itself. The men, for the most part, appeared to be seamen who had given in to the allure of full-time drink, and each woman in the place looked as if she might be had for the price of a beer.

The Executioner led Katz to a table in one corner of the room as a tall man at the bar who wore a black eye patch turned to give them a hate-filled stare. Bolan watched him out of the corner of his eye and saw the bulge of what had to be some type of weapon beneath his grimy brown T-shirt.

Hooking an ankle around the leg of a chair, Bolan pulled it out from beneath the splintered wooden tabletop. He took a seat with his back to the wall.

Katz took the chair to his side, turning it so that he, too, had a sight picture of the room, and the wall behind him.

The Executioner looked across the table at the Israeli and tried hard to suppress a grin. Katz had come to find him unprepared for a swim, and had been forced to change into an extra set of Bolan's clothes in the shabby little wharf-front hotel room the Executioner had been working out of while in Marseilles. The Stony Man Farm tactical adviser now wore an ill-fitting blue work shirt and a pair of khaki work pants that were four or five inches too long.

A waitress wearing a low-cut black top, short red skirt and matching high heels strutted to their table, her hips beating out time to the Parisian folk song that bellowed from the jukebox on the other side of the room. The fact that she was attractive enough to be out of place didn't escape the Executioner's notice. Long raven hair, beyond doubt the cleanest in Le Sorbonne, glistened under the overhead light as it cascaded down her shoulders like a black waterfall. The woman's bright blue eyes were set behind lids with just enough mascara to be alluring, and her red fingernails were carefully trimmed.

The waitress looked down at Katz. "What can I get you?" she asked.

"Beer," Katz said. "Any kind."

The woman turned to the Executioner and smiled, exhibiting two rows of perfect white teeth. Leaning forward, she rested both hands on the table in front of him, and her breasts nearly leaped from the neckline. "And what can I get *you?*" she asked, her double meaning more than obvious.

The Executioner chuckled. "The same. Beer."

The waitress affected a pout as she sashayed away again. Bolan watched her as she returned to the bar and noticed the man still watching them. If anything, his stare looked even more angry than before.

Bolan looked across the table to Katz. Whatever had brought the man in search of the Executioner wouldn't be something he'd want to discuss in front of strangers, so there was no point asking him until the beer arrived. Besides, Katz would get around to the subject when he was ready.

"So how's the advisory position?" Bolan asked.

Katz shrugged as the front door opened and an elderly gray-haired seaman limped in on a cane. The old man took a seat at a table across the room from them as Katz said, "Both good and bad. A little boring compared to what I'm used to. On the other hand, it affords me a little private time. I just returned from visiting my daughter in Tel Aviv."

Bolan smiled. He had never met Katz's daughter, Sharon, but he had heard Katz speak fondly of her many times. Life as a Stony Man Farm operative—whether it be as a member of one of the counterterrorist teams or as an individual warrior like the Executioner—offered little time for family life. Since the death of his son in Israel's Six-Day War, and his wife's automobile accident, Sharon had been Katz's only family.

Bolan was glad his friend was finally getting a chance to make up for the years he'd missed with her. "How is she?" he asked. "She's an archaeologist, right?"

Katz's face lit up like a proud father. "She is fine," he said as the waitress returned to set two glasses of beer on the table. "And yes, she is an archaeologist. She is employed by the Israeli State Antiquities Administration." He paused, lifted his beer and drained half of it.

Bolan took a sip of his own watered-down draft and set it back on the table. "So," he said, sitting back in his seat, "you came to Marseilles, snuck on board the ship and risked your life just to tell me about your trip."

Katz chuckled but his face looked serious. "Hardly." He looked at the ceiling and sighed. "It is difficult to know where to start."

"Pick a place," Bolan said. "If you leave something out, we can fill it in later."

Katz nodded and took another sip of his beer. "You know I have always said Cynthia was murdered."

The Executioner stared down at his beer. Katz's wife of twenty years, American writer Cynthia Armstrong, had run her car off a bridge one cold December night years earlier. Although there had been no evidence of foul play, neither had there been any reason for her to be on the highway between Paris and Versailles at that time of night. Katz's belief that Cynthia had been murdered had been almost an obsession with the man ever since.

When Katz got no answer, he went on. "It *was* murder, Mack. I now have proof."

The Executioner looked up from his beer. In his friend's eyes he saw fire, determination and the glow of a man on a quest. Turning toward the bar, he waved at the waitress. "I think this calls for another beer," he said.

As soon as the waitress served them and left, Katz launched into his story. "A few days ago, about the time you'd have arrived here, Aaron Kurtzman was conducting one of his routine computer intel sweeps at the Farm and intercepted a communiqué from the Mossad to the CIA. It seems a German by the name of Jurgen Schneider had contacted the Mossad, frantically trying to get in touch with me. He said he had information I needed, and he'd only give me personally.''

Katz paused, sipped his beer, then said, ''The rumor with most of my old Mossad buddies is that I'm now with the Company, and since we're usually on good terms, they got in touch with Langley. Anyway, Kurtzman tapped back into the network as if he was the spooks and set up a meeting between me and this Schneider in the Cayman Islands.''

Bolan took a sip of his beer. Across the room the old man who'd come in on the cane was watching them. The Executioner wasn't surprised. He and Katz might not look like models who'd just stepped out of the pages of *GQ* or *Esquire,* but they were different enough to draw attention in a seedy bar like this one. The old man looked quickly away when Bolan met his gaze, and the Executioner turned his attention toward the bar. The man with the eye patch was also staring at them, but he made no attempt to turn away or hide the red rage building on his face. Bolan wondered what had angered him, and decided he'd better keep one of his own eyes on the man.

''I had barely checked into the Holiday Inn in Georgetown under my alias when 'Mr. Wilenzick' got a call from this Schneider. He was there at the Royal Palms but convinced he was being watched. So we agreed to meet at Smith's Cove—you remember that place, I imagine.''

Bolan nodded. He had squared off with blazing

guns against drug-cartel gangsters in the scenic inlet only a few months earlier.

Katz leaned forward, his weathered face a mask of intensity. "Before Schneider hung up," he said in a voice threatening to choke with emotion, "he told me several things. He knew who had killed Cynthia." The Israeli took a moment to compose himself. "I'm sorry," he said. "After all these years I still miss her." When Katz spoke again, his voice was back in control. "Schneider said he knew who had killed her and why, and that it had nothing to do with my professions as soldier or Mossad operative."

Bolan nodded. "So who killed her? And why?"

Now it was Katz who shook his head. "He wouldn't tell me. At least not over the phone. He said the same man was trying to kill him and wanted me to arrange protection. But he did say that the reason she was killed dated back to the German Dachau concentration camp during World War II, and the Bolshevik revolution even before that."

Bolan leaned forward now. "Your father died at Dachau, didn't he?" he asked Katz.

The Israeli nodded. "And he was a Menshevik during the revolution. You familiar with them?"

The Executioner nodded. The Mensheviks had once been a moderate minority faction within the Russian Social Democratic Party. They had split with the Bolsheviks in 1903, and those who weren't absorbed by the Communist Party after the revolution in 1918 were hunted down and systematically liquidated. If Katz's father had survived until Dachau during World War II, it meant he was one of the lucky ones who escaped.

"So you met this Jurgen Schneider at Smith's Cove?" Bolan asked.

"I met his body," Katz answered. "By the time I got there, someone had put a bullet in his head. I'm on my way to Munich, where he lived, to see what I can find out about him."

Before Bolan could reply, the waitress appeared of her own volition and set two more glasses on the table. This time she leaned down and whispered into the Executioner's ear. "I would like to go to Paris. If you help me get out of here, I will make it well worth your while."

Bolan was about to politely decline when a beer glass whizzed past his ear and struck the wall, shattering into hundreds of pieces of glass. Turning in the direction from which the glass had come, the Executioner saw the man with the eye patch lumbering drunkenly toward them.

"You!" the man yelled in a high-pitched voice. "Stand up!"

Bolan stayed where he was but let his hand creep closer to the Beretta. He still hadn't forgotten that the man had something hidden under his filthy brown T-shirt.

The waitress turned toward him, her eyes blazing.

"Louis," she spit angrily, "leave it alone. It is over between us."

"No!" Louis cried, his hand snaking under his shirt as he moved forward toward Bolan. "It will never be over!" When his hand reappeared, it held a dagger.

Bolan reached out, grabbed Louis's wrist behind the blade and bent it back toward him. Keeping the man pinned in the wristlock, he stood, drew back his other fist and smashed it into the drunk's face.

Louis collapsed on the floor, unconscious.

The waitress beamed. "Come," she said, taking Bolan's hand. "I will get my coat and we can be in Paris by morning."

Bolan dropped her hand. "I'm not going to Paris," he said. The Executioner turned to his old friend. "I'm going to Munich." He led the way out the door, stepping onto the cracked sidewalk just as a loud explosion sounded in the distance.

Bolan squinted in the darkness, looking out over the Mediterranean Sea. In the distance he saw the raging ball of fire that had once been the *Jacqueline Marie*.

CHAPTER TWO

Hebron, Israel

One of the world's oldest cities, Hebron had been continuously inhabited since the days of Abraham. Located in a shallow valley, the city nevertheless stood three thousand feet above sea level and over forty-three hundred feet above the Dead Sea fifteen miles to the east. The surrounding hills had long been known for the exceptional grapes they produced, and the local wine made from the fruit was among the finest in the world.

Sharon Katzenelenbogen ran the comb through her long black hair and stared into the mirror. She had learned all these facts and figures as a child in Hebrew school, long before becoming an archaeologist. She also knew that Abraham had first camped in the area immediately after the Lord God promised to give him "all the land which thou seest" and to make Abraham's "seed as the dust of the earth." Her studies in Genesis 13:15-18 had told her that after the promise, the founder of the Hebrew nation had "removed his tent and came and dwelt in the plain of Mamre, which is in Hebron, and built there an altar unto the Lord."

Yes, Sharon thought as she pulled her hair behind her head and tied it in a ponytail. She had learned all this as a child. But she had never dreamed that someday she would actually go to Hebron as part of an archaeological dig team trying to locate that very "altar unto the Lord."

Sharon continued to look into the mirror as she applied a thin coat of lipstick. Normally she wouldn't bother with makeup when she was about to spend the morning digging down through dirt and sand. But this dig wasn't a normal one, and the reason it wasn't made her giggle like a schoolgirl, if only for a moment. Then, even though she was alone, such immature behavior embarrassed her and she stifled the laugh.

Setting down the lipstick, the woman stood, opened the flap of her sleeping tent and stepped out into the early-morning sun. As her eyes adjusted to the light, she thought briefly back to the rare visit she had received from her father the week before. The memory brought a smile to her face. She hadn't spent much time with her father in the past, but she didn't hold that against him. Yakov Katzenelenbogen was an adventurer, and the life of an adventurer afforded little time for family. Sharon knew her father, a French Jew by birth, had been part of the French underground during World War II, a major in the Israeli army and a member of the Mossad. Since then, she knew he had continued to do some kind of intelligence-military work, but the organization in the U.S. with which he was associated was top secret. When he had returned to the United States, Sharon had wept both in sadness at his departure and in joy when he told her he had finally retired from active duty and planned to see more of her in the future.

The day after he had left, the opportunity to go on this dig had come up. Sharon had tried to call and tell her father, but he hadn't yet arrived back in the United States. For all he knew, she was sitting back at her desk in Tel Aviv as bored as usual. There was no telephone in the dig camp, and now she wondered how long it would be before she could share the exciting departure from schedule with him.

Sharon's vision cleared, and she stared off across the flat valley. She wasn't really in Hebron, but a few miles north at the Oaks of Mamre. In the distance she could see the city, the spiral top of the mosque in the center its most prominent feature. The mosque had been built over the Cave of Machpelah, the traditional burial site of Abraham. But Abraham had first camped and built the altar somewhere near where Sharon now stood, and it was for this site that she had argued, cajoled, threatened, begged and finally obtained the grant from Israel's Antiquities Administration to finance the small dig.

The flap of a larger tent twenty yards away

opened, and two men stepped out. The first, an over-weight elderly man with a long beard, wearing a floppy-brimmed white sun hat, khaki cargo shorts and shirt, yawned Sharon's way and waved. She smiled and waved back as the man limped toward the latrine tent in the distance. Dr. Herbert Singer had come from the university in Haifa to help with the dig. In the few short days since they had begun work, he had become almost like a second father to her.

The flap opened again, and a younger man appeared. Sharon felt a jolt of electricity run through her as she watched him step out of the tent. She had only known Jonathan Mayer a few days, too, but she had developed a quick liking for him, as well. With "Yoni," however, the relationship was hardly one of paternal feelings. In truth, Sharon knew it was years since she had been so physically attracted to a man. The realization caused her to blush slightly as Mayer walked toward her, and she wondered if he would notice her self-consciousness.

Stopping a few feet in front of her, he cupped a hand over his eyes and gazed across the valley toward Hebron. "Good morning," he said, his accent betraying the fact that he was American by birth and Israeli by choice.

"Sleep well?" Sharon asked quickly. Her voice sounded odd to her.

Mayer nodded.

An uneasy silence fell over them as Mayer continued to stare across the plain toward Hebron. A quick gust of wind blew past them, and Sharon couldn't help noticing that the man next to her wore either cologne or after-shave today, something she hadn't observed before.

Was he attracted to her as she was to him? She had put on lipstick; she was making sure she looked her best, and it was certainly not for Dr. Singer. Was the scent his masculine version of doing the same thing?

Sharon started to speak, then stopped. She didn't know what she had been about to say, but surely it would have sounded stupid. She started to comment that the day would undoubtedly be a hot one, then decided that, too, would sound ridiculous.

Mayer turned toward her and opened his mouth, but nothing came out, and Sharon felt her skin flush as if it were being pricked by thousands of tiny needles. There was definitely an anxiety on both of their parts. But was it because he was attracted to her as she was to him or because he sensed her feelings, didn't return them and therefore felt uneasy?

Sharon felt her apprehension suddenly turn to anger. She was acting like a childish schoolgirl again.

Mayer finally found words. "Is it today we drive to Tel Aviv to pick up Dr. Werner?" he asked.

The question was ridiculous, as he knew full well that the German archaeologist coming to join the dig wouldn't be arriving for several more days. It had

obviously just been something to say to break the
awkward silence.

"I don't believe so," Sharon said, realizing even
as the words left her mouth that the indefinite answer was as witless as his question had been.

Dr. Singer suddenly appeared from the latrine
tent. Hardly one to be uncomfortable under any circumstances, he walked toward them, zipping his
pants. He stopped a few feet away as Mayer had
done, looked from Sharon to Mayer, frowned, then
smiled.

"Shall we get to work?" he said.

Marseilles, France

THE CONTAINER SHIP still blazed on the water when
Bolan and Katz flagged down a cab. A curious
crowd of seamen, hookers and wharf riffraff gathered to watch as the two men from Stony Man Farm
climbed into the back seat of the vehicle.

Silence reigned over the taxi as the driver left the
seaside area and entered the city of close to a million
people. Although it offered many interesting attrac-
tions to the visitor, perhaps Marseilles's most renowned site was the Château d'If. It was here where
the acclaimed French novelist Alexandre Dumas had
imprisoned his protagonist in the *Count of Monte
Cristo,* and the château caught Katz's attention as
they passed it now.

"I have felt like the count for years now, Mack,"

Katz said, nodding as they drove by. "My body hasn't been imprisoned, of course, and I may have been free to come and go as I pleased. But I have been a prisoner nevertheless. My heart...no, my very soul has been caged by the uncertainty of what actually happened to Cynthia."

Bolan nodded, not knowing what to say.

The cab drove through the dark city, and the Executioner stared ahead into the dim illumination of the streetlights. Over the years he had fought side by side with the man next to him using guns, knives, fists and whatever else they had at their disposal. Together, and along with the other operatives of Stony Man Farm, they had fought the good fight against evil and injustice wherever they found it.

But in the past, it had always been flesh-and-blood enemies who opposed them—adversaries who could be shot, stabbed, punched or kicked. It had never been easy, but the enemy had always been tangible. What Katz was asking of the Executioner now was different.

Yakov Katzenelenbogen wanted to pursue a ghost.

Katz directed the driver east out of the city, and they started along the Riviera proper. Bolan watched his old friend out of the corner of his eye. The Israeli had never made any secret out of the fact that he believed his wife had been murdered. But neither had he dwelled on it, or let it interfere with the missions he was called upon to confirm. He had been forced to live with the mystery, always wondering if the clue would ever come that could lead him toward the truth, and the justice for which Bolan knew he so yearned.

Three highways linked the small towns and coastal resorts along the Riviera, and the cab cruised through the night along the one closest to the sea. Traffic was light, and they passed only a half-dozen sets of oncoming headlights on their way to Toulon. The half moon had risen high in the sky and, along with the bright stars, illuminated the waves as they rolled gently into the coast.

The cab passed through the city of Toulon, still heading east. Bolan had often wondered if Cynthia Armstrong Katzenelenbogen's death had actually been due to foul play or if that was simply the way Katz's unconscious mind had chosen to deal with the grief. Now it looked like the Israeli's wife actually had been murdered. And it looked like there was a chance of finding out who was responsible and solving the decades-old mystery.

If that was the case, the Executioner intended to help.

Any way he could.

A few miles east of La Seyne, a late-model Audi passed them at a high rate of speed, disappearing around a curve ahead. The cab continued on, rounded several more curves, then turned off the highway onto a dirt road.

Thick trees lined the sides of the road as it curved

away from the highway. The boughs rose high over the narrow path, meeting at the center to form a tunnel. The only light in the dark shaft was that of the headlights.

The tunnel of trees finally opened, and the moon appeared again. Bolan saw they had entered a large field cleared of vegetation. The dirt had been packed down to form a short landing strip.

Bolan didn't recognize the Beechcraft airplane idling on the landing strip, but he knew who would be behind the controls. Jack Grimaldi, Stony Man Farm's number-one pilot, would have been the one to bring Katz to the south of France. And he'd be the one to fly them to Munich.

The taxi pulled to a halt just off the road in front of the plane. Bolan and Katz got out, and the Executioner handed several bills back through the window to the driver. The man looked up at him and smiled. His hand closed around the money, then suddenly the fingers relaxed and the bills fluttered down onto his lap.

The smile never left the driver's face as a third eye appeared in his forehead. The cavity filled with blood, then the man slumped forward across the steering wheel.

The horn began to blare as Bolan whirled toward the direction from which the sound-suppressed shot had to have come. When he turned, the big .44 Magnum Desert Eagle leaped into his hand as if having a mind of its own.

"Get down, Katz!" Bolan yelled to the man on the other side of the taxi, but by then the Israeli was aware of the situation himself. Through the window Bolan could see that Katz had drawn his Beretta pistol and was ducking next to the cab.

Though he heard no sound of fire again, Bolan felt the air pressure just over his head change and fell forward onto his belly. Behind him he heard a thump as another round hit the metal door of the cab. His eyes scanned the darkness, trying to pinpoint the source of the attack as he rolled beneath the cab.

Katz was already under the vehicle. "Can you see anything?" he whispered to the Executioner.

Bolan shook his head, knowing there was enough light beneath the cab for Katz to see the movement. He squinted ahead. Through the thick trees that lined the road they'd just left, he saw a flicker of light as another round broke the windshield of the cab. But the light was barely visible; whatever device the gunman was using to quiet his weapon was suppressing the flash, too.

Raising the Desert Eagle, Bolan aimed at the spot where the feeble light had appeared and started to fire. Before he could squeeze the trigger, another flicker showed ten feet to one side.

Bolan lowered his weapon. There was either more than one gunman, or the shooter was moving after his shots to keep them from spotting his position.

From the amount of time between each shot, that made more sense.

Katz had come to the same conclusion. "He's rolling," the Israeli whispered.

Bolan nodded again as he shoved the Desert Eagle back in his holster. They were lucky in the fact that the cabdriver had unwittingly positioned his vehicle between the shooter and the airplane. "Jack!" the Executioner whisper-shouted over his shoulder. "Can you hear me?"

Another silenced round splattered the taxicab.

"Loud and clear, Sarge!" Grimaldi called back.

"You take any hits?" Bolan asked.

"Don't think so," Grimaldi answered. "But it's only a matter of time. That cab isn't big enough to hide all of this bird."

"Get her ready, then," Bolan said.

He turned to Katz. "You go first. I'll give you what cover I can."

The Israeli nodded, holstered his Beretta and began to scoot backward out from under the cab.

Bolan drew the Beretta instead of the Desert Eagle this time. The sound suppressor on the pistol wouldn't hide the muzzle-flash like the one their attacker had on his rifle, but it would be better than the nonsuppressed .44. The big Magnum pistol wouldn't only sound like a cannon, but its flash would be like lighting a bonfire.

Flipping the selector to 3-round-burst mode, Bolan squeezed the trigger as another faint flicker of light appeared at a new position in the trees. He repeated the process twice, then burrowed out from beneath the taxi and turned toward the plane.

The Beechcraft was already starting to taxi as the Executioner sprinted toward it. He felt another round hit the ground as he planted his left foot and zigzagged instinctively away from it.

Katz had the door open. He reached down, grabbed the Executioner's arm and helped him aboard as the Beechcraft picked up speed. A round skimmed across the top of the plane just outside the windshield as they left the ground.

The Israeli grinned at Bolan as the Executioner caught his breath. "This is more like old times," he said.

Grimaldi lifted the plane higher into the air until they were out of rifle range, then leaned across Katz and shook Bolan's hand. "Welcome aboard, Sarge," he said. "It's good to see you." Then, dropping Bolan's hand, he pointed toward the line where the last bullet had skinned across the hull of the Beechcraft. "But you owe me a new paint job."

THE OLD MAN TOTTERED along the cracked sidewalk, leaning on the cane, each step appearing to be a challenge. He paused to catch his breath, then slowly made his way up the rickety steps outside Le Sorbonne. At the door he paused. Leaning heavily on the walking stick, he adjusted the navy blue watch cap over his gray hair.

The old man was worried. Not about what he was about to do—he was a master at his craft, and the apprehension that accompanied dangerous missions had left him years ago. He was worried about something far more basic, something over which he had no control. His mother in St. Petersburg was dying, and he worried that with all he had to do he wouldn't be able to return to his home city for one last visit before she died.

The old man grasped the knob and twisted the door open. His eyes quickly scanned the room, falling for a moment on the table where the Israeli and his big friend sat. Both of the men had arranged their chairs so as to have their backs to the wall. That didn't surprise him. Katzenelenbogen was a trained professional, and the big man—whoever he was— looked to be one, too. That they would take such a precaution was to be expected.

Still, it made the old man smile. At least inwardly he smiled. He was careful not to let the amusement show on his face.

His gaze moved across the room, taking in the rest of the human debris that inhabited the bar. A particularly disheveled form with a black eye patch stood at the bar drinking and glowering toward Katzenelenbogen's table. The old man immediately thought of him as "Cyclops." But why was he watching the Israeli, and why was he angry? Simply a drunk looking for a fight? It seemed the only logical explanation.

The only other open table was across the room from Katzenelenbogen and his friend. That didn't bother the old man. Although he wanted very badly to know what the other two men would be saying, the distance between them wouldn't matter since he was adept at reading lips.

Hobbling across the wooden floor, the old man lowered himself carefully into a chair facing Katzenelenbogen's table. He looked up just in time to see the Israeli answer a question with the words, "Both good and bad. A little boring compared to what I'm used to. On the other hand, it affords me a little private time. I just returned from visiting my daughter in Tel Aviv."

The waitress approached, and the old man ordered a glass of dry red wine, never taking his eyes off the lips of the two men across the room.

"She's an archaeologist, right?"

When Katzenelenbogen replied that his daughter was an archaeologist employed by the Israeli State Antiquities Administration, the gray-haired man shook his head in wonderment at his luck. He couldn't have learned more had he been in a position to simply ask the Israeli the questions to which he wanted answers.

The waitress brought his wine and he took a sip. But who was the big man? he wondered. Where did he fit into the scheme of things? The gray-haired man felt himself frowning. Earlier that evening he had followed Katzenelenbogen to the wharf and watched him sneak on board the *Jacqueline Marie*. He had been surprised when the Israeli came swimming back with the big man. He had then followed them to a cheap hotel where they had changed into dry clothes, Katzenelenbogen obviously wearing his friend's by the fit. Then they had come to this run-down tavern.

The gray-haired man continued to frown as he watched them. The two were old friends; that was obvious by their manner. And he suspected the big man was American—at least the two were speaking English. But he couldn't be sure. That was the one draw back of lipreading—it betrayed no accents.

"So, you came to Marseilles, snuck on board the ship and risked your life to tell me about your trip?" the big man's lips said.

The gray-haired man watched the Israeli force a laugh, then say, "Hardly." He then went on to tell his friend that he believed his wife had been murdered, a piece of information that the big man seemed already to know. The reaction on the big man's face was hard to read, but the gray-haired man suspected the man wasn't as convinced of foul play as was Katzenelenbogen.

The gray-haired man sipped more wine. Katzenelenbogen was right, he thought. She *was* murdered. He could assure him of that.

The old man had done it.

The Israeli went on to tell the story of the past few days: his trip to the Cayman Islands, the murder of Jurgen Schneider. He called the big man "Mack" a time or two. At one point this Mack looked up and caught the gray-haired man looking at them, and the gray-haired man turned away as if embarrassed. And all the while the waitress kept throwing herself at the big man, and the one-eyed monstrosity at the bar kept staring at them in anger.

So that was the answer, the old man realized as he took another sip of his wine. The Cyclops was jealous. He was working up his courage, blustering and convincing himself he could take the big man.

And the big man had noticed. It wasn't obvious, but he was keeping the Cyclops under surveillance, knowing full well what would inevitably happen after the one-eyed man had another drink or two.

The old man drained the rest of his wine. Good, he thought. The Cyclops hadn't only diverted attention from him, but he would provide a little entertainment.

Katzenelenbogen continued to speak to his friend. The gray-haired man was surprised to learn that Schneider and the Israeli had spoken over the phone before their planned meeting at Smith's Cove. But it didn't seem to matter. It appeared the Israeli had learned only that Schneider knew who had killed Cynthia Armstrong and why, but that the German had withheld the answers in exchange for protection. The fact that the big man knew Katzenelenbogen's father had died at Dachau confirmed the gray-haired man's suspicion that they were old friends.

The waitress leaned over, whispering into the big man's ear, and the gray-haired man turned to see Cyclops ready to explode. The man with the eye patch shoved drunkenly away from the bar and moved toward the table. The gray-haired man had seen the weapon hidden beneath the one-eyed man's shirt. From the angle where he sat, it appeared to be some sort of large knife. So the man with the gray hair was hardly surprised when the dagger came out.

The Israeli's big friend grabbed the man's wrist and dropped him with one punch. The old man chuckled.

A moment later the Israeli and his friend began making motions that indicated they'd be leaving soon. The gray-haired man dropped enough francs on his table to cover the wine and a decent tip, then rose on his cane and hobbled out the door ahead of them.

He had parked his Audi on a side street, and the limp disappeared as he hurried toward it. He tossed the cane into the back seat and dropped behind the steering wheel where he could still see the sidewalk in front of the bar. He saw Katzenelenbogen and his friend exit the front door, and almost simultaneously heard an explosion in the distance.

Across the waters of the Mediterranean, he saw a burst of flame and knew it was the *Jacqueline Marie*. At the same time he knew the explosion had been caused by something the Israeli and his friend had done while on board the vessel before swimming back to shore.

The old man laughed out loud. He was dealing with professionals, all right. That should make the game even more interesting.

A taxi picked up the two men a few minutes later. The man with the gray hair jerked the wig from his head and tossed it into the back seat with the cane. As he pulled out and fell in behind the cab, he began to remove the theatrical makeup he had applied to make his face look older.

By the time they had entered Marseilles proper, the gray-haired man was no longer gray-haired and had lost the majority of the makeup-inspired wrinkles. By the time they started along the French Riviera highway, he looked thirty years younger with his stark flat-top haircut. Once again he became Ulric Zhdanov, son of Gregor Zhdanov.

A man with both a legacy and a mission.

As he followed the cab along the highway, Zhdanov donned the shoulder holster that held the Nagant Model 1895 revolver. The 7.62 mm weapon had belonged to his older half brother, and dated back to the early 1920s. Ulric had been instructed by his father that if possible he should use the Nagant to kill Katzenelenbogen. But if the Nagant became impractical, to kill him any way he could. That was the important thing.

But he had no intention of killing Katzenelenbogen until the proper time, which hadn't yet arrived. If it had, he could have easily taken out the man in the Cayman Islands after he'd shot Schneider. He had had a perfect shot as he watched the Israeli examine the German's body through the rifle scope.

No, the man with the flattop thought, Katzenelenbogen had not yet suffered enough. There was other work to do first. Before tonight he had known there was another man who had to die.

Tonight he would kill the Israeli's big friend.

The Audi followed the cab on along the coast. The loss of his friend might not be as sad to Katzenelenbogen as when the man's wife had died, but it would hurt. And it would be something his father would like—having the Israeli suffer the death of a friend. Then, when the big man was dead, there would be only one remaining assassination before the man who had worn the gray wig could kill Yakov Katzenelenbogen and fulfill the destiny his father had raised him to fulfill.

The two vehicles moved on through the night, the assassin staying far enough behind the cab to keep from being noticed, yet close enough that he could keep the other vehicle in sight. He suspected he knew where Katzenelenbogen and his friend were headed—to the isolated landing strip just off the highway. But he could be wrong, and he had no intention of losing the vehicle.

By the time they reached La Seyne, Zhdanov was certain of their destination. He pulled into the oncoming lane to pass, and doing so reminded himself of the night twenty years before when he had fired the Uzi over the roof of Katzenelenbogen's wife's car.

Zhdanov passed the cab and left it in his rearview mirror as he rounded a curve and headed toward the trees that surrounded the landing strip. He pushed the Audi well past one hundred miles per hour for several miles, then pulled off the highway onto the dirt road. He guessed he would have roughly ten minutes before the cab arrived. More than enough time to get set up.

Hiding the Audi in the trees, Zhdanov got out of the vehicle and opened the trunk. He removed a hard plastic rifle case, then glanced at the pile of sandbags next to it. They were used for steadying the weapon in the prone position, but he decided to leave them where they were and slammed the trunk.

At the distance from which he'd be shooting, the sniper rifle could easily handle the job without support. Heinrich had assured him that the scoped Mauser SP-66 had been sighted in properly, and nobody knew small arms like Heinrich. For a moment a flicker of doubt rumbled through Zhdanov. Some of the younger men of the Red Army Faction in Munich had hinted that Heinrich was no longer the man Zhdanov remembered from the Baader-Meinhof days. They said he had changed during the time the Russian had been away.

Zhdanov pushed the thoughts out of his mind and moved quickly to a position near the edge of the trees. In the clearing he could see a Beechcraft Baron aircraft waiting on the landing strip. Dropping to a prone position, Zhdanov opened the rifle case. He removed the weapon and began to thread the sound-flash suppressor onto the end of the barrel. That done, he removed the plastic covers from the scope and prepared to wait.

It wasn't long before the cab pulled off the highway onto the dirt road. A moment later it parked in front of the airplane.

Through the scope Zhdanov watched the Israeli's big friend get out of the cab and pay the driver. He centered the crosshairs on the back of the big man's head, took a deep breath, let half of it out and gently squeezed the trigger.

The Mauser bucked slightly against his cheek. Zhdanov continued to watch through the scope and was surprised when the big man didn't fall.

A moment later the cabdriver fell against the steering wheel, and the horn broke the silence of the night. The big man whirled toward him, drawing a pistol.

Zhdanov centered the crosshairs on the man's chest. Again he pulled the trigger, and again his round missed. Rolling two feet to his side, he aimed and fired again. In the dim light it was impossible to tell exactly where the round went, but it was obvious it hadn't struck its target.

The big man dropped beneath the taxi.

The assassin cursed under his breath as he continued to roll and fire, roll and fire. The telescopic sight was off; that could be the only answer. Heinrich hadn't sighted in the weapon as he'd said, or else he had done it incorrectly.

Return fire came from beneath the cab, forcing Zhdanov to roll more frequently. The big man was good, and he was aiming at the tiny bit of muzzle-flash he had to be able to see through the trees. Zhdanov continued to fire, trying different points of aim in the hopes that a round would accidentally strike home.

It didn't. And a moment later he watched impotently as Katzenelenbogen and his friend leaped onto the plane and disappeared into the dark sky above.

Zhdanov stood, anger flooding his veins like an injection of poison. He was angry at the Israeli, and angry at the man's friend. But most of all, he was angry at his old friend Heinrich Stubrel.

He thought of his mother on her deathbed in St. Petersburg, and how he had planned to go visit her and tell her how things were progressing. Tell her how things were falling into place as planned, and about the unexpected dividend of killing the Israeli's friend. His mother wasn't as obsessed by his quest as his father had been, but she deserved to know that it was about to be accomplished before she died. Now, however, the visit would have to wait. And waiting meant an even greater chance that the old woman would be dead before he got to her.

Zhdanov walked back to where he had hidden the Audi. No, his mission had to come first. And before he visited his mother, Zhdanov believed that Heinrich Stubrel had some explaining to do.

CHAPTER THREE

Bolan had strapped himself in next to Grimaldi as the plane leveled off. Katz had taken the back seat. Now the Israeli caught his breath, then leaned forward. "Any idea whether that had to do with Cynthia's murder and my deal, or your drug-smuggling operation?" he asked.

The Executioner turned and rested an arm over the seat. "My guess is that whoever it was wanted me," he said. "None of the shots seemed directed at you."

"That's what I thought, too," Katz agreed. "On the other hand, the guy was such a bad shot it's hard to tell."

Bolan felt his eyebrows lower over his nose. "Maybe," he said. He wasn't so sure; it really didn't make a lot of sense. Whoever had fired at them from the trees had known his business. He had picked a perfect spot to set up, and had been quite adept at firing, then rolling to keep the Executioner from pinpointing his position. That was the work of a professional, and poor marksmanship didn't fit the rest of the profile. There had to be some other reason the man had missed so many easy shots, something Bolan and Katz had no way of knowing.

The Beechcraft Baron followed the Mediterranean coast over Cannes and Nice, and somewhere during the night the waves lapping below the low-flying craft became those of the Ligurian Sea. At Geneva, Grimaldi turned east-northeast, and both Bolan and Katz took advantage of the downtime to catch a nap.

The Executioner had played the game too long to foolishly think there would be much time for sleep in the next few days. Once a mission began, you did what had to be done when it had to be done. That didn't involve punching a clock and keeping banker's hours.

Bolan woke briefly as they neared Milan, looking down to see the chain of lakes that stretched deep into the mountains. There was enough light, and the aircraft was flying low enough, that he could barely make out some of the vineyards and elaborate villas atop the rolling hillsides. Closing his eyes, he dozed again.

Sometime later the Beechcraft hit an air pocket and jerked him back awake. He turned to see that Katz had slept through the bump, then gazed out the window and looked down on the glistening white slopes of several ski resorts. He glanced at his watch, then turned to Grimaldi and said, "Innsbruck?"

The pilot nodded.

The Executioner watched through the window as they glided over the Sill Valley just south of the city. The moonlight reflected off the snow, and he could easily make out Brenner Pass. Innsbruck was surrounded by jagged Alpine peaks, and in the distance he could see the Stubai Valley. Stubai, the showplace of Austria's Tirol area, boasted eighty glaciers and forty mountain peaks over ten thousand feet high. Tourists flocked to shoot pictures of its scenic beauty year-round.

Bolan had been there himself in the past. But his visit had hardly been what you'd call a vacation. He had finally cornered a band of drug and gun smugglers in the Stubai, and though he had taken many shots, they hadn't been with a camera.

Bolan closed his eyes again. "Wake me when we get near Munich, Jack," he told Grimaldi.

Again the pilot nodded and flew on.

It seemed like only seconds later when the Executioner felt a hand on his shoulder. He opened his eyes.

"Okay, Sarge. Reveille."

The Executioner rubbed his eyes. He felt better, even though the sleep hadn't been much. Looking through the windshield, he could see Munich in the distance. Reaching forward, he unclipped the microphone from the radio mounted on the Baron's dash and held it to his lips. "Stony Man One to Stony Man Base," he said. "Come in, Stony."

Letting up on the button with his thumb, he

waited as his words shot up to the satellite relay in space before making their way back down to the Shenandoah Mountains in America. The message, as well as the reply from the Farm, would be scrambled in case any unauthorized parties were listening in.

"Stony Man Base to One," Barbara Price's voice came back a few seconds later. "We hear you, Striker."

Bolan pictured the honey blond mission controller seated at her console for a moment, then said, "Barb, patch me through to Aaron, will you?"

"Affirmative, Striker," Price said. "Hold on."

The Executioner heard a series of clicks as Price connected the radio to the intercom system, then Aaron "the Bear" Kurtzman said, "Hello, Striker. What can I do for you?"

Behind him Bolan could hear Katz still snoring softly. "Can you get me a Munich address for Jurgen Schneider?" he asked the Farm's chief cybernetics specialist and computer genius.

On the other side of the Atlantic, Kurtzman chuckled. "Sounds as if Katz caught up to you."

"He did," Bolan answered. "We're about to touch down. How long will it take you to get the address?"

"However long it takes me to look down at the yellow legal pad I just wrote it on," Kurtzman said. "I figured you two would be headed that way so I got busy early."

"Good job. What is it?"

Kurtzman read off an address on Tult Strasse at Maria-Hilf-Platz. "Apartment 8."

"You get any other information on the man?" Bolan asked.

"Yeah, I did. I had a hunch and tapped into Munich city files. Schneider had no family, so the government is stuck with the body. They're having it shipped back, and when they get around to it they'll sell anything of value that he owns to try to defer costs." He paused, then added, "Bureaucracy being what it is, it'll probably be weeks before they get around to doing all that. The apartment should be clear. But be careful—you never know."

"Affirmative, Bear," Bolan said. "Thanks."

"One other thing, Striker," Kurtzman said. "You know the Maria-Hilf-Platz area?"

Bolan frowned. Kurtzman's tone of voice told him this was more than a casual question. "I've been there," he said. "It's near the Deutsches Museum."

"Ever been there in April, July or October?" Kurtzman asked.

Bolan's frown deepened. "I don't remember."

"Then you haven't," Kurtzman said. "If you had, you'd remember."

The Executioner looked at Grimaldi, who shrugged.

"What are you getting at, Bear?" Bolan asked.

"Oh, you'll see," the computer man replied with

a chuckle. "Have fun. Stony Man Base clear." He broke the connection.

Bolan clipped the microphone back to the panel in front of him. He didn't know what Kurtzman had been referring to, but whatever lay ahead presented no danger. The men and women of Stony Man Farm weren't above playing a little joke now and then, but they didn't fool around when it came to serious situations.

Grimaldi worked the controls, and as the morning sun rose over the horizon the Beechcraft began its descent toward Munich.

Munich, Germany

"IT IS CALLED Auer Dult," the cabdriver said in his thick Bavarian accent. "It occurs three times a year, and each time draws 450,000 Germans." He looked up into the rearview mirror and smiled at the people in the back seat. "It has been said that there breathes not a soul in Munich who has not been to the Dult at least a dozen times."

The cab turned the corner and entered the section of Munich known as Au, at Maria-Hilf-Platz. Bolan stared out the window. Up and down the street he saw what looked like the world's largest flea market. Booth after booth was crowded with men, women and children buying antiques, jewelry, straw items, clothing, toys, cheese, sausage, pastries, souvenir

T-shirts and practically every other item one might imagine.

Next to him in the back seat of the cab, Katz chuckled. Leaning slightly toward Bolan, he said, "This is what Aaron meant. I have heard of this festival but never been to it."

The cab slowed as several wooden street barriers appeared. "I am sorry," the driver said, "but I can take you no farther. The streets are closed to vehicles until after the Dult."

Bolan and Katz got out, and the Executioner paid the driver, the act reminding him of what had happened to the last cabbie he had paid. Instinctively he looked over his shoulder. There was little chance that the sniper even knew that he and Katz had come to Munich, let alone would have been able to follow them this quickly. But if he had, it was useless to look for him. The driver had said the Dult attracted nearly half a million people, and it looked to Bolan as if they had all crammed into the block where he and Katz got out of the taxi.

The Executioner led them through the swarm of loud, happy people looking for bargains. The air held the mixed scents of wursts, popcorn, cotton candy and human sweat, and even though it was barely after 0900 hours, the aroma of beer hung strong with the other smells. Bolan jostled his way past a huge tent the size of a building and saw that the tables set up inside were filled with beer drinkers. Elbowing on, he and Katz passed a pony track, a Ferris wheel and other carnival rides. Organ grinders, complete with monkeys holding tin cups, seemed to be on every corner, and several small bands belted out lively oompah music.

Bolan came to the corner of Tult Strasse and turned, shoving on past the booths and stands. Everyone bumped into everyone else in the hectic throng, but it seemed to be expected and no one took offense.

At 207 Tult Strasse was a run-down two-story wooden-frame apartment building with a common entrance in the front. Leaving the horde of Auer Dult celebrants, the Executioner led Katz up a short flight of cracked concrete steps and into the hallway. The four doors on the ground floor were marked 1 through 4. A stairway sat in the center of the hall, and Bolan started upward, the loud creaking of the rotting wood beneath his feet making him grateful that a stealthy approach wasn't called for in this instance. A common bathroom stood just to the side of the second floor, and through the open door the Executioner could see the ancient claw-foot tub. He found apartment number 8 in the southwest corner facing the street.

Katz stepped in next to him. Just to make sure no government officials were inside, Bolan knocked. When no one answered, he knocked again.

"Want me to do the honors?" Katz asked.

Bolan nodded and stepped back.

Katz pulled a credit card from his billfold and

inserted it between the door and frame. A second later the cheap snap-lock clicked open, and they were inside.

Jurgen Schneider might not have died in his apartment, but it smelled as if someone had. Mold hung so thick in the air it could almost be seen, and after the third sneeze Katz pulled a handkerchief from his pocket and held it to his nose.

Bolan walked to the window, opened it and let some fresh air come in along with the sounds of Auer Dult on the street below. He turned to survey the small one-room apartment.

Schneider had lived a Spartan life. Tile covered the floor of the rear third of the room and held a refrigerator, cabinets and a sink. A hot plate rested on the countertop and appeared to be the only method of heating food in the apartment.

The rest of the room was a living-sleeping area with one armchair, a roll-out couch, a coffee table and a desk. Set in the far wall was a small closet. A plain black rotary telephone stood on a scarred end table with one drawer. The apartment was devoid of decoration, with the exception of a photograph in a cheap black plastic frame that stood in the center of the coffee table. "Not much here," Katz said. "Looks to me like the German government is going to get stuck with a funeral bill."

Bolan nodded. He picked up the photograph and examined it. It showed a middle-aged man wearing what he recognized as a West German prison guard uniform. Holding it up for Katz's inspection, he said, "This Schneider?"

Katz squinted at the picture. "Very possible, although it's hard to tell. The man was much older when I saw him. Not to mention dead, with quite a bit of his face blown away."

"He say anything about being a prison guard?"

"No," Katz said. "But he didn't say he *wasn't* ever a prison guard, either."

Bolan set the picture down, walked to the kitchen area and opened a cabinet. Inside he saw an unmatched assortment of glasses and coffee cups. The next cabinet offered up a similar collection of bowls, dishes and other containers.

Behind him the Executioner could hear Katz open the closet door. He turned to see the Israeli rifling the pockets of several threadbare suits that hung in the tiny room.

Bolan continued digging through the cabinets. He finished the search and opened the refrigerator. Three bottles of beer and a half-eaten, molding cheesecake were its only contents.

The Executioner heard a drawer slide open behind him and glanced over his shoulder to see Katz next to the end table that held the phone. He had barely turned back around when the Israeli said, "Hey, Mack."

Bolan shut the refrigerator door again and turned.

By now Katz was kneeling on the floor next to the phone on the end table. He had dumped the contents of the drawer onto the tattered carpet and begun digging through a mess of papers, rubber bands, paper clips and other odds and ends. In his hand he held a wrinkled yellow sticker. "Take a look," he said, rising to his feet.

Bolan walked over and took the note, which read 706 Goethe Strasse. And after that, the same scribbly hand had written Baad.-Mein. The Executioner frowned. "Baader-Meinhof?"

Katz shrugged. "Looks like it to me."

"But they haven't been active for years," Bolan stated. "Most of them either got killed or went to prison. What was left became the Red Army Faction."

Katz's gaze narrowed. "Yes, but they were going strong in the days when Cynthia was murdered," he said.

Bolan pocketed the note and moved over to the desk as Katz continued to look through the pile at his feet. Opening the middle drawer just beneath the top, he found old bills, receipts and other items of no value. Three drawers were set in the right-hand side of the desk, and the top one proved equally uninteresting. But in the middle drawer the Executioner came across a worn and ragged black address book. He removed it and opened it carefully.

Addresses and phone numbers had been written in the same shaky handwriting that had written "Baad.-Mein" and the address on the sticker. The entries had been made with various types of pens and pencils, and here and there an address and phone number had been crossed out and new ones entered.

Bolan glanced through several pages, not recognizing any of the names. Right now the book was of little use, but in the hours and days to come, after they'd investigated any other leads they came across in the apartment, it might prove invaluable. Carefully he slipped the shabby volume into his pocket.

Closing the middle drawer again, the Executioner opened the bottom. More junk covered the top of what looked like a photo album. Reaching past the debris, he extracted the book and opened it.

The volume did contain photos mounted behind a protective plastic sheet. The first page held pictures of a young man in his late teens who looked like he might well be a younger Schneider. But when the Executioner removed the photo from the plastic and flipped it over he saw "Helmut Kaufman, 18" scribbled on the back.

Bolan scrutinized the pictures for any clue as to the time frame. In each photo Kaufman wore a plain white shirt and khaki slacks, drab items of clothing that might never be trendy but never went out of style, either. The Executioner squinted at the backgrounds of the pictures. No hint as to what year the pictures had been taken there.

The Executioner returned his attention to the name and age on the back of the one photo. Regardless of what it said, he couldn't get over the fact that the man on the other side resembled Schneider. Walking the album over to the coffee table, Bolan compared the pictures to that of the man in the prison-guard uniform. Again many years separated the pictures. It was impossible to be certain.

The Executioner took a seat on the couch and began to thumb through the rest of the album. Some pages showed an even younger version of Kaufman. Others showed him in his twenties. In a few he could be seen posing proudly with a sturdily built, moderately pretty woman who seemed to have a penchant for austere suits.

"Katz," Bolan called.

The Israeli looked up.

The Executioner showed him the album. "The woman's clothes," he said. "What year?"

Katz studied the pictures for a few minutes. "I'm no fashion expert, but my guess would be late thirties or early forties. The hairdo looks right for that time period, too, and if you'll look close you'll see she's wearing a snood."

"A what?" Bolan asked.

Katz laughed. "I guess that's a little before your time, all right, Mack. A snood was a kind of hair net they wore back then."

"Take a close look at this guy," he said. "The back of one of the pictures identifies him as Helmut Kaufman. But could it be Schneider?"

Katz studied the ageing photos for several seconds. Finally he shrugged and said, "Maybe."

Bolan closed the photo album. "You find anything else interesting?" he asked.

Katz shook his head as he piled the rubble on the floor back in the drawer, rose and stuck it back in the end table. His face showed that his mind was miles away—at a different time, in a different place.

With a woman who had been his wife.

Bolan closed the photo album and stood. Katz had learned to live with his sorrow over the years, and like all wounds, the one caused by Cynthia's death had scarred over. But Jurgen Schneider had reopened that wound, and the Executioner knew it would never heal again until Katz had tracked down whoever was responsible for his wife's death and exacted justice. Until then, the best thing to do was try to keep Katz's mind off it.

The Executioner was trying to think of something to say that would do just that when they heard the voices in the hallway outside.

A moment later there was a scratching sound in the lock as a key was inserted into the door.

The one-room apartment offered little chance of concealment. Bolan grabbed Katz and half pushed him toward the closet. He drew the sound-suppressed Beretta and ducked behind the front door a split second before it opened.

Two men entered, not bothering to close the door behind them. Bolan could see only their backs. One of the men, fat, unkempt and wearing tight brown slacks and a soiled white shirt, held a huge key ring in his hand. The other man wore a cheap blue suit and carried a clipboard. Who they were couldn't have been more clear.

The fat man was the apartment manager. The other was a government bureaucrat who had come to see if Jurgen Schneider had anything worth selling.

The two stopped in the center of the room, still facing the other way.

"Like I told you," the manager said. "There is nothing of value to you."

The voice of the man in the cheap suit was suspicious. "Are you sure you did not pay this place a visit before I arrived?"

Bolan evaluated the situation as the manager protested his innocence. The men might not check the closet and find Katz, but that made little difference. There was only one way in and the same way out of the apartment, and as soon as they turned to leave they would see *him*. The possibility of them physically detaining the Executioner was laughable, but they would report the incident to the police, who would then be on the lookout for men matching his and Katz's descriptions.

The Executioner knew he couldn't kill them— they were average everyday citizens, not the enemy. But he couldn't let them go, either. And he had to decide just what he was going to do fast.

"We might as well leave," the man in the cheap suit said as Bolan moved up behind him. When he turned he found himself looking into the suppressor of the Executioner's Beretta. He froze, his mouth dropping open, speechless.

The manager turned. "What's—?" he started to say when the Executioner drew the Desert Eagle with his other hand and jammed it under his nose.

Katz had to have had the door cracked open because by now he had come out of the closet with his Beretta drawn. "What do we do with them?" he asked Bolan. "Dump them in the river?"

Bolan had to suppress a smile. The statement had been made for effect, as a control over the two men. Katz would no sooner kill a couple of helpless men like this than Bolan would. "It's too far away," the Executioner answered. "But we aren't that far from the dump."

Tears were forming in the eyes of the city official. "Please," he said. "We haven't done anything."

"Don't hurt us," the apartment manager pleaded. "Please, just take what you want and let us go."

Bolan took a step back, but kept the guns trained on the men. "Take off your clothes," he ordered.

True terror now appeared in the eyes of both men.

"Do not worry," Katz said. "Both my friend and I prefer women."

The two men's heads swung toward the Israeli.

"Here's the deal," Bolan said, and the two men's heads jerked back to him. "We don't want to hurt you, but we can't let you go reporting us to the police."

"I promise we will not—"

"Just shut up and listen," Bolan growled. "Promises aren't worth a dime under these kinds of conditions. We're going to tie you up and then leave. Taking your clothes just helps us slow you down a little more after you work free."

"Can't you just tie us tighter?" the manager asked.

Bolan was losing patience. "Friend, I can tie you so tight that you'll lie up here and starve to death if that's what you want. But I'm trying to avoid killing you." He stepped forward again and pressed the Desert Eagle between the man's eyes. "But I'm getting real tired of explaining all that to you, and just shooting you isn't beginning to seem so bad anymore."

Fifteen seconds later, the two men were naked.

Bolan and Katz used the men's neckties and belts to bind their hands and feet, then tore strips of cloth from their shirts to fashion gags. They left them lying on their bellies on the carpet.

"How long do you think we have before they get loose?" Katz asked as, the men's clothes under their arms, they left the apartment and stepped out into the hall.

Bolan closed the door behind him, making sure the lock snapped into place. "Depends on how smart they are."

"Then they very well might starve up there," Katz declared.

Bolan grinned. "They'll be free by morning. Then they'll have to call someone to bring them some clothes. That'll buy us even more time before the cops get our descriptions." He started toward the stairs, then stopped suddenly as the door to the apartment across the hall opened.

An old gentleman, probably in his eighties, stepped out into the hallway. He wore a long frayed overcoat, gray fedora and carried a cane. His wrinkled eyes opened wide when he saw Bolan and Katz. "Are you come to see Jurgen?" he asked.

Bolan glanced at Katz out of the corner of his eye. He could tell the Israeli was thinking the same thing he was. This man obviously knew Schneider and might be able to tell them something. "Yes," the Executioner said. "Do you know where he is?"

"The manager told me he died," the old man replied. He had the face of someone who had lost his last friend, and perhaps he had.

"Could you tell us about him?" Bolan asked.

"Who are you?" the old man asked suspiciously.

Katz stepped forward. "I was with the prison system for a short while," he said. "Jurgen and I were friends. Please, if we could only have a few moments of your time…"

"I was leaving to get something to eat," the old man stated, still looking suspicious.

"We'll take you to dinner," the Executioner offered. "Any place you'd like."

The old man's eyes opened almost as wide as

when he'd first seen them in the hall. The offer was more than he could turn down. "Yes, all right," he agreed. "My name is Goertzen. Victor Goertzen."

Together the Executioner, the Israeli and Victor Goertzen walked down the steps and returned to the festival atmosphere of Auer Dult.

AFTER ANDREAS BAADER and Ulrike Meinhof had been captured and committed suicide in prison during the mid-1970s, the remnants of the Baader-Meinhof Gang had developed into the Red Army Faction—RAF. Eventually it merged with the 2nd June Movement. Most active in 1977, the RAF had then temporarily fizzled out, only to come back to life with new zeal and leadership in the 1980s.

On August 31, 1981, a Red Army Faction car bomb at the USAF European headquarters in Ramstein wounded twenty people. The next month the RAF ambushed U.S. General Frederick J. Kroesen, firing an RPG-7 rocket at his armored Mercedes. The general escaped with minor injuries. Lying low until 1985, they then teamed with the French Action Directe to send a long and tautological communiqué to the press. The communiqué announced the formation of the political military front in Western Europe with NATO proposed as its main target for new terrorist attacks. Within the next two weeks, both French General René Audran and Ernst Zimmermann, president of the West German Aerospace and Armament Association, had been shot. Sporadic car bombings, shootings and other acts had run hot and cold ever since.

Through it all, leaders had come and gone. But one man had remained the same. Ever since the days of Baader and Meinhof themselves, Heinrich Stubrel had been in charge of both small arms and explosives for the radical German groups regardless of what they were calling themselves that year. And through it all he had always lived in the same place—the Pension Kopromed on Bayer Strasse. Just across from the Munich railroad station, the thirty-two-room pension had been in his family for five generations and provided the perfect cover—not to mention an income—for his gun and bomb experimentation and manufacturing.

Ulric Zhdanov had been Heinrich's friend for nearly a quarter of a century.

Two of the younger Red Army Faction men, who had been staying at Stubrel's pension the past several months, had been waiting for him when he'd touched the Piper Cub down a half hour earlier. They had arrived in a BMW and an Audi, and he had left the plane in their hands and taken the BMW. They would see to servicing the aircraft, then return to the city in the Audi.

Zhdanov frowned as he drove. He didn't know exactly where the Israeli and his big friend had gone, but he suspected they had come to Munich to see what they could find out about Schneider. If so, they would go to Schneider's apartment.

If they had done that, it was ironic that Zhdanov was even now probably only a few miles away from them. He needed to get to his mother in St. Petersburg as soon as possible, but when he finished here, with Stubrel, he would drive to the old apartment building where Schneider had lived. It wouldn't delay his trip home that much longer, and who knew? Perhaps the Fates would smile on him and he would get another shot at Katzenelenbogen's friend.

The BMW passed the Pension Kopromed, and Zhdanov glanced up at the four-story building before pulling into the train-station parking lot. He sat behind the wheel for a moment, collecting his thoughts and giving himself a moment to cool down. Stubrel's failure to sight in the Mauser had allowed the Israeli's friend to escape, and under other circumstances might have gotten Zhdanov killed. He was angry with his old friend, and he had a right to be, but uncontrolled anger was never productive.

He took a deep breath. Part of what had happened was his own fault, and he would have to accept that fact. He had been warned that Stubrel was no longer as dependable as he had been when Zhdanov had been active in the "old days." The Russian had chosen to ignore the warning, and had only himself to blame.

Zhdanov sighed. He had seen Stubrel only once since his return—when he'd picked up the rifle— and his old friend had appeared fine, if considerably older. So Zhdanov had preferred to believe the rumors about heavy drinking were jealousy on the parts of the younger RAF men. In other words, he had allowed sentimentality to cloud his judgment.

Killing the BMW's engine, Zhdanov continued to sit for a moment. The first shot out of the Mauser had convinced him he should have listened to the warnings. The memory caused his outrage to return, and he took another deep breath, reminding himself again that anger would only get in his way. It was always better to remain calm, sacrificing the self-indulgent desire to ''feel'' one's success at a task until after the task was complete. Better just to do it coolly, calmly, without emotion and make sure things got done correctly.

When he was certain he had his anger under control, Zhdanov exited the vehicle. Opening the trunk, he pulled out a long cardboard box. Inside the box was the hard plastic rifle case that contained the Mauser, but the case was too obviously a weapon container to carry openly.

He could have abandoned the Mauser in France, but he wanted Stubrel to see it, to see the evidence that his irresponsible lie about sighting in the scope might well have gotten his old friend killed.

Zhdanov carried the box across the street to the pension, his mind traveling back over the years to his first meeting with Heinrich Stubrel. He had been a young man then, and it had been only a few weeks since he'd escaped the Soviet Union and hooked up with the Baader-Meinhof Gang. His father had recently passed away, and he had come to the gang to get the training he knew he would need to carry out the promises he had made to the man. Andreas Baader had assigned Stubrel as one of Zhdanov's first teachers.

The Russian smiled at the memory as he reached the steps of the pension. Stubrel had taken Zhdanov under his wing and taught him everything he knew about small arms and explosives. Stubrel was a good fifteen years his senior, and their relationship had become that of an older and younger brother. Zhdanov had lived here at the pension and been like one of the family. Stubrel had been Zhdanov's mentor, but somewhere along the line, the student had become more proficient than the teacher.

Zhdanov mounted the steps to the pension's entry hall, balanced the box on his shoulder with one hand and pushed through the door into the lobby. An unusual place, the wallpaper hadn't been changed since Stubrel's mother had put it up years before. It pictured huge boulders and trees, making the lobby seem as if it were out of doors. Zhdanov could remember when Elsie Stubrel had chosen the strange wallpaper, also remembered teasing her about it.

For a moment Zhdanov paused, staring at the wallpaper. It had become yellow and stained over the years since he'd been there. A tear formed in his eye. He had missed his own mother during his years in Germany. Elsie had realized that and taken him in, becoming like another parent. Then she had died while he was away, but he hadn't learned of her death until his return to Munich a few days earlier.

To him, her death was new, and he grieved for her now.

Wiping the moisture from his face with the back of his hand, Zhdanov turned toward the desk. Huge hanging plants, in baskets fastened to the ceiling, made a straight path across the room impossible. Zhdanov had to rest the box lower on his shoulder as he cut back and forth through the indoor jungle until he'd reached the front desk. A closed door stood behind the desk. Zhdanov knew that it led to a combination office-apartment where Stubrel and his mother, and now Heinrich alone, lived.

Zhdanov rang the bell on the desk, but the door didn't open. A few moments later he tried again, but receiving no response, pushed through the swing gate to the rear of the counter. The door in the wall was unlocked, and the Russian let himself in.

He found Heinrich Stubrel passed out drunk on his back on the couch.

Zhdanov shook his head at the sight. This was what the younger Red Army Faction men had warned him about. Since Elsie's death, Stubrel's drinking had gotten more and more out of hand. He could no longer be counted on. Worse than that, he had become a liability in that he talked when he drank.

The Russian glanced around the small apartment where he had spent so much time years earlier. He could almost see Elsie's ghost in the kitchen preparing dinner. She had kept the place immaculately clean, but now it looked as if a herd of winos had moved in. Fast-food containers, empty paper sacks, beer, wine and spirit bottles littered the floor. The stench of stale alcohol and body odor permeated the air. On the coffee table in front of the couch was a half-empty liter bottle of vodka.

The Russian dropped to one knee between the table and couch and reached out, gently shaking Stubrel by the shoulder. The ageing RAF man snorted drunkenly and rolled to his side, facing away from Zhdanov.

"Wake up, Heinrich," the Russian said.

His answer was an unintelligible mumble.

Zhdanov shook his head. "Wake up, Heinrich. It is Ulric. I must show you something." He reached inside the cardboard box, extracted the rifle case and opened it.

Heinrich Stubrel burped, and the scent floated nauseatingly through the room.

Zhdanov shook his old friend again. "Heinrich," he said, louder this time, "you must awaken. You have made a very bad mistake of which you must be made aware."

Stubrel rolled onto his back again and opened his eyes. His glazed pupils floated like tiny black islands in a sea of red. "Mother?" he said. "Is that you, Mother?"

"No," Zhdanov said. "It is Ulric."

Stubrel smiled. "Ulric," he repeated. "My friend. My little brother. You are back."

"I have been back for over a week," Zhdanov said disgustedly. Then his voice softened. He lifted the scoped Mauser SP-66 and held it up where Stubrel could see it. "You said you had sighted in this weapon, Heinrich."

Stubrel tried to focus his eyes on the rifle. "It was not accurate?" he slurred.

"No."

The man closed his eyes again. "Perhaps I forgot." His eyes still closed, he whispered, "Ulric, there is beer in the refrigerator. Would you get me one?"

"You have had enough."

"Please…Ulric…" Heinrich pleaded. "I need it."

Zhdanov leaned the Mauser against the couch and rose to his feet. Wading through the mess of trash on the floor, he entered the small kitchen and opened the refrigerator. It contained only two bottles of beer. Finding a bottle opener on the counter next to the refrigerator, the Russian lifted both caps. He took a small sip from one of the bottles as he walked back into the living room.

Stubrel was sitting up when he returned. Zhdanov saw that more of the vodka had disappeared from the bottle on the coffee table.

Stubrel reached quickly for the beer Zhdanov held out in front of him. Lifting it to his lips, he tilted his head back, drained the liquid and looked hopefully at the bottle Zhdanov still held.

The anger in Zhdanov's heart was suddenly replaced by a black feeling of hopelessness for his old friend. He handed Strubel the other bottle and watched the man smile.

"Oh, Heinrich," he said, his heart breaking, "I must do something to help you."

Stubrel drank slower this time. Shaking his head, he said, "Do not worry about me, Ulric. I will be fine. I will get myself put back together." He looked up into his friend's eyes. "You can count on me, Ulric. I will help you carry out what you promised your father you would do."

Zhdanov didn't answer as Stubrel leaned forward, took a long drink from the vodka bottle and fell backward on the couch, asleep again.

The Russian had learned how to control anger, so it didn't affect his work. He had learned to control his other emotions, as well. Much as he had done earlier in the BMW to get a rein on his fury, he now took a deep breath. The black feeling of depression he felt for his old friend and mentor disappeared.

Zhdanov lifted the Mauser from where it still leaned on the couch. He rested the barrel of the rifle on the bridge of Stubrel's nose, but the man was too drunk to wake up. The Russian shook his head. He had a mission to accomplish, a promise to keep, and he couldn't let emotion, be it anger or compassion or any other sentiment, get in his way.

"Goodbye, Heinrich," Zhdanov said. "At this range, your incompetence with the scope will not matter." He pulled the trigger, and the rifle cracked loudly against the narrow walls of the apartment.

Zhdanov dropped the rifle to the floor next to the couch and looked at his watch. If they had come to Munich, the Israeli and his friend would go to Schneider's apartment.

If he hurried, he might still catch them there.

Moving through the kitchen, the Russian entered the tiny bedroom and opened a closet door. He pried away the molding around the floor of the far wall, then slipped the hidden panel out and rested it against the side wall.

Before him, Zhdanov saw a small armory.

With the skill, knowledge and precision that Stubrel had taught him years before, he began to pick out the weapons he guessed he might need. Knowing that an incompetent drunk who would forget to sight in a sniper rifle might well forget that guns wouldn't fire without bullets, he began to check each weapon to make sure it was loaded. He finished the inspection by dropping the magazine from a High Standard .22-caliber target pistol fitted with luminous night sights and a sound suppressor, noting the CCI Mini Mag round at the top of the box, then pulling the slide back far enough to see brass in the chamber.

Satisfied that Stubrel's incompetence wouldn't foil him again, Zhdanov shoved the weapon into his waistband and lifted the box.

CHAPTER FOUR

Victor Goertzen led Bolan and Katz through the carnival-like atmosphere of the ongoing Auer Dult. Many of the vendors who were selling their wares on the streets and sidewalks could have had successful careers as stand-up comedians. One man, the sign over his awning-covered stand reading Der Billige Jakob, fired insults and witty one-liners at all who passed, causing the audience that had gathered around him to roar with laughter as they bought his umbrellas, belts and other odds and ends.

"Good day, Victor!" Jakob yelled out, looking up as the old man, Bolan and Katz neared.

"Good day, Jakob," Goertzen replied.

"Can I interest you in an umbrella today?" Jakob asked.

"No, Jakob."

"A billfold perhaps?" Jakob said.

"No, thank you," Goertzen answered.

The crowd quieted, realizing Jakob was setting up for another joke.

"A young woman, then?" Jakob asked the old man, and the crowd laughed.

"No, no," Goertzen said as they drew abreast of Jakob's awning.

The crowd hadn't realized the joke had a second part.

"No young woman?" Jakob asked, timing it perfectly as the old man led Bolan and Katz past him. "I am sorry, Victor, I am all out of young boys!"

This time the crowd went into hysterics.

The old man's eyes lit up for a moment, and he laughed along with the others. Then a dullness seemed to come over him again as if he weren't quite sure where he was.

Bolan studied the man's face as they walked on. He seemed to be coherent one moment, then a thousand miles away and thirty years in the past the next.

Goertzen led them away from the Dult and down a side street. Gradually the jovial, carnival-like noises dwindled in the distance behind them. Bolan continued to study the old man. While he had seemed to make sense when they'd spoken back in the hall across from Schneider's apartment, the Executioner suspected it had been a moment of clarity in what was otherwise a quickly deteriorating brain. Goertzen's appearance, while not particularly disheveled, showed signs of a wandering mind. The vest he wore beneath his jacket had been buttoned crookedly, and he'd forgotten to tie the laces of his left shoe. He had puttered along on his cane all the way through the Dult, and as they walked now the rubber tip fell off and the steel point began to clap noisily against the concrete. Victor didn't even notice.

The Executioner turned, retrieved the rubber tip and replaced it for him.

But Goertzen knew where he wanted to eat and, four blocks from the Dult, he led them through a door into a small cafeteria. Grabbing a tray, he shuffled along the line, pointing and calling out to the servers who stood behind the steaming pots of food.

Bolan and Katz followed suit, and soon the three of them were sitting at a corner table eating a hearty meal.

The Executioner watched the old man eat. Goertzen looked as if it were the first meal he'd had in days. At least the first that hadn't come out of a can and been heated over a hot plate like the one they'd seen in Jurgen Schneider's kitchen.

The old man didn't speak until he had finished eating and stuck a toothpick into his mouth. Then he leaned back and said, "So, you are friends of Greta?"

Bolan and Katz exchanged glances. "Greta?" Bolan asked.

The old man looked surprised. "Yes, Greta," he said. "My wife. Perhaps you are in the painting class with her at the university?"

Bolan frowned. Goertzen had forgotten that they had come because of Jurgen Schneider. But what puzzled the Executioner was the fact that he had gotten the feeling that the man was a widower. Perhaps it was the man's age combined with his crookedly buttoned vest and the fact that he had been on his way to eat alone when they'd met him that led Bolan to that assumption. In any case, the Executioner supposed he had to have been wrong.

"I'm sorry," Katz said. "But no, we do not know your wife. We were friends of Jurgen Schneider. We want to talk to you about him."

"Jurgen?" Victor said. "He lives across the hall. I can take you there."

Bolan leaned toward the man, more convinced than ever that the man was the victim of Alzheimer's disease or some other form of senility. "You told us you had heard Jurgen died," he said gently.

The old man's brow furrowed in thought, as if he were trying to remember something that wasn't quite coming. "Jurgen is dead?" he repeated.

Katz nodded. "Yes, and we are friends of his and would like to talk to you." The Israeli shot a glance toward Bolan with an expression that asked the Executioner if he thought the interview was worth pursuing.

Bolan shrugged. There was no way of knowing. But besides the address on the yellow sticker—an address that might have absolutely nothing to do with what they were interested in—they had no other leads. They might as well invest a little more time in Goertzen.

"Victor," the Executioner began, "have you had enough to eat?"

The old man nodded.

Bolan reached into his pocket and pulled out enough money to cover their bill. "Then maybe we should go back to your place where we can speak more privately."

Goertzen nodded.

Bolan and Katz flanked the old man as they walked back down the street to the Auer Dult area, then back up the steps of the apartment building. Goertzen stuck a key in the lock and ushered them inside.

The interior of the old man's apartment was the mirror image of Jurgen Schneider's. If anything, it was dirtier.

"Please have a seat," Victor said, pointing to a worn couch. He looked toward the kitchen end of the room. "Greta," he said, "we have company. Could you put on some tea, dear?"

Bolan and Katz both followed the old man's gaze to the far end of the room where the refrigerator and sink stood. There was no one there.

"Oh, Greta, if I had known, I could have picked some up on my way back." He turned to Bolan. "I am sorry but Greta informs me we are out of tea. Could I get you a glass of water? A beer, perhaps?"

Bolan shook his head. "No, thanks, Victor. Just some information. Please, sit down and talk to us."

The old man nodded and sat in a wooden, straight-backed chair.

"Did you know Jurgen Schneider well?" Bolan asked.

"Ah yes, Jurgen and I play pinochle every Tuesday morning," Goertzen replied, smiling. "I always win."

His use of the present tense when referring to Schneider told Bolan the old man had again forgotten that his neighbor was dead.

The Executioner decided to try another tack. "You always beat him, huh?"

Goertzen's eyes lit up in delight. "Yes, yes. Jurgen is not a very good player."

"Do you two play alone?" the Executioner asked.

"Sometimes Dieter joins us."

"And who is Dieter?" Bolan prompted.

"Dieter is Jurgen's friend. He comes to visit. He is even worse at pinochle than Jurgen."

Bolan leaned forward. This might be the break he needed. "And what is Dieter's last name?" he asked.

"Roden," Victor said. "Dieter Roden."

Bolan slipped Schneider's address book out of his pocket and handed it to Katz. He heard the Israeli begin rustling carefully through the ragged pages. "Victor, do you know where Dieter Roden lives?" the Executioner asked.

The old man looked puzzled. Before he could speak, Katz tapped Bolan on the shoulder. "There is no Dieter Roden listed," he said, glancing at the address book.

"Of course not," Goertzen said, his eyes now amused. "Dieter Roden has been dead for over thirty years. He was my uncle—my mother's brother." He paused. "Did you know him?"

Bolan remained patient. Dealing with the old man was frustrating, but that was hardly the old man's fault. "We were talking about another Dieter," he said quietly. "The Dieter who plays pinochle with you and Jurgen Schneider."

"Ah!" Victor said. "Dieter Heinz!"

Katz turned several pages, then shook his head again.

"Victor," the Executioner said patiently, "are you sure that it is Dieter Heinz who is the pinochle player?"

The old man looked away from Bolan, a tear forming in the corner of his eye. Like so many older men and women whose minds were leaving them, he still had enough left to know he was slipping. It was a painful situation, and the Executioner felt compassion for Goertzen.

Bolan could hear Katz still rustling through the pages of the address book. "Victor," he said gently, "it's important or I wouldn't ask. Does Dieter Heinz play pinochle with you and Jurgen?"

"Dieter Heinz was my dentist," he said.

Bolan didn't like to keep asking the man questions that brought him pain, but he had no other choice. "Victor," he said, "think hard. The man who plays pinochle with you and Jurgen. What is his last name?"

The answer came from Bolan's side rather than the chair across from him. "Bernhardt," Katz said. "Is it Bernhardt, Victor?" Then, under his breath to Bolan, he added, "It is the only Dieter in the book."

Victor's head jerked back. "Yes!" he said excitedly. "Dieter Bernhardt!" Then, with one of the sudden mood swings so characteristic of his disease, he added, "Dieter Bernhardt. The man does not know the queen of hearts from the knave of diamonds!" He began to chuckle.

"Do you know where we can find Dieter Bernhardt?" Bolan asked.

"I have only seen him here, across the hall at Jurgen's." He paused, and the clouds suddenly fell over his eyes again. "Jurgen has been gone for several days. Do you know when he will be back?"

The Executioner turned to Katz. "Is there an address with the name?" he asked.

Katz nodded.

Bolan stood. Walking across the room to where the old man slumped in his chair, he reached into his pocket and pulled out several hundred marks, shoving them into the old man's hand. "Thank you, Victor."

The old man looked up and smiled through the clouds in his eyes. "I would never turn down a request for help from a friend of Greta's," he said.

"Do you enjoy the art classes as much as she does?"

"Yes," Katz said. "But she paints much better than either of us."

The old man smiled proudly.

Bolan and Katz moved across the room. The Executioner opened the door to the hall and ushered Katz through.

THE RAUCOUS Auer Dult atmosphere showed no signs of quieting as Bolan and Katz returned to the street. An organ grinder playing a jazzy version of "Cha Cha Polka" approached, suddenly switching to "Rosamunde" as he passed them on the sidewalk.

Bolan waited for the man to get far enough away that Katz could hear him, then said, "The way I see it, we've only got two leads."

Katz nodded. "Dieter Bernhardt and the Baader-Meinhof address," he said. He pulled a package of unfiltered Camel cigarettes from somewhere inside his jacket, stuck one in his mouth and struck a match.

The Israeli drew deeply on the cigarette, then let the smoke out, glancing up at the Executioner. "One a day," he said. "I allow myself one a day." He paused, took another drag, then said, "If I try for two, shoot me." He paused. "But not until after this is all over."

Bolan nodded. "Which address is closer?" he asked.

Katz reached into another pocket and pulled out a folded map of the city. He moved to the edge of the building as he unfolded the map, leaning his back against the ageing wood.

Bolan watched his old friend squint as Katz's eyes darted about the map. "Dieter Bernhardt," the Israeli said. "It's on the river."

According to Jurgen Schneider's address book, Dieter Bernhardt lived in room 4 at the Pension Sonnenheim. Bolan and Katz flagged another cab and made their way across Munich to 45 Klenzestrasse.

The Executioner studied the outside of the pension as Katz paid the driver. It was a plain but agreeable place, and he saw several men and women of various ages coming and going out of the front entrance. The Sonnenheim appeared to appeal to both young travelers just there for one night and older, retired people staying on a more permanent basis.

Bolan led the way inside and rapped on the wooden door of room 4 with his knuckles. When he got no response, he knocked again.

The Executioner waited, but no one called out or opened the door. He was about to knock again when he saw the faint light visible through the peephole darken.

"Herr Bernhardt," he said softly. "We are friends of Jurgen Schneider. Please let us in."

A long period of silence followed.

"Please," Bolan said again, "Herr Bernhardt, I know you are there. I can see you at the peephole. We need to talk to you about our mutual friend."

After another pause a trembling voice said, "If you want to know about Jurgen, go ask him your questions. If you are really his friends, you will know where to find him."

Bolan hesitated, then said, "I'm sorry to be the one to tell you, but Jurgen is dead."

The silence now was so still as to be almost audible. "Dead?" the old man behind the door asked.

"Yes."

Another pause, then, "How can I be sure you are a friend of Jurgen's?"

"You said if we were his friends, we would know how to find him," Bolan answered. He recited Jurgen Schneider's address. "We just came from there where we met Victor, the man who played cards with you and Jurgen."

The man behind the door still wasn't convinced. "These things you could find out without being a friend."

Leaning close to the door, the Executioner took a chance. "Helmut Kaufman," he whispered to the place where the door met the frame. As he said the name, he wondered what it meant.

The sound of a dead-bolt lock sliding out met his ears. Slowly the door swung open.

Bolan and Katz stepped into the high-ceilinged room as an old man wearing a tattered cardigan sweater and equally worn brown slacks stepped back. Small frameless octagonal spectacles covered his eyes. One hand hung at his side, the other hidden behind his back.

The Executioner looked past the man to a gold-framed bull's-eye mirror on the wall behind him, and saw in the mirror that the man was hiding an old toggle-bolt 9 mm Luger pistol.

Katz closed the door behind them.

"You won't need the Luger," Bolan said quietly. "We just want to ask you about Herr Schneider."

For a moment Bernhardt's eyes widened in surprise as he wondered how the Executioner had not only known that he held a weapon but the type of pistol, as well. Then he turned, looked at the mirror and shook his head. "I am such an old fool," he muttered under his breath. "And I am sorry. If you want to kill me, I suppose there is little I can do about it—even with a gun. Neither my mind nor my body work as they once did."

"No one wants to hurt you," Katz said. "Please, may we sit down?"

Bernhardt pointed to a short couch that faced his bed and said, "May I offer you something to drink? A beer, perhaps?"

"Sure," Katz said.

Bolan nodded.

Bernhardt dropped the gun on the white coverlet spread across the bed as he walked past it to a small refrigerator. Opening the door, he pulled out a tall bottle of Chimay ale. From a shelf above the refrigerator, he took down three fruit jars, set them on top of the short cooling box and poured the ale.

"I am sorry I have no real glasses," he apologized. "I am on a pension, and money is tight." He tottered over with two of the jars, gave one to Bolan and the other to Katz, then returned for his own before taking a seat on the bed facing them.

Katz raised his fruit jar. "To Jurgen," he said.

"To Jurgen," Bernhardt repeated, and the three men drank. "Please tell me what happened." The wrinkled eyes looked like they might break into tears at any moment.

"He was murdered," Bolan said. "He had gone to the Cayman Islands to give my friend some kind of information." He glanced to Katz, then back to Bernhardt. "Someone shot him before he could do that."

Bernhardt took another gulp of beer, and now a lone tear did form in his left eye. "Jurgen was all I had left," he said. "My last friend."

"How long had you known him?" Katz asked.

Bernhardt let a small tired sigh escape his lips. "Since Dachau," he said, looking down to the fruit jar clasped in both hands between his legs.

Bolan and Katz exchanged glances, and the Executioner remembered that Schneider had told the Israeli that Cynthia's murder had nothing to do with anything Katz had done personally; rather, it involved Dachau and the Bolshevik revolution. But one thing confused him: Dachau had been a prison camp for Jews. It was rare when prisoners of other nationality were kept there, and even more strange that two Germans—as Schneider and Bernhardt obviously were—would be incarcerated at Dachau.

Katz was thinking the same thing and asked the question. "You and Schneider were both prisoners at Dachau?"

Bernhardt looked up. "No, we worked there."

Bolan leaned forward slightly in his chair. "You and Jurgen Schneider were guards?" he asked.

"Helmut—Jurgen's name was Helmut Kaufman then—was a guard," Bernhardt said. "I was in charge of bookkeeping." He paused. "But I thought you knew that. You said Helmut—"

"I saw the name on the back of a picture at Schneider's apartment," the Executioner explained. "The picture looked like it might be a younger Schneider. It was a wild guess."

"It was correct," Bernhardt said. "Jurgen's real name was Helmut Kaufman. Mine was Werner von Studnitz."

"You changed your names after the war to escape prosecution at Nuremberg," Katz ventured. There was a hard edge to his voice as the words came out.

Dieter Bernhardt bristled slightly. "Hardly," he said. "We changed our names because we wanted to start new lives after the war. We were both tried at Nuremberg and cleared of all offenses. Many former Jewish prisoners testified in our behalf." He took another drink of his beer. "Would you like to hear why?"

"Very much," Katz said, sounding like a man who only half-believed what he was hearing.

Bernhardt continued to stare at his half-empty fruit jar as he began to speak. "Neither Helmut nor I could endure what was happening at Dachau," he said. "So we devised a plan to enable as many Jews to escape as possible. I doctored the books, making it look as if as many prisoners as I dared had been transferred to other camps. Helmut, working closely with one of the prisoners, found ways to get them out of the camp and then out of the country."

"You had an underground railroad working?" Bolan asked.

"Yes," Bernhardt said. "Most of those who escaped were taken into Switzerland by Germans sympathetic to the Jews. Other times they were taken to Russia where Yakov had contacts. In either case—"

"Wait a minute," Katz cut in. "Who did you say had contacts in Russia?"

"Yakov," Bernhardt replied. "The Jewish prisoner who worked closely with Helmut."

"Yakov Yakobovich Katz," the Israeli said.

Bernhardt looked up in surprise. "Why, yes!" he confirmed. "How did you know?" He stared at Katz, squinting through his spectacles. Before Katz could answer, he said, "My God. Yakov, is it you?"

Katz shook his head. "No, but I am his son."

Bernhardt nodded. "Of course. Your father would

be far older, of course. And died at Dachau.'' The old man drained the rest of his ale, then stood slowly and shuffled back to the refrigerator to pour more. ''I saw him die.''

Bolan and Katz waited quietly. The Executioner wondered if alcohol might have been the medicine Bernhardt had used to soften the horrors he had been part of at the death camp.

Katz waited for the old man to resume his seat on the bed, then said, ''You actually saw my father die?''

Bernhardt nodded and took a big gulp of ale.

''If you witnessed the death, you must have played a more direct part in it than just recording it as a bookkeeper,'' Katz said, and Bolan could sense the anger rising in his tone again. ''To actually see him die, you had to have been one of the guards in charge of the gassing.''

Bernhardt stared at Katz blankly. ''I'm sorry, you are confusing me.''

Katz's voice grew even harder as he said, ''Bookkeepers didn't go down to watch the prisoners die in the gas chambers, did they?'' he asked. ''Those were the guards—the men directly responsible for the millions of deaths. You're a liar, Bernhardt. I don't know how you passed yourself off at Nuremberg but—''

Bernhardt frowned and held up a hand. ''Wait,'' he said. ''You believe your father was killed by the poison gas at Dachau?''

Katz sat silent for a moment. "Of course. Are you telling me that's not the case?"

The old man took another drink and shook his head. "Not at all," he said in his tired, shaky voice. "Yakov Yakobovich Katz was murdered. He was stabbed in the exercise yard by another prisoner."

ULRIC ZHDANOV PILED the weapons he had chosen into the cardboard box he'd used to camouflage the rifle case. Leaving Stubrel's apartment, he crossed the lobby and stepped out onto the porch to see an old woman struggling up the steps. Zhdanov recognized her; she was one of the many pensioners who had nothing to do with, nor was even aware of, the terrorist connections at the Kopromed.

Setting the box on the porch, Zhdanov hurried down the steps and helped the woman to the top.

"Thank you," the woman said, out of breath. "You are a fine young man."

Zhdanov smiled at her. In a strange way she reminded him of both Elsie Stubrel and his own mother.

The Russian lifted the box again and hurried down the steps as a cab passed on the street in front of the pension. He walked hurriedly to the BMW, stowing the box in the trunk before sliding behind the wheel. Twisting the key in the ignition, he pulled out onto the street.

A glance at his watch told Zhdanov that the two young terrorists, in whose hands he had left the

Piper Cub, had had more than enough time to service it. That belief was confirmed two miles later when he met the Audi in the oncoming lane and caught a quick glimpse of the familiar faces as they flashed past. For a second he hesitated. They were returning to the Pension Kopromed, which meant the plane was ready and he could leave immediately to visit his mother. But a quick trip to Schneider's apartment would throw him back less than an hour. It would be worth the delay if he could get another shot at the Israeli's friend.

Zhdanov parked near the Deutsches Museum, and stared unhappily at the celebration across the street. The glorified flea market meant he would have to walk a half mile both ways through the crowd of crazed shoppers. The side trip to Schneider's apartment, which he had guessed would delay him only an hour, might well now take two or three.

For a moment Zhdanov considered pulling out of the parking space and heading back to the airport. No, he had come this far. He would see if the two men were at the apartment.

Zhdanov reached under the front seat for the Nagant, then stopped. He was only obliged to kill the Israeli with the ancient Russian revolver, and even then his father had told him to use it only if practical. To use the Nagant would be symbolic, but practicality had to take precedence over symbolism. In any case, it wasn't yet time to kill Katzenelenbogen, and he had a much better weapon for the man's friend—the High Standard .22 pistol with the attached sound suppressor. He made sure the pistol was hidden under his jacket before getting out of the car.

The Russian pushed, shoved, elbowed and cursed his way through the throngs of people until he reached the ageing apartment building Schneider had called home. He had been there once before— just before he had gone to the Cayman Islands. Zhdanov had gone to kill Schneider for what the old man knew, and had he not been half a step behind, he would not have had to go to the Caymans at all.

And the Israeli wouldn't know something was up.

Zhdanov smiled as he walked up the steps to Schneider's apartment. Katzenelenbogen knew only part of what was going on, and perhaps that part would even make the game more interesting.

Stopping in front of the door, Zhdanov pressed his ear to the splintering wood. Inside, he could hear strange muffled noises.

Someone was there. The two men? Maybe.

Zhdanov tried the knob. It held fast. He looked at the lock, which was the simple snap variety. Gripping the knob with both hands, he twisted violently and the lock broke. In one smooth motion he drew the .22 from his belt and shoved the door inward.

The Russian went in low, the pistol held before him at eye level. He needn't have bothered, he saw, as his eyes swept the room.

The Israeli and his friend weren't there. But they had been.

Two nude men lay next to each other on the floor, bound and gagged.

Four eyes stared at him in terror as Zhdanov closed the door behind him and walked over to where the two men lay. Dropping to a squatting position, he chuckled. "Is this a game you two play often, or has someone done this to you?" he asked. He jerked the gag from the face of an obese man.

"Thank God you have come!" the man said.

"Who did this to you?" Zhdanov asked.

The man who was still gagged mumbled. Zhdanov left the cloth around his face in place. "I asked who did this to you," he said again to the fat man.

"I do not know. Two men...they were here when we arrived." He paused to catch his breath. "I am the manager of the building. This man represents the government."

"What did the two men look like?" Zhdanov asked, knowing the answer before he asked.

"Are you with the police?" the manager asked, his eyes shifting to the pistol still in Zhdanov's hand.

"Yes," Zhdanov said. "Now answer my question. What did they look like?"

The fat apartment manager described the two men Zhdanov sought.

"What did they want?" Zhdanov asked. "Why were they here?"

More muffled noises came from the man who still wore the gag.

"Aren't you going to untie us?" the fat man asked.

"Not if you do not start answering my questions without my having to ask them each twice," Zhdanov replied.

"I don't know why they were here or what they wanted," the fat man stated. "Now, please. Untie us!"

"I think not," Zhdanov said. "You make too much noise." He replaced the gag around the man's mouth.

Two sets of smothered complaints came from the floor as Zhdanov rose to his feet and looked around the apartment. There were signs that the place had been searched—a drawer open here, a chair slightly off the indentations it had made in the carpet there.

What had the two men found? Anything? It was impossible to know.

Zhdanov returned to the men on the floor. This time he ungagged the other one. "How long ago did they leave?" he asked.

The man shook his head. "I have no way of knowing. I could not see my watch!"

"Do not shout," Zhdanov said in a low, threatening voice. He jerked the gag from the other man. "How long?" he asked again.

"I do not know, either!" the fat man said. "Untie us!"

"I am a government official!" the smaller man shouted. "I demand...no, I *order* you as an officer of the law to untie us immediately."

Zhdanov looked down at the two nude, helpless men on the floor. He would leave Germany immediately, and the description of him that they gave police would make little difference. Still, there was no point taking a chance.

"Untie us!" the fat man yelled again.

"I will have your badge for this!" the government man threatened.

"I am sorry to tell you I lied," Zhdanov said. "I am not a police officer."

For a moment confusion filled both faces. Then the confusion was replaced by fear. "Then, who are you?" the government man asked.

"Just a man who does not like your noise," Zhdanov said. Slowly and methodically, he lifted the pistol and placed a single .22-caliber round between the government man's eyes.

By the time the shot had coughed through the sound suppressor, the fat man was screaming.

Zhdanov shook his head in mock sorrow. "Your noise will bring others. Then I will have to kill them." He pulled the trigger again, and a small red dot appeared on the fat man's forehead. "If I do, it will be your fault," he said to the corpse.

The apartment manager's eyes rolled back in his head. He didn't answer.

Zhdanov crossed to the front door quickly. What

he had told the fat man hadn't been an idle threat. The two men had been loud, and nosy neighbors weren't something the Russian needed right now.

Cracking open the door, Zhdanov peered out. Directly across the hall he saw an elderly gentleman standing in the doorway, a puzzled look on his face. "Jurgen?" the old man asked.

Zhdanov extended his arm through the opening and pulled the trigger again. His third round was off slightly as the old man chose that moment to step out into the hall.

The elderly head bobbed down slightly as he stepped, and instead of catching the old man between the eyes, Zhdanov's .22-caliber round skimmed across the top of his skull.

It was still enough to knock the man to his back on the floor. Zhdanov stepped out into the hall and moved over him, looking down at the face that was now even more bewildered. The old, cracked lips twisted into a tired smile, and then softly, almost inaudibly, the old man uttered a woman's name.

Zhdanov pulled the trigger again, and the eyes closed. He entered the old man's small apartment and searched the closet and under the bed to make sure there were no other witnesses. The apartment was empty, and he returned to the hall, stepping over the old man's body as he headed for the stairs.

CHAPTER FIVE

Yakov Katzenelenbogen stood up, feeling as if someone had just pulled the rug out from under his feet and slapped him across the face at the same time. All of his life he had known that his father had died at Dachau. That was all he had known, and therefore he had naturally just assumed that he had been gassed along with the thousands of other Jews who had died in the concentration camp. Now it appeared that was not the case.

"Tell me about it," Katz said quietly.

Bernhardt shrugged. "As an accountant, I did not work that closely with the prisoners. I did not know your father as well as Helmut—or Jurgen—did. But I know that he was instrumental to the escape of dozens of men and women, and that Jurgen thought highly of him." Bernhardt paused for another drink of ale. "But let me backtrack a moment, if I might. As I said, neither Jurgen nor I could abide what was happening at Dachau. You must realize that when we, like so many other young men, joined the Nazi Party and the army we never dreamed that such atrocities could ever happen. Not in Germany, at least. Not in our country.''

Bolan nodded. ''It can happen anywhere. As the saying goes, all it takes is for good men to do nothing.''

''Yes,'' Bernhardt agreed after another gulp of ale. ''And these outrages do not happen overnight. It is like boiling the frog.''

Katz felt a puzzled look creep over his face.

Bolan was familiar with the proverb. ''Throw a frog in a pot of boiling water, and he will immediately jump back out,'' he said. ''But put him in when the water is room temperature, then heat it slow enough, and he'll boil before he realizes what's going on.''

''Precisely!'' Bernhardt exclaimed. ''That is exactly what happened. Little by little, Hitler escalated his abominations, killing Jews, then Gypsies, anyone he felt contaminated the master race.'' He drank again. ''But I am telling you nothing you do not already know.''

Katz sat back down. ''Tell me more about how my father died.''

''As I have already said, he was helping Jurgen. Together they would arrange work details so that certain prisoners were always at the back of the crew, or out of sight in one way or another. Remember that what you see regularly is what you miss when it is gone. When Jurgen and your father felt that the guards had grown accustomed to the absence of certain faces, Jurgen would arrange for them to escape. Sometimes they would hide under the trash in garbage trucks. Sometimes in other vehicles leaving the camp. Sometimes they escaped in other ways—whatever opportunities presented themselves were taken advantage of. For a while we even had a tunnel." He paused to drink again. "Jurgen would tell me who was leaving, and I would falsify papers that verified a legitimate transfer to some other prison. Just in case one of the guards noticed."

"Why didn't my father go?" Katz asked.

"Many times Jurgen and I urged him to do so," he said. "'You have done your part, Yakov, now *go*,' we said. But he always refused, preferring to remain and help others escape. And perhaps it is best that he did."

"Why?" Katz asked.

"He would surely have been missed," Bernhardt explained. "All of the guards knew him. You see, they were afraid of him."

"Why?" Katz asked. "Under the circumstances, how could they possibly have feared him?"

Bernhardt stood and wobbled to the refrigerator. He held up the empty bottle of ale, then dropped it into the trash next to the refrigerator and pulled out another. "May I get either of you another drink?" he asked over his shoulder.

Both men declined.

When he had uncorked the ale, Bernhardt returned to his seat on the bed. "Your father scared them because he had no fear of death. He knew he was going to die—there was nothing he could do to change that. And with that knowledge came a courage the likes of which I have never seen before or since." The old man took a big gulp of ale, then continued. "Often Yakov would cause trouble just to divert attention from the other prisoners. Or to distract the guards from the fact that a few more faces had disappeared during the night."

"So they killed him?" Katz asked.

"No, no. Your father was a true artist. He knew exactly, instinctively, just how far he could push without crossing over the line where they *would* have killed him. Each time his foot slipped over that line, he jerked it back a half second before they cut it off."

Katz felt a surge of pride flow through his chest. He looked into the ancient, wrinkled eyes, now watering with the effects of the ale. A few moments earlier, when he had suspected that Dieter Bernhardt was lying about the part he'd played at Dachau, he had been ready to lean forward and strangle the old man. Not just for his father, but in retaliation for what had happened to millions of his people in camps like Dachau.

Now Katz saw the pain in the man's face. For half a century the man had lived with the horrors he'd not only seen, but been forced to take part in, and no amount of ale would ever erase those nightmares.

Katz watched as tears began to flow down the old man's cheeks. "I am sorry," he whispered. "God in heaven, help me, I am so sorry." He closed his eyes, and his chest began to jerk.

Katz leaned forward and took the old man's hand. "You did what you could," he said. "You risked your own life."

"So many died..." Bernhardt sobbed. "So many..."

"But some lived," Katz said. "Some lived because you risked your own life to help them." He paused. "I am proud to know you, Dieter Bernhardt. I wish I could have told Jurgen Schneider—Helmut Kaufman—the same thing."

Bernhardt opened his eyes and started to take another drink. He looked at the glass, then set it on the floor in front of him.

"You have not yet told me how my father died," Katz prompted.

Bernhardt looked up. "One day a truck transporting Soviet prisoners arrived at Dachau," he said.

"Russian Jews?" Katz asked.

"No, they were military prisoners," Bernhardt replied. "Soviet soldiers. The truck was experiencing engine trouble, and the prisoners were temporarily detained at Dachau en route to another site. Your father and another man seemed to know each other, and at first it looked as if there might be some trouble between them. Then they appeared to become friendly." He looked down at his ale but left it where it was on the floor. "Then one day I left my office, and as I was walking across the yard I heard a commotion. A large group of the Soviets were huddled together, and when they dispersed, your father lay on the ground, a knife in his heart."

"Who did it?" Katz demanded.

"I do not know," Bernhardt said. "And Jurgen did not see it happen, either."

"Was there any kind of investigation?" Katz asked, knowing the answer without being told.

"No," Bernhardt said. "In the words of the commandant, 'It was just another Jew.'"

"You have no idea who killed my father?" he asked again.

"My guess is that it was the man I spoke of. Gregor something. I am sorry, my mind is not what it once was. I do not remember his last name."

"Dieter," Katz said, "twenty years ago someone murdered my wife. Now it looks like they're trying to kill me, and it's tied into all this somehow. Do you have any idea how?"

The old man shook his head.

"Is there anything else you can tell me? Anything at all that might help?"

The old man shook his head. "Not that I can think of," he said. "I am sorry."

Katz stood and shook the old man's hand. "Dieter, I thank you."

As Katz followed Bolan out the door, he saw the old man reaching for the ale glass on the floor.

THE EXECUTIONER FLAGGED a passing cab and directed the driver to Bahnhofs Platz, giving the man an address a block beyond the one on Jurgen Schneider's yellow sticker. Arriving in a cab would draw attention, and if remnants of the old Baader-Meinhof Gang indeed resided at the address, attention was the last thing they needed.

The Pension Kopromed stood directly across from the train station, and Bolan and Katz watched through the windows as they drove past a sign announcing it. An elderly woman was making her way painfully up the concrete steps to the pension. As the cab passed, a middle-aged man with a dark flat-top haircut and carrying a large cardboard box came out of the front door. He set down the box long enough to help the woman the rest of the way up the steps.

Bolan and Katz got out a block later and paid the driver. "Anything unusual you saw?" the Executioner asked as they started back down the street.

Katz shook his head. "Looked like any other pension from where I sat."

"Yeah," Bolan agreed as they walked along the railroad station, "but I've got a feeling there's more to it than that." He paused. "There wasn't a room number with the address," he said.

"No," Katz agreed. "Strange."

They reached the Kopromed a few seconds later and climbed the steps. Both the old woman and the younger man had gone on about their business somewhere, and the porch and foyer were deserted. Bolan led the way through a maze of hanging plants to the desk and rang the bell.

The sound rang shrilly in the oddly decorated antechamber.

When no one answered the bell, Bolan leaned forward and rang it again. This time when there was no answer, he turned to Katz.

The Israeli glanced at the door behind the desk and nodded.

Bolan let his hand inch closer to the Beretta in the shoulder rig as he pushed through the half door to the area behind the desk. The door in the far wall was unlocked, and he drew the weapon as he shoved it open.

The man on the couch had seen better days. But for better or worse, he'd seen all the days he was going to see.

"Damn," Katz said as the Israeli closed the door to the foyer.

Bolan looked down at what was left of the man on the couch. The entire upper right quarter of his head had blown away with the bullet one had to assume came from the Mauser SP-66 sniper rifle lying on the floor next to him. Though it would have been difficult to achieve, the man might have committed suicide.

The Executioner dropped to one knee and reached down, lifting first the right, and then the left hand of the corpse on the couch. Carefully he studied the thumbs, forefingers and the web of the hands for marks. He found none. Nor were there any blood splatters or tissue fragments on the man's hands.

Katz had been following the Executioner's movements. "This guy didn't kill himself," the Israeli said.

"No," Bolan replied, rising back to his feet, "he didn't." He surveyed the living room. "Let's take a look around."

The two split up as they had done at Jurgen Schneider's, each following his own instincts as to where to search. Bolan walked through the kitchen into a small sleeping area that was even grubbier than the front room.

Like the rest of the house, it appeared that the occupant was trying to carpet the floor with trash. Wine and beer bottles, cans, empty cigarette packages and overturned ashtrays left only patches of the colorless carpet visible.

The Executioner had started toward a splintering chest of drawers when he saw the closet door ajar. Instinct led him that way, and he opened it to see the gaping holes in the wallboard just inside.

Bolan stepped into the closet, the Beretta leading the way. But there was no need—whoever had killed the man on the couch had already taken what he wanted and left. The Executioner saw the false wall lying against a shoe rack. He holstered the pistol and stuck his head through the hole.

Inside, he saw a large room. As his eyes adjusted to the dimmer light, he saw Argentinean Halcon, Australian Austen and British Sterling submachine guns hanging from hooks on one wall. Mixed in with them were Heckler & Koch, Colt and Kalashnikov automatic rifles. Pulling a penlight flash from his pocket, he stepped into the hidden armory and shone it on a stack of see-through plastic storage boxes against an adjacent wall. Pistols of every make and model were visible inside.

Bolan moved the beam to the ammunition crates across from the pistols, then turned to the areas on both sides of the opening. The contents of those crates had been noted with a red marking pen, and according to the words, in German, the boxes contained Belgian Trialene, Soviet SZ-3 demolition charges, FAMAE 78-F7 hand grenades.

Hurried footsteps sounded behind the Executioner, and he whirled, the Beretta leaping into his hand once again.

"We've got company," Katz whispered. "Somebody just stuck a key in the door."

Bolan turned back to the wall of rifles and subguns, lifting a Sterling from its hook and opening the bolt. The weapon was loaded and chambered, and he handed it to Katz. The next Sterling proved loaded, as well, and the Executioner took it for himself.

"So let's give them a warm reception," Bolan said as he led the way out of the closet. He crept back through the bedroom with Katz at his heels, entered the kitchen and turned toward the living room.

The two men just inside the door both wore blue jeans and unbuttoned OD army fatigue jackets. More prominent than their clothes were the expressions of shock on their faces as they stared down at the corpse on the couch.

"Damn!" the taller of the two men said. "Has the old drunk killed himself?" Just then he saw Bolan appear and looked up.

Both men were in their early twenties, but they had been well trained. They went for the pistols in their waistbands with the speed that came with smooth precision, and a smooth precision that only came with hour upon hour of practice. They were fast, but not fast enough.

Katz had stepped out to the Executioner's side. Both soldiers raised their Sterlings as if the movement were part of some well-choreographed and rehearsed ballet. The subguns began to stutter as 9 mm rounds chugged from the barrels, riddling the two terrorists who were less than ten feet away.

The men in the fatigue jackets looked like marionettes at the mercy of some crazed puppet master as they jerked and danced with each round. The assault lasted less than two seconds, and then the men collapsed to the floor.

Bolan and Katz walked quickly forward and knelt by the men. One of them—about twenty-five with a wispy red goatee and thin mustache—was still breathing. But his breaths came in short painful pants. He stared up at the ceiling, and the Executioner could see that he didn't have long.

"Who are you?" Bolan asked.

"Hans..."

"Who are you with?" the Executioner asked. "What group?"

The man didn't answer. But tears began to form in his eyes. "Am I dying?" he whispered.

"Yes," Bolan said. "You are. This is your last chance at a clear conscience. Now tell me who you're with."

"RAF."

Bolan wasn't surprised. "Who killed the man on the couch?"

The young terrorist shrugged, and the movement brought a grimace of pain. "Ulric," he said. "It must...have been Ulric."

"Ulric who?"

Hans took a long deep breath. His eyes clouded over, and Bolan could see he was about to go. "Ulric...Zhdanov..."

"Is he the man who tried to kill us in France?"

"He just returned...from France." The man's breaths became shorter and faster, then suddenly slowed again. Bolan knew he had only seconds.

"Why does he want to kill us?" the Executioner asked.

The man didn't respond.

Bolan reached out and squeezed the young man's shoulder. "Hans," he said again, "why does Ulric Zhdanov want to kill us?"

"I...do not know. He is deranged, possessed by something.... It has something to do...with his father...." Hans closed his eyes.

Bolan took Hans's wrist and checked the pulse. It was barely perceptible. "Where is Ulric now?" he asked.

The young terrorist didn't answer.

Bolan shook Hans again, then peeled open the man's eyelids. Leaning in close to his ear, he said, "Hans, where has Ulric gone?"

"I...do not...know. We serviced his plane...."

"Where?" Bolan asked. He knew he had only seconds now. "Where was the plane serviced? Where has he gone?"

"Perhaps...to visit his mother...."

"His mother? Where?"

"Russia."

Katz had remained silent throughout the deathbed interview, but now he reached forward and grabbed Hans by both shoulders. "Was it Ulric who killed my wife?" he demanded.

Hans took another deep breath and let it out.

"Tell me!" Katz yelled, shaking the man again.

"Did Ulric Zhdanov kill Cynthia Katzenelenbogen?"

Hans lay perfectly still.

"He's gone, Yakov."

The Israeli let out a deep breath and shook his head in frustration.

Bolan stood. "We'll find him," he promised. "We'll find this Ulric Zhdanov, whoever he is. And if it wasn't him who killed Cynthia, he'll know who did."

The Executioner paused. "And when we find him, Katz," he said, "there will be a reckoning. You have my word on that."

Russia

ULRIC ZHDANOV CAUGHT a cab at the airport and gave the driver the address of the retirement village. He settled back as the taxi pulled away and the snow began to drift down through the foggy St. Petersburg night. He watched the white flakes fall during the forty-minute drive into the city that had been called Leningrad when he had been a child, and reflected on all he had missed during his twenty years away.

By the time the cab reached the inner city, a heavy blanket of white lay on the ground. Zhdanov smiled as they began to pass the brightly painted buildings that were such a rare mixture of Western European and Russian architecture. The radiant colors would have looked ostentatious anywhere else in the world. But under the northern light that fell over St. Petersburg, and reflected off the snow-covered ground, they were truly beautiful and reminded him of how long he had been gone.

The driver guided the cab onto Nab Sinopskaya, and they began following the Neva River. They passed the Alexander Nevsky Monastery, then the Smolny Convent before winding back west. The taxi slowed, turned off the major street and began winding its way through a light-commercial section of the city.

They emerged into a district of multifamily housing, and Zhdanov got his first glimpse of where his mother had lived for the past four years. The Boris Yeltsin Retirement Village consisted of five separate areas. The first was a long row of apartment buildings for retired couples. Each apartment featured emergency switches in every room in case the occupants encountered illness or injury. The second row of apartments was for single men and women, and many former occupants of the couples apartments moved there when their partners died. On the other side of the singles flats stood a nursing home, and just beyond that a hospital. The fifth section of the village stood on the other side of the street—a cemetery.

The Yeltsin Retirement Village was patterned after similar installations in America, Zhdanov had been told. He stared at the various components as they passed. Old people started at one end of the complex and ended life at the other, he noted, and the idea struck him as both a joke and a tragedy.

The cab stopped in front of the hospital. Zhdanov handed several bills over the seat to the driver and got out, pulling the muffler tighter around his neck. On his head he wore a traditional Russian rabbit hat, the earflaps down over his ears and neck as he hurried through the slush on the sidewalk and up the steps.

Zhdanov removed the hat as soon as he'd entered the hospital, running his fingers through his hair. He scanned the lobby, seeing a sign that read Information, and hurried over to the old woman who sat behind the desk.

"Natalia Zhdanov," he said. "I need her room number, please."

"One moment," the woman replied, and began to twirl a circular card file on the desktop. She finally stopped on one of the cards, frowned and looked up. "Are you a family member?" she asked.

"I am her son."

"Mrs. Zhdanov has been moved to the intensive-care unit as of this morning. First hall to the left, then take a right. You will see the sign."

Zhdanov pivoted on the balls of his feet and hurried down the hall. He entered a door into the ICU waiting room and started toward a pair of gray swing doors set in the far wall.

An attractive, dark-complected young woman wearing a white uniform came through the doors as he approached, forcing him to take a step back. Both of them stopped in surprise.

"May I help you?" the nurse finally asked.

"I am here to see my mother," Zhdanov said. "Natalia Zhdanov."

The nurse shook her head, and her coal black hair whipped around her face. "The priest is with her now."

"What?"

"Earlier this evening she called for a priest. He has come to visit her."

Zhdanov started to step around the nurse, but she moved to block his path. "ICU visiting times are for ten minutes only on odd-numbered hours. You will have to wait."

Zhdanov smiled his most charming smile. "Please," he said. "My plane was late in arriving. And business forces me to leave again soon. Couldn't I just see her for a moment? If the priest is here, it might well be my last chance." He forced an exaggerated expression of agony and remorse onto his face.

The nurse relinquished. "I suppose so. Wait for the priest to leave, and don't let the head nurse know I gave you my permission. As far as I am concerned, I have not seen you."

"You have my word," Zhdanov promised.

The nurse headed down the hall. Zhdanov took a seat on the couch in the waiting room. If his mother had called for a priest, it meant the time was near.

Ukrainian by birth, Ulric had never been as close to his mother as he had to his father. Perhaps that was because she didn't share her husband's and son's passion for the mission that Ulric was finally about to complete after a twenty-year diversion. But Ulric loved his mother nonetheless, and her passing would sadden him.

Five minutes later a man wearing the traditional garb of a Uniate Church of the Ukraine priest came out the gray doors. He paid no attention to Zhdanov as he hurried away down the hall.

Zhdanov rose from the couch and pushed through the swing doors, moving quietly by the partitions that separated the beds. Labored breathing came from behind several of the white curtains, and the smell of disinfectant, old age and death itself threatened to overcome him.

Zhdanov found his mother in the third bed to the right of the door. Natalia Zhdanov lay on her back, tubes running in and out of her body. Her chest heaved as she struggled for life. Her eyes were closed in sleep.

Moving silently, Zhdanov opened the drawer in the nightstand next to the bed and found a phone book, notepad and several pencils. He flipped through the pages of the directory until he found the number he wanted, then wrote it on the top page of the notepad beneath two numbers his mother had evidently called. Setting the pencil and notepad on the nightstand next to the telephone, Zhdanov dialed the number.

He had just completed his call, torn off the page with the phone numbers on it and dropped it in the trash when his mother's eyes opened.

"Mother," Zhdanov said as he set the receiver back in the cradle and took her hand.

The old woman looked up and smiled. "My son. Is it really you?"

Zhdanov nodded.

"What took you so long to arrive?" she asked.

"I am sorry, Mother," Zhdanov said. "I did not know you had become so ill. When I left two weeks ago, you were fine."

Natalia shook her head. "I was dying," she said. "You knew that."

Zhdanov felt the guilt creep over him, and along with it came the anger he always experienced along with the shame. "Mother, I—"

"The priest just left."

"Yes, I saw him."

"You have been away from me for twenty years," Natalia said. "Is it too much to ask that you spend my last hours with me?"

"I am sorry. I had business. You know that."

A new fire came into Natalia Zhdanov's eyes. "It must stop! This killing must stop!"

"Mother," Zhdanov soothed, "please do not excite yourself." He hesitated, then said, "I must keep my vow to Father."

"Do you love me, Ulric?"

"Of course, Mother," Zhdanov said.

"Then stay with me. Do not allow me to die alone. Abandon this senseless vendetta of your father's."

"I cannot," Zhdanov said.

"Those you plan to kill had nothing to do with what happened so many years ago," Natalia whispered. "One of them was only a child. The other had not yet been born."

"But it was my father's wish," Zhdanov protested. "And I gave my word."

"It was not fair of him to ask such a thing," Natalia said. "You are not bound to it."

"I am."

"I ask you something now, Ulric," the old woman said. "I ask you to stay with me until I die. It will not be long now."

"Mother, I cannot. The Israeli was difficult to locate. If I lose track of him now, I may not find him again."

A new sadness came over the woman's face. "So you would allow me to die alone while you keep your promise to your father?"

"I must," Zhdanov said.

"We all love and we all hate," she whispered to her son. "It is only human." She stopped speaking suddenly, coughing, her eyes bulging and her back rising off the bed with the effort.

"Mother..." Zhdanov leaned forward.

The coughing stopped, and the old woman fell back again. "Ulric, if you leave, it means your hatred is stronger than your love," she said in a weak voice. "That is evil."

"I must go now, Mother."

The old woman stared at him but didn't answer.

Zhdanov placed his mother's hand on the bed, turned and walked out of the ICU unit. He hurried back through the lobby, nodding at the woman behind the information desk before leaving the hospital through the same front entrance he'd come in.

He was halfway down the steps when he saw them coming down the sidewalk.

Zhdanov turned his head quickly to the side and walked calmly down the steps, turning onto the sidewalk away from the pair. As the snow fell on his shoulders, the fingers of his right hand unbuttoned his overcoat and snaked inside, resting on the butt of the .22-caliber pistol.

Zhdanov crossed the street toward the cemetery and cast a quick glance over his shoulder. He saw them going up the steps to the hospital. Confident they weren't watching, he continued on, stepping over a short hedge that circled the cemetery and ducking behind a four-foot granite grave memorial.

He drew the pistol and smiled. Somehow they had learned who he was and come looking for him at his mother's. How they had obtained that information he didn't know, but it didn't matter. It would even make the game more interesting.

Zhdanov knew that fate had given him another chance to get the Israeli's friend, and he would take advantage of it. Hidden behind the monument, he would wait until they came back out of the hospital and put a silenced bullet into the head of the big man. He would then escape across the cemetery before Katzenelenbogen had time to figure out what had happened.

He pulled the muffler tighter around his throat and settled in to wait. And as he waited, two things became abundantly clear to him.

First he knew he had seen his mother for the last time. She would be dead by the time he could return.

And second Natalia Zhdanov was right.

Ulric Zhdanov had a far greater capacity for hatred than he had for love.

CHAPTER SIX

In the seat directly behind the Executioner, Yakov Katzenelenbogen had sat silently contemplating things during the flight from Munich to Moscow. Now, as Jack Grimaldi dropped the Beechcraft through the sky toward the airport, the Israeli spoke up. "We better get back on the horn to the Farm and find out what they've done," he said. "We need to know what kind of reception we'll be facing below."

Before Bolan could answer, the radio on the control panel in front of him suddenly came to life.

"Stony Man Base to Stony One." It was the voice of Barbara Price. "Come in, Stony One."

Bolan reached forward and lifted the microphone from the clip, first checking the red light that signified that the radio scrambler was on. They were about to enter Russia illegally, and the last thing he wanted was for Russian intelligence to intercept the satellite-relayed conversation. "Stony One here," he said, satisfied that the light was blinking. "Go ahead, Barb."

"What's your location, Striker?"

"Descending right now."

"In reference to your request," Price said, "we just received word back from the White House. The President has paved the way for you. Russian customs officials believe you're Justice Department agents on your way to the new DEA office in Moscow." She paused. "You shouldn't have any trouble."

"Affirmative. What has Aaron found out?"

"Hold on."

Bolan heard a series of clicks over the airwaves, followed by several short staccato bursts of static. Then Aaron Kurtzman came on the air. "You there, big guy?" Kurtzman asked.

"Roger," Bolan said. "You get anything on Zhdanov?"

"Oh, yeah. Took me a while, but I finally hacked into both the Russian and German networks. You ready?"

"Shoot."

"Ulric Gregor Zhdanov," Kurtzman said. "Born January 15, 1950, in Leningrad. Escaped the Soviet Union in August 1972, and wasn't heard of again until January 1975 when he was arrested with three other men in Munich on murder charges."

"Who'd they kill?" Bolan asked.

"A German diplomat by the name of Feodor Shatz," Kurtzman replied. "The three men arrested with Zhdanov were all known by the German police to be Baader-Meinhof members.''

There it was again, the connection between Baader-Meinhof and Red Army Faction. ''Was Zhdanov part of the group?'' Bolan asked.

''Suspected of being. No proof. But he was sentenced to life imprisonment with the others anyway. That's where he's been for the past couple of decades.''

''What's he doing out now if he got life?'' Bolan asked. Before Kurtzman could answer, he added, ''Never mind. Germany has its share of knee-jerk bleeding-heart parole-board members, too, right?''

''You hit the nail on the head with a big hammer there, Striker,'' Kurtzman said.

Next to Bolan, Grimaldi turned and said, ''We'll be on the ground in less than a minute, Sarge. Unless you want the whole Russian army listening to all this, you'd better bring it to a close.''

Bolan had kept the mike keyed as Grimaldi spoke, and Kurtzman heard. ''Okay, I copied,'' the Farm's computer man said. ''Clear customs and then get back in the air for St. Petersburg.''

''You got a line on Zhdanov's mother?'' Bolan asked as the wheels touched down.

''According to the German prison files, she was last living at the Boris Yeltsin Retirement Village on the river.'' Kurtzman read off an address and apartment number.

The plane taxied to a halt on the runway. Through

the window the Executioner saw two Russian customs men in green uniforms walking toward them. "Okay, Aaron," he said. "We'll get back to you. One clear."

"Base clear."

Bolan replaced the mike and opened his door as the customs men arrived at the plane. The larger of the two smiled, showing a mouth full of silver-and-gold bridgework. "Passports and U.S. Department of Justice credentials, please," he said in heavily accented English.

The Executioner removed the appropriate identification from the storage compartment in front of him and handed the documents out of the plane.

The customs man scanned them briefly, then stamped the passports and handed them back. "You stay in Moscow?" he asked.

Bolan shook his head. "No," he said. "We go on to St. Petersburg. Do we need any other papers?"

The customs man shook his head. "No! No!" he said. "No more Soviet Union. America and Russia, big friends now. No travel pass necessary." He closed the door of the plane and stepped back, waving.

Bolan lifted the microphone and requested permission for takeoff in Russian. A few minutes later they were back in the air.

The flight to St. Petersburg took a little over an hour. A light snow had begun to fall by the time they touched down and rolled to a halt.

The Executioner glanced at the Beechcraft as he prepared to deplane. They had been using the nondescript aircraft in order to keep a low profile, but he had a feeling things were about to heat up. If they did, speed would be more important than anonymity. "Jack," he said as he opened the door, "get back on the horn to Stony Man and make arrangements to get us a faster fly, will you? This Beechcraft is like holding on to the tail of a pregnant duck."

The Stony Man pilot frowned. "Charlie," he said, referring to the Farm's number-two pilot, "stashed a Learjet near Helsinki last month. I can be across the gulf and back in two shakes."

The Executioner nodded. "Do it," he said, and got out.

Bolan and Katz showed another Russian official their stamped passports, and a few minutes after that they were in the back seat of yet another cab, heading along the Neva River toward the Boris Yeltsin Retirement Village.

"Your first time St. Petersburg?" the driver asked.

"No," Bolan said.

"Oh, you here before?"

When Bolan didn't answer, the man shrugged and gave up his attempt at small talk. They rode in silence.

It was Katz who broke the silence a few blocks later. "January 1975," he said in a low voice.

Bolan turned toward him. "What about it?"

"That's when Zhdanov was arrested," the Israeli said, staring straight ahead.

"And?"

"That's roughly a month after Cynthia was killed," Katz said. Now he turned toward the Executioner. "That means he could have been the one who killed her."

"It means he could have, Katz. It doesn't mean he did."

"But he did," Katz insisted. "I know it. I feel it. Right here." The Israeli thumped his chest with his left fist. "It's almost like Cynthia is calling out from the grave to tell me."

Bolan didn't answer. He didn't particularly believe in such things, and he knew Katz didn't, either. On the other hand, both soldiers had seen too many unexplainable things happen over the years to completely discount such possibilities. And the Executioner was getting the same funny feeling that it was this Ulric Zhdanov behind Cynthia Katzenelenbogen's death. He doubted it was Cynthia's ghost speaking to either of them—more than likely something had registered in both his and Katz's subconscious minds that led them to believe it was true.

The snow began to fall harder as they neared the retirement village. The driver spoke again. "Which part of the Yeltsin Village?"

"Building 2," Bolan directed.

"That's in the single-person section," the driver

replied. He pulled through the iron gate surrounding the village and up to a row of apartment buildings.

Bolan paid the man, then he and Katz walked down the sidewalk abreast to the second building, turned and entered a common hallway. Kurtzman had told them that apartment 23 on the second floor belonged to Natalia Zhdanov. They found the elevators, and Katz leaned forward, punching the Up button.

The elevator had been designed for people who were no longer in any hurry and quite possibly walking with canes, crutches or riding in wheelchairs. It was slow in coming. The doors were even slower in opening, and took what seemed like five minutes to close.

Like the other apartments, 23 was marked with large numerals. Bolan reached inside his jacket, his fingers wrapping around the butt of the leathered Beretta. He had no idea whether Ulric Zhdanov was inside, but if the Russian wasn't there, the Executioner didn't want to give the man's mother a heart attack by shoving a gun in her face.

With his free hand Bolan knocked on the door. When he got no response, he knocked again, louder. A minute later he looked down at the dead-bolt lock and pulled a set of picks from his jacket. The lock was good, and it took two minutes to get in.

The musty smell of the apartment reminded the Executioner of Jurgen Schneider's tiny room in Munich.

"Mrs. Zhdanov?" he called out as they entered.

No one answered.

The two men took a quick look around. A thin layer of dust covered the furniture, and when Bolan opened the refrigerator door he found that most of the food inside had molded.

"She hasn't been here for a while," Katz said. "But the guy back at the pension said Zhdanov had gone to visit his mother."

"He said 'perhaps,'" Bolan reminded the Israeli. He frowned. "Why would Zhdanov drop whatever mission he's on and come home to visit his mother?"

Katz frowned, then realization spread across his face. "The woman's old or she wouldn't be here."

Without further words the two men hurried out of the apartment, locking the door behind them. They passed the elevator this time, found the stairs and hurried down two at a time.

On the sidewalk once again, Katz said, "Do we try the nursing home first?"

Bolan shook his head. "My guess is that if she'd moved there they'd have cleaned out her apartment. I'd say she skipped that stage and went straight to the hospital." They walked swiftly past the nursing home and turned down another sidewalk that led to the hospital. In the distance they saw a man in a black muffler and rabbit-fur hat hurry out the front door, descend the steps and turn down the sidewalk away from them.

A vague, uneasy feeling came over the Executioner as he and Katz mounted the steps to the hospital's front entrance. He couldn't put a finger on it, but something was bothering him.

Inside, Bolan led the way to the information desk. The woman seated there smiled up at him. *"Da?"* she said.

"Natalia Zhdanov," Bolan said politely in Russian. "May I have her room number, please?"

"She's been moved to intensive care," the woman said without looking at the register in front of her. "Only family is allowed to visit. Are you family?"

Bolan nodded. "Yes," he said, continuing to speak in his best Russian. "I am her son." He glanced at Katz. "This is my uncle."

The woman smiled and gave the Executioner directions to ICU. He and Katz had started down the hall when they heard her speak again.

"None of you look alike, you know," the old woman said pleasantly.

Bolan stopped and turned. "Pardon me?"

"You, your uncle, your brother," the woman said. "None of you look alike."

The Executioner walked back to the desk. "My brother was here?" he asked.

"Why, yes," the woman said. "He went in a few minutes ago."

"Is he still here?" the Executioner asked.

The woman shrugged. "I didn't see him come out, but I was indisposed for a few minutes."

Bolan forced a smile. "Well, I'll go see." He led the way around a corner. Glancing quickly up and down the hall to make sure no one was watching, he started to reach into his coat for the Beretta, then hesitated. There was a good chance that he and Katz were about to come face-to-face with Zhdanov, but the crowded confines of the ICU was no place to risk a stray shot.

Drawing the Applegate-Fairbairn fighting knife, the Executioner hid it discreetly behind his wrist in a contoured ice-pick grip. Out of the corner of his eye, he saw Katz palm a blade, as well.

The nurse who came out of the swing doors as they approached carried a transparent plastic trash bag filled with trash. "Visiting time does not begin again for another thirty minutes," she said.

Bolan smiled as he moved his knife hand farther behind his back. "I'm on a tight schedule and came to see my mother," he said. "Couldn't you make an exception?"

"Mrs. Zhdanov?" the nurse asked.

Bolan frowned. "Why, yes. How did you know?"

"Because I've already heard that line once tonight," the nurse said with a smile. "You Zhdanov boys are smooth talkers." She looked him in the eye. "And not half-bad-looking, either." She paused and shook her head. "Oh, go on in."

The Executioner hesitated briefly at the swing

doors, then pushed through, his knife ready to spring into action. A quick scan of the room told him it wouldn't be necessary. The only occupants were in the beds.

Bolan shoved the knife back into his belt sheath. He moved to his left, making his way along the line of patients, looking at the names on the charts that hung from the foot of each bed.

"Mack," he heard Katz whisper, and turned.

The Israeli stood at the foot of a bed that held an elderly woman with tubes running in and out of her body. Next to the bed was a nightstand that held a telephone, a pencil and a notepad.

Bolan took up a position on one side of the bed with Katz on the other. Though her eyes were closed and she appeared to be asleep, the woman's breathing was labored, her chest heaving with each effort. The Executioner had started to place a hand on her shoulder when her eyelids rose. She looked first at Bolan, then Katz.

"You have come looking for Ulric," she said. Her voice was filled with certainty, the words a statement of fact rather than a question.

The Executioner nodded. "Do you know where he is?"

The old woman shook her head. "He has left. Where he is going, I do not know." She turned back to Katz. "You are the Jew," she said, with the same tone of confidence.

"I am Jewish, yes," Katz said.

"It was your wife who Ulric killed, then," the woman said.

Katz leaned in closer. "Yes, but why? Was he trying to get to me? What had I done to him?"

The woman broke into a coughing fit. When she had finished, she whispered, "It was not anything you did. It was…what your father did."

"What?" Katz said, leaning in even closer now. "What did my father do?"

The color in the woman's face was fading fast. Her voice grew suddenly weaker. "Your father," she croaked in a low guttural tone. "Yakov Yakobovich Katz…"

"Yes, he was my father. What did he do?"

The old woman gasped for air, then said, "After the revolution…when the Mensheviks were on the run from the Bolsheviks, he murdered my husband's first wife and firstborn son." As if driven suddenly by another force, she now rose to a sitting position and grasped Katz's hands. "So Gregor killed your father," she gasped. "And he poisoned Ulric's mind from the day he was born." A choking sound escaped her lips, and the woman began to cough again. "He killed your wife, and he plans to kill you. But the killing must stop!"

Katz gripped her tightly by the hands. "Where has he gone?"

Natalia Zhdanov started to speak again, but another series of choking sounds cut her off. Her eyes widened, then relaxed. A smile of peace replaced the pain on her face as she fell back on the bed.

She died still holding Yakov Katzenelenbogen's hands.

Bolan watched as Katz gently placed the old woman's hands on the bed at her sides. The Israeli muttered a few words in Hebrew that the Executioner took to be a prayer, then looked up. "I don't believe it," he said. "My father was a Menshevik. I don't doubt that he killed his share of Bolsheviks after the revolution when the Communists were trying to wipe out all of the moderate socialists. But he never murdered anyone. Particularly not some child or woman."

The Executioner nodded.

"If he killed these people, he had good reason," Katz went on.

Bolan didn't answer. For a moment, as he contemplated the situation, he felt far older than the seasoned warrior who stood facing him. The simple fact of the matter was that Katz had never known his father very well, that the Israeli's impression of the man came primarily from stories told to him by family and friends. When Katz said his father could never have murdered anyone, he was picturing a personality that came secondhand from those stories. Human nature dictated that dead loved ones be eulogized, sometimes to the point of sainthood. Such glorified memories were rarely founded in fact.

The truth of the matter was, Bolan knew, neither

he nor Katz had known Yakov Yakobovich Katz. The man might have been capable of murder. All families had their black sheep and skeletons in the closet. Katz's father might have been one.

Yet the Executioner's gut-level instinct told him that was not the truth, that the blood that flowed through the veins of the honorable Israeli who now stood before him had come from his father, and that the elder Katz, too, had been an honorable warrior.

"Where has he gone?" Katz asked, thinking out loud.

Bolan walked to the nightstand next to the bed, glancing down at the telephone, pencil and notepad. The top page of paper was blank, but he could see the indentations that had pressed through from the preceding page. The Executioner looked down at the empty trash can next to the stand, then remembered that the nurse had been collecting the garbage when they'd arrived.

Lifting one of the pencils, Bolan held it at an angle and began lightly rubbing the lead across the top page of the pad. A few moments later three numbers appeared in white below the brownish gray lead. The first two had been written in the jittery handwriting of an elderly person. The third number had been written with a steadier hand.

Bolan lifted the telephone and handed it to Katz. "Your Russian accent is better," he said. He tapped in the first number and waited.

Katz frowned, said, "Sorry, I have gotten the

wrong number," and hung up. He looked at the Executioner. "The Uniate Church of the Ukraine," he said. "The woman knew she was dying. She must have called for a priest to administer the last rites."

Bolan nodded as he tapped in the digits of the second number.

Katz held the receiver to his ear for perhaps a minute, then replaced it again. "No answer," he said.

The Executioner dialed the last phone number and handed the receiver to Katz. He watched the stern concentration on the Israeli's face as he said, "My name is Ulric Zhdanov. I have lost my ticket and cannot remember which flight I'm booked on." There was a pause, then Katz said, "Yes, thank you, I'll hold." He held the receiver away from his mouth and whispered, "Lufthansa Airlines. Zhdanov is going somewhere. They're checking their computer for me now."

"Let's see if we can make some sense out of all this," Bolan said as they waited for the airline representative to come back on the line. "Zhdanov believes your father killed his half brother and his father's first wife." He glanced down at the dead woman in the bed. "So Zhdanov killed your father when he bumped into him later at Dachau. It sounds like that wasn't enough revenge for him. His whole family was dead, so he wanted all of your family dead, too. But why indoctrinate his son to finish the vendetta? Why didn't he come after you himself?"

Katz shook his head. "I don't know. Something, though. Something we don't know about yet. It's like Ulric running Cynthia off the road twenty years ago, then getting arrested on other charges with the Baader-Meinhof Gang before he could come after me. That delayed his mission for two decades while he was in prison."

Bolan nodded. "Yes, but where does Jurgen Schneider fit into all this?"

Katz shrugged, then held the receiver tighter to his ear as the airline representative came back on the line.

Bolan watched his friend's expression of concentration change to surprise, then concern. "Yes," he said. "Thank you. I will pick the ticket up at the desk."

Katz hung up the phone, looked up at the Executioner and drew a deep breath. "He plans to kill me, all right," he said. "But not yet."

The closest thing to fear the Executioner had ever seen in Katz now appeared on the older man's face. "Zhdanov wants the whole Katzenelenbogen family, Mack," he said. "He got Cynthia, and now he's booked on a flight to Tel Aviv."

Katz started for the door. "He's going after Sharon next."

THE SNOW CONTINUED to fall in great white flakes as Ulric Zhdanov crouched behind the four-foot-tall granite monument. It felt as if the temperature had dropped another ten degrees since he'd left his mother's ICU bed in the hospital across the street.

But the Russian wasn't cold. The anger and hatred instilled in him as a child by his father kept him warm.

From birth Zhdanov had been indoctrinated with stories of his half brother, Ivan, and his father's first wife, Melaniya. He had been told how Yakov Yakobovich Katz had broken his father's heart when he murdered them, and that because of the same Jew, Ulric would never meet his brother.

Zhdanov wrapped the muffler tighter around his neck, more out of habit than need. The fact that his father wouldn't have married his mother had Gregor Zhdanov's first wife not died, and that Ulric himself would therefore not exist, never occurred to him. He had been programmed from birth to hate the memory of Yakov Yakobovich Katz and to gear his life toward wiping out the man's legacy. His hatred hadn't died during the twenty years he had spent in prison; rather it had flourished, festering in his soul until it was all the fuel he needed in the falling snow in the cemetery across the street from the hospital.

Zhdanov continued to watch the front steps of the hospital, ducking behind the monument whenever a car passed on the street. He ducked particularly low when a Russian police car passed, its red-and-blue lights flashing as it sped toward some emergency.

A taxi pulled up and parked along the curb to wait for a fare. Zhdanov ducked again, peering around the side of the stone to watch. When the driver lifted a newspaper to his face, blocking his view of the cemetery, the Russian rose once more.

Zhdanov surveyed the terrain in front of him. He had taken refuge behind the first granite marker tall enough to hide him from view, and was approximately ten feet inside the low hedge that ran the circumference of the cemetery. Another twenty feet or so of street led to the curb, then perhaps twenty more to the steps of the hospital. The Israeli's big friend would be a fifty-foot shot, at most. It shouldn't be difficult for a man of Zhdanov's ability using an accurate target pistol.

A sudden uneasiness started at the pit of Zhdanov's stomach and quickly spread throughout his body. He remembered the faulty sights on the sniper rifle he had obtained from Heinrich Stubrel. The High Standard target pistol had come from the same hidden armory at the Pension Kopromed, and he'd had no opportunity to check the sights himself.

Well, Zhdanov thought, there was no time like the present. The pistol had been fitted with a sound suppressor, and neither the taxidriver nor anyone else in the area would hear his test rounds.

Leaning forward, Zhdanov used the top of the monument as a rest for his hands. Lining the luminous bar-dot-bar sights up on a streetlight half a block beyond where the taxi was parked, he gently squeezed the trigger.

The pistol coughed. The streetlight popped, and

the light went out as tiny particles of glass rained to the street.

The Russian dropped behind the monument, peering over the top as the cabdriver lowered his newspaper and glanced over his shoulder at the noise. To him, it had to have appeared that the light had simply burst from faulty wiring and too much pressure. No big deal.

The newspaper rose again over the man's face.

Zhdanov smiled. The sights on *this* weapon were true.

Settling in again to wait, the Russian thought of the Israeli's daughter. After he shot the big man in a few minutes, he would fly to Israel to kill her. Then there would be only Yakov Katzenelenbogen left to make Gregor Zhdanov's reckoning complete. Ulric would kill Katzenelenbogen with the same Nagant revolver that the Jew's father had used to kill Ivan and Melaniya.

And then it would be over.

A moment of fear suddenly shot through the Russian. What would he do then? All of his life he had worked toward this mission. The childhood indoctrination by his father, his escape from the Soviet Union in order to obtain the training he would need to carry out his duty—all had been a means toward this end.

What would he do when it *had* ended?

The fear quickly subsided as Zhdanov saw the front door of the hospital open and the Israeli and his friend come out. They hurried down the steps side by side, Katzenelenbogen blocking a shot of the big man.

Zhdanov frowned. Why did they hurry so? Had his mother told them where he was going? That he was about to kill the Israeli's daughter? No, that was impossible. She had been asleep when he made the call to the airline; of that he was certain.

The phone number, Zhdanov realized as he watched the two men bound down the steps. He had thrown the piece of paper on which he had written it into the wastebasket by the phone. They had found it, called the number and learned he had a reservation on the next flight to Tel Aviv.

Zhdanov was glad he had ordered the RAF men to arrange a backup plan to get to Israel. The Israeli would surely go to the airport, even by himself. A confrontation there might force Zhdanov to kill the man ahead of schedule, and that would mean that Yakov Katzenelenbogen would never suffer the knowledge that his daughter, too, had been killed.

That was important. He needed to grieve the loss of a child just as Gregor Zhdanov had grieved.

As the two men neared the cab, the Israeli broke off to circle to the other door. The big man leaned forward to open the door on his side.

Zhdanov centered the luminous green dot of the front sight between the shining emerald bars behind it and lined them up on the side of the big man's head. Gently his finger moved back on the three-pound trigger.

The High Standard pistol skipped lightly in his hand.

A tiny hole appeared in the taxi door just below the big man's chin.

Zhdanov looked down at the pistol in shock. His hold had been true—of that he had no doubt. And the weapon had been sighted in properly; he had tested it.

What had happened?

By the time he tore his eyes away from the pistol and looked back to the street, the big man had fallen to the ground next to the taxi. A 9 mm Beretta pistol, wearing its own sound suppressor, had appeared in the man's hand as his eyes darted back and forth trying to pinpoint the source of the shot.

On the other side of the cab, the Israeli had drawn a gun, as well.

Zhdanov cursed under his breath. His shot had hit perhaps three inches low and slightly to the right of his point of aim, so as he lined up the pistol again, he adjusted for the discrepancy. Another squeeze of the trigger sent a second .22 round flying from the barrel of the target pistol.

Where, Zhdanov couldn't say. He only knew it didn't strike the big man on the ground next to the taxi.

The big man had to have seen movement of some type behind the gravestone because he now swung his Beretta toward Zhdanov. Three fast rounds struck the marker in front of the Russian, careening off the stone with more noise than the suppressed rounds had made during ignition.

Zhdanov fired again. Again he missed. This time the round struck the door of the taxi two inches above the big man's head. The Russian cursed in frustration. It made no sense. If the sights were off, they would send the bullet in the wrong direction, but it would be the *same* wrong direction with each shot.

The Russian didn't know why the pistol wasn't firing accurately after he'd just tested it, but now was no time to find out. He would have to check the weapon later to see what was wrong.

A sudden pause in the return fire from the street caused Zhdanov to frown. What was the big man doing? Moving forward, perhaps? His chest against the stone, he peered around the edge to see that the man hadn't moved but that the Beretta was now gone and a different pistol was in his hand.

A moment later, it sounded as if a nuclear bomb had gone off. The monument against Zhdanov's chest shook as if were an erupting volcano.

A fast series of more explosions, and the granite began to crack.

Turning, the Russian crawled away from the monument on all fours as the explosions behind him continued. He heard the stone give way, crumble and fall as he rose and sprinted away, dodging other markers and running like a halfback who'd broken through the line to open field.

As he made his way toward the other side of the cemetery, Zhdanov had two regrets. He regretted that he had once again missed killing the big man.

But even more than that, he regretted that he couldn't kill the bumbling, incompetent, alcohol-saturated Heinrich Stubrel more than once.

CHAPTER SEVEN

The tiny hole appeared in the taxi door just to the Executioner's side. Even with no telltale sound, he recognized what it was immediately.

"Get down, Katz!" he yelled as he twisted toward the general direction from which the shot had to have come. By the time his chest hit the pavement, he had already drawn the Beretta and thumbed the selector to 3-round-burst mode.

Bolan scanned the area. From the angle at which the bullet—small caliber, .22 probably—had twisted the metal as it entered the car door, he could tell the round had been fired from across the street in the cemetery. But where in the cemetery? All he could see was row after row of granite monuments that rose anywhere from two to eight feet in the air from the carefully tended plots.

The sensation of a bee zooming past his head registered in the Executioner's mind, and he felt the air pressure as another silenced round passed. Across the street he caught a flicker of movement behind one of the monuments closest to the low hedge that ran along the curb.

Turning the Beretta that way, Bolan held the trigger back and sent a 3-round burst into the stone. The 9 mm hollowpoints did little but screech as they zoomed off in another direction.

"Katz! You okay?" The Executioner jammed the Beretta back into his shoulder rig and rolled slightly to one side, unleathering the Desert Eagle.

"I'm okay," the Israeli replied. "Where is he?"

"Cemetery across the street. Closest marker to the hedge. Can you see it?"

"Not from where I am now. Let me move—"

"No! Stay where you are," Bolan said. "We'll make *him* move." He pressed the release button by the trigger guard, dropped the magazine of .44 Magnum rounds from the Desert Eagle and stuck it into the side pocket of his jacket. Reaching to his waistband, he pulled another box mag from a carrier on his belt. The sharp conical tip of the full-jacketed armor-piercing round at the top of the stack glistened under the streetlight as he shoved the new load into the Eagle.

Bolan saw a face dart around the left side of the monument as he lined up the sights. It jerked back just before he pulled the trigger.

The first round out of the big .44 pistol was the bullet that had already been chambered, and it flattened against the stone, zinging off like the 9 mm slugs had. Bolan's hands followed the recoil, then brought the weapon back down and zeroed in on the monument once more. He pulled the trigger again, then again and again, using a steady stream of fire at the center of the stone to crack and then crumble the barrier.

The final armor-piercing round from the big Magnum pistol sent the top half of the monument flying in brick-sized chunks. The Desert Eagle's slide locked back, empty.

Bolan slammed a fresh magazine back into the weapon. He thumbed the slide, chambering a round, as he saw a man rise to his feet some distance behind the collapsed monument. The man wore a dark overcoat and black Russian rabbit hat, and the Executioner suddenly remembered seeing him come out of the hospital as he and Katz had entered.

Although it hadn't registered at the time, it was the man's face that had given the Executioner the uneasy feeling as they'd walked up the steps to the hospital. Now he knew why. He had seen the face before, but without the hat.

It was the same man who had come out of the Pension Kopromed in Munich as they'd driven by; the same man who had a flat-top haircut and carried a large cardboard box that had to have contained the weapons he had taken from the hidden compartment in the pension. The same man who had killed the drunk on the couch.

Ulric Zhdanov.

"It's him, Katz!" the Executioner shouted as he bounded to his feet. "Let's go!"

KATZ SPRANG to his feet, knowing that Bolan had to mean Zhdanov. The Israeli glanced into the cab long enough to see the back of the driver's head. The terrified man had flattened out across the front seat and was desperately hugging the upholstery with both arms.

The Executioner was already ten feet ahead of him, halfway across the street when Katz hit the curb. Deeper in the cemetery, the Israeli could see the shadowy figure of a running man. He watched Bolan vault the hedge and sprint past the collapsed monument behind which Zhdanov had evidently hidden, then followed the Executioner around markers and monuments as they pursued their prey.

Katz felt his breath come in sharp pants as he ran, silently cursing the age that no man escaped. Ahead he could see Bolan. The younger soldier had increased his lead to twenty feet or so.

The Israeli closed his eyes for a moment as he sprinted through the night, pursuing the man who he now knew had killed his wife. Born a Jew but raised in a Jesuit school, Katz now prayed to the God to whom he had been introduced in both religions. "Give me the strength, Lord," Katz said quietly under his breath. "Don't let these aging bones fail me until they've served out the justice Cynthia deserves."

And with these words, Katz felt a new strength come over him. As he ran on, the gap between him and the Executioner didn't narrow. But neither did it increase.

Lights stood here and there throughout the cemetery, but the fleeing form ahead of the Stony Man Farm warriors stayed clear of their illumination. At one point Katz saw Bolan suddenly leap into the air like a broad jumper, then take off again without breaking stride. Glancing down as he neared the spot where he'd seen the Executioner jump, Katz saw a freshly dug grave, ready for someone's service the next day. He also went airborne, clearing the hole and running on.

Ahead Bolan suddenly stopped, diving behind a marble statue of the Madonna and child. Taking the cue, Katz flew forward onto his belly, sliding along the grass as he felt the pressure of several rounds fly over his head. He crawled forward as he saw Bolan rise to a kneeling position behind the statue and lift both hands.

A soft cough replaced the deafening pistol roars Katz had heard earlier, meaning Bolan had replaced the Desert Eagle with the Beretta again. As he fired, Katz crawled forward. "Can you see him?" he asked.

Bolan nodded, gesturing in the semidarkness toward a large concrete building thirty yards ahead. Dim lights ringed the roof, casting eerie shadows over the area that fit the graveyard ambience perfectly. "He's behind that mausoleum," the Executioner whispered. "At least he was a second ago." He paused. "You circle right. I'll go left. But keep behind cover and don't move in too fast. If I could see him when he ducked behind the building, he'll be able to see us."

Katz nodded.

Bolan disappeared to the left, darting from behind the statue to a large square stone, then moving on to disappear into the darkness. Katz kept his gaze glued to the center of the mausoleum, enabling him to watch both sides of the building with his peripheral vision, as he moved off to the right. He stopped briefly behind a six-foot-tall double marker and squinted through the darkness. Though dim, the lights along the roof illuminated the structure sufficiently that he felt confident he would see Zhdanov if the man showed his face on either side of the building.

What worried him was that that might not happen. Those same lights that enabled Katz to see the sides of the mausoleum would enable Zhdanov to see them approach the building. This made a "rush" out of the question. Knowing this, the Russian might well take advantage of the time he knew he had before Bolan and Katz could gradually move in. What Zhdanov might be doing, even now, was making his way straight back away from the mausoleum, hidden from Katz's and Bolan's lines of vision by the building itself.

If that was the case, the Russian might well escape before he or Bolan reached an angle where they could see what was happening.

Katz kept low as he moved on through the night, gradually moving forward and closer to the left side of the mausoleum. Somewhere, on the other side of the concrete building, he knew Bolan was doing the same.

By the time Katz had drawn even with the side of the mausoleum and taken cover behind a marble headstone, he knew in his gut that Zhdanov was gone. He moved on until he could see the rear of the building, then drew in a short deep breath when he saw a figure move around the corner from the other side.

Katz let the breath out slowly as he recognized Bolan's silhouette in the darkness. Moving quietly from behind the marker, the Israeli made his way toward the mausoleum.

Bolan turned his way quickly, raising his Beretta, then lowering it again when he recognized Katz.

"He's gone?" Katz asked.

The soldier nodded. "But he had to have taken off straight back, and he's had to move quietly, which means he can't have moved fast." Bolan scanned the darkness. "Move ten yards back to your right," he said. "I'll take the left again. Let's go."

The two warriors spread out and took off.

ZHDANOV WASN'T surprised when he heard the sound of running footsteps behind him. He had known the men would pursue him.

What surprised him was how quickly they had come. Surely they had to be aware that the advantage in such a race was his. There were any number of markers and other objects large enough for him to hide behind and set up an ambush. Yet the Israeli and his friend came on as if they had no fear whatsoever.

The Russian ran on, sidestepping the markers and vaulting a freshly dug grave he didn't see until the last second. He chuckled to himself, hoping the two men wouldn't spot the hole and fall in. In any event he needed to slow them, and when he saw the mausoleum ahead he knew how.

The Russian skidded to a halt next to the concrete building, rounded the corner, then stepped into the open far enough to aim the .22. He doubted he would hit anything with the gun, and again he hated and cursed Heinrich Stubrel. But the two men didn't know that the weapon had problems, and a shot or two in their general direction should slow them. And who knew? Maybe he'd get lucky like he had when he'd shot the streetlight.

Zhdanov had barely had time to steady his arm on the side of the mausoleum when the big man came into view. The Russian saw his shadow leap into the air and knew he had seen the open grave. The big man ran on as Zhdanov saw a smaller shadow jump the hole behind him.

The Russian fired, the .22 missing its target but coming close enough that the big man knew he'd been shot at. Zhdanov stayed in sight at the side of the mausoleum long enough for the man to see him, then ducked back as the man fell behind a statue to return fire. Just before he disappeared, the Russian saw Katzenelenbogen appear and go to the ground.

Zhdanov took only long enough to make sure the two weren't foolhardy enough to charge the mausoleum, then started away from the building. He walked sideways, his pistol aimed back toward the mausoleum and ready to fire should either man show his face.

When he was far enough away that he knew his running footsteps couldn't be heard, Zhdanov turned and began to jog toward the far side of the cemetery. He couldn't keep the smile off his face. Yes, he had missed the big man yet again, but the man wasn't an integral part of the mission—only an additional benefit. If he killed the big man, fine. If not, fine.

It was Katzenelenbogen and his daughter who were important. And Ulric Zhdanov intended to send them both to meet the woman he had killed twenty years earlier.

Ahead, Zhdanov could see a tall statue of Christ to one side of his path. On the other side was an equally large image of St. Peter. Farther on, between the two statues, he could see the lights along the street on the other side of the cemetery. He knew what lay on the other side of the street—several blocks of commercial area that included cafés, night-spots and specialty shops.

He would make it, he knew. The Israeli and his friend had probably worked their way to the rear of the mausoleum by now and learned that he was no longer there. But they couldn't be much closer than that. As soon as he hit the street, he would duck into the first café or other establishment he came to, then go out the back door. It would be as if he'd vanished into thin air.

Satisfaction flooded the Russian as he sprinted between the statues of Christ and St. Peter, and he glanced over his shoulder in triumph.

It was at exactly that moment when he realized the earth was no longer beneath his feet.

Zhdanov felt himself falling and knew immediately what had happened. Another open grave, another plot ready for a burial in the morning. The shadows of the tall statues on either side had hidden the hole from his view, and he cursed himself and his inattention as he fell.

A moment later the Russian's left foot hit the soft earth at an angle.

Zhdanov suppressed the cry of pain that threatened to spill from his lips as his ankle twisted beneath him. His forward momentum carried him on, and his head struck the side of the dirt hole. Clods exploded into clouds of dirt as he rebounded back to a sitting position, feeling both angry and stupid at the same time.

For a moment he sat dazed. Then, as the haze of dirt settled back to the bottom of the grave, he forced himself to rub his eyes and look upward.

The stars above the cemetery twinkled as if mocking his carelessness.

Zhdanov fumbled through the dirt around him until he found the .22-caliber High Standard. He shoved it into his waistband and stood, trying to put his weight on the ankle he had twisted. He grimaced in pain and sat back down. The ankle wasn't broken; he was fairly certain of that. But it was sprained, and he'd stand no chance now of outrunning his two pursuers. No, he would have to stay where he was and hope they missed him. Or hope that he could shoot them with the unreliable .22 when they looked down into the grave.

Jerking the pistol out of his waistband, Zhdanov dropped the magazine from the gun. It might well have gotten clogged with dirt during his fall, and the last thing he needed was to blow himself up with a burst barrel. He worked the slide, holding his hand in position to catch the chambered round as it flew out, then held the weapon up toward the sky.

Enough light filtered into the grave that he could see the stars through the barrel. Clear.

The Russian had started to reload the weapon when his index finger brushed the tip of the .22 round that had come from the chamber. He frowned, holding it up to the light. A round-nosed lead bullet. He couldn't read the brand on the end of the brass case, but it was *not* a CCI Mini Mag like the one he had seen at the top of the magazine when he'd inspected the weapon back at Stubrel's apartment.

Flipping the remaining rounds out of the magazine, Zhdanov found a variety of brands and bullet shapes.

Again the Russian cursed Heinrich Stubrel's drunken incompetence. But at least he finally had the answer to the pistol's erratic shooting. The gun had been sighted in for whatever load had been in the chamber when Zhdanov shot out the streetlight to check it. But the magazine was filled with a variety of rounds with different weights and velocities. Each would print differently on a target.

At sufficient range, anyway. If the Israeli or his friend looked down into the grave, Zhdanov would be shooting only a few feet. It would make no difference at that distance, and he quickly reloaded the magazine and chamber.

A few minutes later the Russian heard the sounds of footsteps approaching in the distance. He moved onto his back, facing the direction from which the footsteps came, and aimed the pistol straight up into the air.

Zhdanov took a deep breath, and waited.

THE EXECUTIONER MOVED as swiftly as possible, walking the fine line between speed and stealth as he moved through the cemetery. Thirty feet away he could see the dark form of Yakov Katzenelenbogen doing the same thing. It was impossible to know precisely what route Zhdanov would have chosen as the Russian made his way out of the cemetery, but it had to be one that would have been hidden by the mausoleum. And that meant a fairly narrow line of flight to the street on the other side of the markers.

Bolan gripped the Beretta in his right hand as he moved forward, fully aware that each rectangular marker, each statue of Christ, the Virgin Mother or one of the saints might hide a waiting assassin. But there was no other way to handle the situation. If he didn't want the Russian to escape, he had to continue forward and hope that his reflexes, training and experience were enough to see him through any trap that Zhdanov might set.

And if those reflexes, training and experience weren't enough? Bolan asked himself. Then he would die.

The thought of impending death didn't bother the Executioner other than how it might affect the mission at hand. Long ago, when he had lost his family to the hands of violent men, he had resolved that if their deaths were to be avenged it would have to be he who avenged them. At that time the Executioner had resigned himself to the fact that death, for him, would more than likely come violently, as well.

Such was the nature of the game he played; such was the destiny of the warrior.

Since accepting that fact, death had carried with it no fear, and Bolan had fought the good fight as a man who considered himself already dead and living on borrowed time. He didn't want to die. But if this was to be his time, so be it. He only hoped he would have the chance to help his friend avenge the deaths of *his* loved ones first.

The Executioner moved on through the cemetery, the lights on the other side becoming brighter. He glanced across the grounds toward Katz again. The Israeli was much the same as him, he knew. Katz might not be quite as fast as he once was or quite as strong. If he had been, he wouldn't have retired as leader of Phoenix Force and taken on the adviser's spot at Stony Man Farm. But that didn't mean the Israeli was no longer a formidable warrior. Bolan would still pick Katzenelenbogen as his backup any day of the week.

Bolan looked ahead and saw a white marble statue of Christ in the dim moonlight. Ten feet away, closer to the path Katz was following, was a similar icon of St. Peter. The areas to the sides and in between the statues were dark, and the Executioner moved on.

Bolan hadn't known Katz's wife, Cynthia, but it seemed they had enjoyed the ideal marriage. In many ways Bolan knew the Israeli still mourned and missed her. Katz was human, however, and didn't enjoy being alone. During the years since Cynthia's death, he had kept several mistresses. But emotionally he had remained at arm's length from his lovers, reserving his love for his daughter, Sharon.

Ten minutes later Bolan and Katz reached the low hedge that ran along the curb on the other side of the cemetery. Hiding their weapons beneath their jackets, they looked across the street to the many shops, cafés and bars. Men and women crowded the sidewalks.

"It's hopeless," Katz said. "He could have gone in any of them."

"And then gone out the back," Bolan said. "By now he's left the area."

"Dammit, Mack," he said. "We were so close...so damn close."

Bolan started across the street toward a row of cabs. "We're still close," he said. "He doesn't know we know he's going to Tel Aviv."

"The airport?" Katz asked.

The Executioner nodded as he opened the back door of the nearest cab. "We'll catch him before he gets on the plane."

THE .22 TARGET PISTOL aimed upward, Ulric Zhdanov lay still on his back as he heard the footsteps approach. At first it sounded as if they came from the right side of the grave. A moment later he'd have sworn they were approaching from the left.

Then it hit him. There were two sets of footsteps, and they were coming from both sides of the grave. The two men had fanned out to examine a wider path through the cemetery.

Slowly Zhdanov disengaged the manual safety on

the .22. He continued to aim it up at the stars, determined to put a round into whichever face showed itself first.

The two sets of footsteps seemed to draw even with the grave, and Zhdanov's fingers tensed around the grip of the pistol. It would be only seconds now. They would see the freshly dug hole in the ground and come to inspect it.

But the steps moved on.

Zhdanov frowned. Had they missed seeing the open grave? It was possible. After all, he himself hadn't seen the hole until he'd fallen into it. But he had been looking behind him when he fell, and his pursuers would be concentrating on what was ahead. No, they were simply playing a game with him. Making him think they were moving on past the grave when in actuality they would double back any second now and appear from the other side.

Zhdanov sat up, then twisted onto his back again so he was facing the other direction. Again he waited.

Again the footsteps didn't come.

Finally he rose to a squatting position and slowly raised his eyes over the edge of the grave. Perhaps twenty yards ahead, next to the hedge that ran along the street, he could see the two men talking. Vaguely, a few words of their conversation drifted back on the wind.

"...still close...going to Tel Aviv...."

"...airport..."

"...before he gets on the plane."

Zhdanov raised the pistol over the side of the grave and tried to line up the target sights on the back of the big man's head as the men crossed the street. The shot was blocked by a low-hanging tree branch. He watched as the men entered a cab.

So they did know he was going to Tel Aviv. Perhaps his mother had told them. More likely they had found the piece of scratch paper where he'd written the number. Whatever it was, it didn't matter. They were going to the airport.

When the taxi was out of sight, Zhdanov shoved the pistol into his waistband, reached up and pulled himself out of the grave. He started to limp toward the hedge, feeling like a fool for spraining his ankle. Then curiosity got the better of him and, even though each step sent lances of pain shooting up his leg and down into his toes, he turned and retraced his steps toward the mausoleum.

Fifty feet past the grave into which he'd fallen, Zhdanov turned another about-face. Ahead he could see the statue of Christ on one side of the hole, and St. Peter on the other. But the peculiar light drifting through the trees scattered throughout the cemetery kept the grave unseen in the shadows.

Taking the course that he suspected the man who had approached on the right had used, Zhdanov walked toward the image of Christ. He passed the statue slowly, squinting, trying to make out the open grave on the other side. Even as he passed, the dark shadows of the cemetery kept it hidden.

Walking back to his starting point, Zhdanov went left this time, walking toward the statue of St. Peter this time. Again the shadows kept the grave invisible.

A grin spread across his face as Zhdanov limped past the open grave toward the short hedge. He had learned early on from both Baader and Meinhof that one should always have an alternate plan, and those were words of advice he had heeded. He had already made emergency backup plans with just such an alternate route to Israel, and it would get him there almost as fast as the direct flight from St. Petersburg. But first, luck had provided him with yet another chance to kill the Israeli's friend—at the airport.

Which should be easy. Neither man would know Zhdanov had suspected them of finding the phone number of the airline when they came barreling down the hospital steps. Neither would they know he had overheard their conversation by the hedge, which confirmed that they knew he was going to Tel Aviv. They did know he would recognize them, which meant they would either disguise themselves or try to hide from him at the airport. He also suspected that they now knew what he looked like, so he would have to overcome that obstacle, as well.

Zhdanov stepped over the hedge gingerly with his sore ankle and started to cross the street, then on a lark, turned back for one final look at the two statues next to the grave that had hidden him.

"Thank you, Jesus," Zhdanov said, then he threw his head back in laughter as he limped across the street to the waiting line of cabs.

CHAPTER EIGHT

The suitcases in their hands were empty as Bolan and Katz walked casually through the ticket counter area toward Concourse A. The strong odor of fresh paint filled their nostrils as they neared the wide corridor. Turning a corner, they passed several men in white coveralls and caps who were painting the walls. Both the men's caps and the breast pockets of their coveralls bore the emblem of the maintenance contracting company employed by the airport, a flying red-winged Pegasus.

Bolan and Katz moved on, finally finding the door they were looking for down the concourse. Ten yards farther they could see the line of passengers waiting their turn to pass through the metal detector before making their way to the boarding gates.

Bolan stopped in front of the door. The sign, in Russian, read Personnel Only.

Katz kept an eye on the uniformed security police working the metal detector and X-ray machine as the Executioner transferred his suitcase to his left hand. He tried the door with his right. Locked.

"Keep me covered," Bolan whispered as he pulled the set of picks from his pocket. "This shouldn't take more than thirty seconds." Katz backed up in front of him, blocking the view from the security station. The men, women and children hurrying toward the various gates and flights had other things on their minds and paid no attention to the two men at the closet door.

As soon as the lock snapped open, Bolan and Katz slipped into the closet. They found everything they needed hanging on the wall. Several pairs of white work coveralls bearing the red Pegasus crest hung from nails. Bolan dug through the coveralls until he found a set that fit over his weapons and clothes. The legs were a little short, so he rolled up his slacks, stuffing them into his socks beneath the cuffs.

Katz pulled a similar pair of coveralls from a nail on the wall and slid them over his own clothes. A row of white caps, also exhibiting the red-winged horse, sat on a shelf above the nails. Bolan and Katz helped themselves.

Bolan pulled a push broom and dustpan from spring clamps screwed to the wall, then dropped them into a tall rubber trash can on wheels. Katz found a mop, then filled a bucket with water in the large industrial sink. He added a cleaning and disinfecting agent he found in a metal can nearby, and a moment later the two men were back out on the concourse and making their way toward gate A-8, where Zhdanov was scheduled to take off in an hour.

The two men slowed their pace as they neared the metal detector, then sped up again when a redheaded security officer wearing an eight-point cap nodded them through. The detector beeped as Bolan pulled the rubber trash can carrying the metal handled broom and dust pan between the sensors, then sounded again when Katz came through the arch with the metal bucket and mop. Along with the cleaning equipment came the assortment of concealed guns and knives the men from Stony Man Farm carried under their coveralls. But the uniforms did the trick. The security officers chalked the metal detector's reaction up to what they could see and ignored both beeps.

The smell of fresh paint returned to their nostrils as Bolan led Katz on along the concourse. As they passed gate A-5, they saw that the steel-framed seats had been unbolted from the floor and stacked along the wall. More men in the white uniforms were busy stretching new carpet on the floor. Others painted the walls while yet more were busy washing the windows that faced the runways.

Bolan and Katz stopped at the rows of seats surrounding gate A-9. The sign above the check-in counter announced that a flight from Helsinki would touch down in ten minutes, then continue on to Moscow.

But the gate that interested the Executioner was

A-8, directly across the hallway. It was from here that the Lufthansa flight to Tel Aviv would take off. The Executioner began to sweep the area around the seats, nodding and smiling to passengers who awaited the flight to Moscow. He kept one eye on the concourse and the security officers around the metal detector. Katz positioned himself in a corner of the waiting area where he could keep watch, as well. The Israeli dipped the mop into the bucket, squeezed it out in the press clamped to the side and began to scrub the tile.

Bolan continued to sweep, periodically gathering the piles of debris in the dustpan and dumping them into the trash can. Zhdanov would come soon; the Executioner could feel it. The Russian had no reason to believe that Bolan and Katz would be here, so it was even possible that he would come unarmed in order to avoid problems with security. Of course, he would need weapons once he reached Israel, but those would be easy enough to obtain at that end.

Ulric Zhdanov was obviously a well-established international terrorist, meaning he could take advantage of the world-wide terrorist network that linked European groups like the Red Army Faction to their counterparts in the Middle East. Someone—from Hezbollah or Al Dawa or Islamic Jihad or some other such organization—would be more than willing to provide the Russian with all the firepower he needed once he arrived.

The Executioner knelt, lifted another pile of dust,

chewing gum wrappers and other litter into the dust-pan. He hoped that would be the case—that Zhdanov would come unarmed, and that he could take the man alive. Zhdanov had killed Katz's wife, and he would have to pay for that. Justice needed to be served, and "an eye for an eye" was the only way that would happen. On the other hand, the occurrences involving the Katzenelenbogen family and Zhdanov's were a baffling puzzle that still had many missing pieces. Katz's father killing Gregor Zhdanov's first wife and his son seemed to have started the ball rolling, but what were the details around the killings? Jurgen Schneider, a.k.a. Helmut Kaufman, had been a friend to Yakov Yakobovich Katz at Dachau, and had been there when Gregor Zhdanov murdered the man. But where did the former Nazi prison guard fit into the picture in regard to *Ulric* Zhdanov? In fact how did Schneider even know that Ulric existed?

Bolan wanted an opportunity to complete the puzzle before Katz enacted the justice he so richly deserved. It appeared at this point that the only man who could fill in those missing pieces was Zhdanov himself, and the Russian couldn't do it if he was dead.

With one eye still on the hallway, the Executioner continued to sweep. Through the window he saw the incoming flight from Helsinki touch down and taxi toward the gate to pick up the passengers waiting to board for Moscow. The Executioner watched the

WELCOME TO THE
CASINO!
Try your luck at the Roulette Wheel ...
Play a hand of Twenty-One!

How to play:

1. Play the Roulette and Twenty-One scratch-off games, as instructed on the opposite page, to see that you are eligible for FREE BOOKS and a FREE GIFT!

2. Send back the card and you'll get hot-off-the-press Gold Eagle books, never before published! These books have a cover price of $4.99 each, but they are yours to keep absolutely free.

3. There's no catch. You're under no obligation to buy anything. We charge nothing — ZERO — for your first shipment. And you don't have to make any minimum number of purchases — not even one!

4. The fact is, thousands of readers enjoy receiving books by mail from the Gold Eagle Reader Service™ before they're available in stores. They like the convenience of home delivery, and they love our discount prices!

5. We hope that after receiving your free books you'll want to remain a subscriber. But the choice is yours — to continue or cancel, any time at all! So why not take us up on our invitation, with no risk of any kind. You'll be glad you did!

Play Twenty-One For This Exciting Free Gift!

THIS SURPRISE
MYSTERY GIFT
COULD BE
YOURS FREE WHEN
YOU PLAY
TWENTY-ONE

It's fun, and we're giving away **FREE GIFTS** to all players!

PLAY ROULETTE!

Scratch the silver to see where the ball has landed—7 RED or 11 BLACK makes you eligible for TWO FREE novels!

PLAY TWENTY-ONE!

Scratch the silver to reveal a winning hand! Congratulations, you have Twenty-One. Return this card promptly and you'll receive a fabulous free mystery gift, along with your free books!

YES!

Please send me all the free books and the gift for which I qualify! I understand that I am under no obligation to purchase any books, as explained on the back of this card.

Name (please print clearly)

Address   Apt.#

City   State   Zip

The Gold Eagle Reader Service : Here's how it works:

plane through the window as he dropped to one knee
and began collecting debris in the dustpan again.

Soon, Bolan knew, a man would come. A man
whom the Executioner might, or might not, have to
kill.

THE OLD MAN'S HAIR was gray. Deep crow's-feet
were etched into the corners of his eyes, and he
walked with a slight limp. Usually when he wore
this disguise, the limp was a hoax. Today, however,
his ankle was actually sprained—not as badly as
he'd feared the night before—but injured nonetheless, and the limp was real. The rubber tip of his
cane tapped along in front of him as he crossed the
airport toward Concourse A.

The old man's mind was on the two men he knew
would be waiting for him at gate A-8. But for a
moment he drifted back to the night not long ago in
Marseilles, when he had first seen the Israeli's
friend. Zhdanov had been dressed as he was now,
and he wondered for a brief moment if either man
would remember him from the Le Sorbonne tavern.

Zhdanov shook his head as he passed several men
painting the walls. Anything was possible, but it
wasn't likely that either Katzenelenbogen or the
other man would recall his face from the dockside
bar. They had been too preoccupied with what they
had been discussing, and Le Sorbonne had been like
a carnival side show of human aberrations. Zhdanov,
in his old-man disguise, had faded into the wood-

work compared to freaks like the man with the eye patch who had pulled the knife on Katzenelenbogen's friend.

Ahead on the concourse, the Russian saw the line of men and women waiting to pass through the security checkpoint. He approached, took a place at the end and waited his turn, watching as the passengers ahead of him handed carry-on items to an officer who passed them through the X-ray machine on a conveyor belt. The passengers themselves stepped through the metal detector. When his turn came, Zhdanov handed his walking stick to a stocky female officer who tried to twist the knob off to see if a sword or other weapon might be concealed inside. Finding that the ends were solid, she dropped it on the conveyor belt, then looked back to Zhdanov, glancing down at the leg on which he'd been limping. "Sir," she asked, "do you need help walking through the metal detector?"

Zhdanov gave her his most grandfatherly smile. "No, no," he said. "As long as it is not too far, or up stairs, I am fine without the cane." He stepped forward, pulling a key ring, money clip with paper money and a handful of coins from his pocket, then set them in a small plastic bowl next to the arches.

The Russian passed through the metal detector with no problem.

Putting his possessions back into his pockets, Zhdanov accepted the cane from a male officer working the other end of the conveyor belt, then limped down the concourse. He kept his gaze on the floor to further disguise his features, but his eyes darted back and forth across the wide hallway.

They were here; he knew it. He could feel it in his blood. Somewhere, although he hadn't yet spotted them, the two men were waiting to kill him. He passed gates 1 through 7. Some of the waiting areas were deserted with no flights scheduled to arrive or depart for some time. Others bustled with activity as passengers received boarding passes at the check-in booths, or greeted loved ones on incoming flights. Gate A-5 had been closed completely while more of the men in white coveralls painted and laid new carpet on the floor.

When Zhdanov reached A-8, both it and the gate directly across the hallway were crowded. People in both waiting areas sat reading magazines, newspapers and paperback books or carrying on conversations in low tones. The Russian saw two more of the white-clad maintenance men sweeping and mopping, their backs to him as he passed. He moved on, scanning the rest of the gates before coming to the end of the concourse.

A small kiosk stood just off the concourse near the end, and Zhdanov stopped long enough to buy a newspaper. He carried it under the same arm that held his cane as he moved to the men's room located between gates 12 and 13 and took a place at the end of a long urinal. Only one other man—looking even older than Zhdanov himself—occupied the other end of the trough. The Russian waited until the old man had rezipped his pants, washed his hands and left the room before moving along the toilet stalls checking for shoes. The rest room was empty.

Zhdanov opened the doors to one of the empty stalls, stepped inside and locked it behind him. Taking a seat on the toilet, he reached into his sock and pulled out a fiberglass-filled plastic knife known as a Delta Dart. Almost eight inches long, the knife had a spikelike Zytel blade that offered three and a half inches of penetrating power that could be driven through hollow-core doors, yet weighed only seventenths of an ounce.

Reassured that the small dagger hadn't fallen out of his sock, Zhdanov reached into the inside pocket of his sport coat and pulled out what appeared to be an ordinary plastic hairbrush. But when he grasped the bristles in one hand and jerked on the handle with the other, the brush broke into two pieces and the handle became a needle-pointed stiletto. Nicknamed "the Honey Comb," the stiletto weighed slightly more than two ounces. Constructed of a similar plastic called Rynite, it was like the Delta Dart in that it was primarily a thrusting weapon. And it shared another similarity with the dart.

It would pass unnoticed through metal detectors.

Zhdanov stuck the stiletto back in his jacket, then rolled up the newspaper and hid the Delta Dart inside. Again he wedged it under his right armpit, on the side that carried the cane. From this position he could draw the weapon from its newsprint sheath with his left hand. The paper would fall to the floor, and he would still have the walking stick as a bludgeon in his right hand.

The Russian left the toilet stall and moved to one of the mirrors over the sink. As he double-checked his wig and makeup, he shook his head at his reflection. What had he overlooked? The men were here; he could feel them.

So why couldn't he see them?

The answer dawned on him as he straightened the gray wig. If *he* could wear a disguise, why couldn't they?

Zhdanov retraced his steps down the concourse. So what kind of disguises would the two men choose? What was he looking for? Old men like himself? Women, even? It could be anything.

As he neared gate A-8 again, Zhdanov heard the roar of a jet landing on the other side. He looked over through the windows behind him and saw a plane taxiing off the runway toward the terminal. At almost the same time, something familiar appeared in the corner of his eye.

The hair on the back of Zhdanov's neck stood on end as the thought tried to register in his brain. What had he just seen?

Zhdanov scanned the waiting area of gate A-9 as the jet approached the window. He saw old women, young women and old and young men. He saw every age human between one month and ninety.

Some were alone; others were in couples. Others were members of larger families or other groups. But none looked like they might be Yakov Katzenelenbogen or his friend.

Then Zhdanov's eyes fell on the back of the workman kneeling with the dustpan.

The Russian's heart quickened. He didn't recognize the back—he hadn't seen enough of Katzenelenbogen's friend to know him from that angle. But what he had just seen—what had just registered in his mind as out of place—was the way the man had knelt forward with the pan. It hadn't been with the tired, bored awkwardness of a janitor. The movement had been masculinely graceful, like that of a professional athlete or martial artist. It had demonstrated the same skill and coordination Zhdanov had witnessed in the Israeli's friend when he avoided the Russian's earlier assaults.

Zhdanov stared at the back of the workman's neck as the man in white swept the dust into the pan. This man was big enough to be the Israeli's friend; his back was broad and strained against the too tight coveralls.

The Russian's eyes fell lower to the workman's ankles. Not only were the coveralls too tight across his back, but they were also too short, and the man had rolled up the legs of the pants he wore beneath them in an attempt to camouflage the fact. This made the coverall pants legs bulge.

The bottom line was that these coveralls didn't belong to the man who wore them.

Zhdanov looked up quickly, scanning the waiting area. He remembered he had seen two men in white coveralls working at Gate A-9 when he passed earlier, and now he spotted the one with the bucket in the far corner by the door.

He had no problem recognizing this man. Yakov Katzenelenbogen was still mopping the floor, but this time the man faced Zhdanov.

The Russian smiled in anticipation. He couldn't have asked for better luck. The big man knelt on the floor less than ten feet away, his back to Zhdanov. Yet the Israeli—whom Zhdanov wanted to spare until later—was on the other side of the crowded waiting room. The Russian could move in behind the big man, draw the Delta Dart and plunge it down through the white coveralls into the broad back. If that didn't completely take care of the man, he had the walking stick and spiked Honey Comb as backups.

There would be witnesses, there would be screams and there would be hysteria. But it would all work in Zhdanov's favor. Before Katzenelenbogen had time to figure out what had happened and get through the panicking people in the waiting area, Zhdanov would be long gone.

Reaching inside the rolled-up newspaper, Zhdanov wrapped his fingers around the grip of the Delta Dart and moved forward.

LIKE AN ANIMAL catching the scent of a hunter in the woods, or a soldier sensing the presence of the enemy in the jungle, Bolan perceived the danger behind him before he saw it.

The Executioner continued to sweep the trash into the dustpan. As he heard the jet approaching the loading ramp, he casually glanced up at the huge windows that looked out onto the runways. On the other side he saw the plane as it neared. But in the glass's reflection he could see the passengers in the seats around him. Seated next to where he knelt he could see a middle-aged woman with graying hair and a bright red scarf. He could see himself on his knees, the broom in one hand, the metal dustpan in the other, and the large rubber trash can next to him.

But most of all he could see the old man standing behind him—the old man who was *staring* directly at his back.

Bolan vaguely remembered the old man limping past on his cane a few minutes earlier. He still carried the cane and had added a rolled-up newspaper under his arm.

As Bolan watched in the window, the old man suddenly moved forward with a speed and agility that contradicted his age and the cane. His left hand snaked into the newspaper under his arm. It reappeared a split second later gripping a thin black blade like an ice pick. The old man brought the blade high over his head as he reached the Executioner.

Bolan moved as the weapon started downward, rising from his knees. The movement thrust him forward and away from the descending blade just enough to ruin the angle of attack. He felt the knife pierce his coveralls but not the jacket beneath them. The blade snagged in the heavy material, and he felt it ripped from his attacker's fingers as he twisted around.

A stifled scream came from the woman in the bright scarf next to Bolan. The cane came flashing toward Bolan's head at a ninety-degree angle as he turned. He dropped below the blow, feeling the wind as it flashed over his skull. Crouched, he shot a left jab forward. But he was too far away and the punch was overextended; by the time it reached the old man's jaw, it had lost ninety percent of its force and barely fazed the man.

The cane came back at Bolan's head from the opposite direction. By now the Executioner was close enough to see that the crinkly skin at the corners of the man's eyes had been created with theatrical makeup, and that the gray wig was slightly askew. This "old man" wasn't really old, and the Executioner knew who he was.

Zhdanov brought the cane around lower this time, anticipating that Bolan would duck. With no time to move out of the way, the Executioner raised his shoulder slightly, taking the force of the blow on the triceps muscle. His arm felt as if it had been scorched by a red-hot frying pan, but the weapon missed bone.

By now the shock of what was happening had worn off of the passengers. A few more screams— not so stifled now—erupted from shocked women. One young man wearing the uniform of a Russian air force pilot tried to step in and caught a cane in the mouth for his trouble. He stumbled toward Bolan, blowing out white teeth and blood as if they were popcorn covered in ketchup.

Bolan had been about to step forward to punch again when the young pilot got in his way, forcing him to abort the attack or hit the kid. This gave Zhdanov time to step back and draw a hairbrush from inside his coat.

The Executioner frowned as he tried to shove the young pilot out of his way, then he saw what the brush concealed as Zhdanov tore the bristles away from the sharp spike.

The Russian came at the Executioner with a vengeance now, using classic stick-and-dagger techniques. The cane moved forward in a series of figure eights, driving Bolan backward into the crowd of passengers. The Executioner tried to get his hand inside the coveralls for a weapon, but Zhdanov kept the pressure on, forcing him to continue backing up.

Out of the corner of his eye, the Executioner saw Katz on the far side of the waiting room. The Israeli had drawn his Beretta 92 and raised it to eye level.

He dropped the weapon again as some innocent citizen evidently blocked his shot.

Bolan heard a shout, then a curse, as he bumped into someone behind him. The next thing he knew he had tripped over the fallen form and was falling backward.

The fall turned out to be the chance he needed, providing extra distance between him and Zhdanov. In one smooth movement the Executioner's hand shot inside the coveralls and jerked the Beretta 93-R free. Falling to his back, he rolled on, popping back to his feet with the 9 mm select-fire pistol braced in both hands.

Zhdanov stood ten feet away, still armed only with the cane and plastic comb-dagger. Bolan leveled the pistol's sights on the man. There was only one problem.

The Russian had his cane pressed into the throat of the middle-aged woman in the bright red scarf, the ends of the walking stick held in the crooks of his elbows. His right hand pressed the tip of the pointed plastic stiletto into her jugular while his left rested against the back of her head.

Bolan's hand froze on the trigger. The cane served to hold the woman in place while the plastic dagger could pierce her throat in an instant. Particularly with his other hand on the back of her head, where Zhdanov could push as he thrust the blade upward.

The Russian had the woman in a position of immediate peril. Unless Bolan shot the man squarely in the brain stem, Zhdanov could kill her with his dying breath. And Zhdanov was no fool. His face—and the brain stem behind it—were hidden low behind the woman's shoulder.

The Executioner glanced to his side and saw that Katz had no better shot than he did.

The standoff began.

CHAPTER NINE

A slight trickle of blood began to drip from the woman's throat onto the bright red scarf around her neck. The rest of the passengers waiting at gate A-9 had hit the floor or taken refuge behind the seats.

Outside the area, on the concourse proper, activity had come to a halt. The men and women who hadn't already run to safety in another part of the airport had frozen in place. This applied to the security officers at the checkpoint, as well as to passengers.

"Drop the dagger, Zhdanov," Bolan ordered. He kept the Beretta's sights just above the woman's shoulder where he could see the top of the Russian's head. A lone eye peeked over the shoulder or to the woman's side occasionally, taking a visual reading of the situation but never remaining in Bolan's sights long enough for the Executioner to get off a safe shot. And a shot at that angle over the hostage's shoulder would do little more than scalp Zhdanov. Anything lower would hit the woman.

The woman herself was stiff with fear.

"No, *you* drop your gun," Zhdanov countered. "And how do you know my name?"

"We know more than you think," the Executioner said. "Now drop the weapon or I'll shoot." Behind the Russian, on the concourse, he saw one young security officer begin to creep from the area of the metal detector toward them.

"Go ahead and shoot. You will probably hit her. Even if you get me, I'll have time to kill her. If you are as able a warrior as you appear to be, you know that." He paused and chuckled sardonically. "And if you are not, you will find out."

"Then we've got a problem," Bolan told him. "Because if I drop my gun, I've got no doubt you'll kill her anyway." Behind Zhdanov he could see the security officer creeping silently closer. The young man drew a Tokarev pistol from the holster on his hip.

Bolan watched the officer with his peripheral vision, not wanting to tip off Zhdanov to what was happening behind him. The Executioner also remembered how he had learned of Zhdanov's presence behind *him* a moment before—the reflection in the big windows looking out over the runways. He wondered if the Russian could see the windows from where he was, and if he had thought to check them if he could. With most of his vision hidden behind the woman, Bolan doubted that Zhdanov would be able to see the uniformed man's reflection approaching. But the Executioner wanted to keep the Russian talking—keep his mind occupied—to increase the odds of the young officer's success.

"And that's right, we know your name," Bolan said.

"How nice," Zhdanov answered. "What else do you know about me?"

From across the room, Bolan heard Katz's voice. "We know that your father was Gregor Zhdanov. And that he murdered *my* father at Dachau."

The security cop was less than ten feet from Zhdanov and his hostage now.

"He did not murder your father!" the Russian said. "He gained justice for his first wife and my half brother!"

Bolan saw the police officer behind Zhdanov hesitate, wondering whether he should try a shot with the hostage so close. Then a look of determination came over the young man's face, and he raised his gun over his head like a club as he moved in.

The movement had to have caught Zhdanov's eye in the window because he whirled in a flash. Keeping the woman wrapped in one arm, the plastic dagger still in her throat, he brought the cane around in an arc to crack into the security officer's temple.

The young man's arm froze in midair.

Zhdanov dropped the cane and reached up, grabbing the Tokarev as the young officer slithered to the floor.

The Russian turned and replaced the plastic dagger with the pistol. He had kept his hostage between him and the Executioner the whole time, never giving Bolan a shot. The woman struggled halfheartedly for a moment, then froze again when Zhdanov shoved the gun tighter under her chin. "Now," he said sarcastically, "where were we? Ah, yes. You were saying that if you drop your weapon I would kill this woman anyway. You were right. Now you must worry that if you drop it I will shoot *you* before I kill her."

Tears began to roll down the hostage's cheeks. Her mascara smeared, and it looked as if she had two black eyes. Otherwise, she remained as still as a pillar of salt.

"So it doesn't seem that this discussion has gotten very far," the Executioner said.

"Tell me how my father killed your brother and his mother," Katz ordered. "Give me the details."

"You do not deserve the details, Jew!" Zhdanov roared. "How did you know about Dachau?"

"If I tell you that, will you tell me what I asked?" Katz asked.

Zhdanov paused. "Yes."

"Jurgen Schneider told me the situation went all the way back to Dachau and to the Russian Revolution before that. Then another man—a man who worked with Schneider at Dachau—told us of the stabbing."

Zhdanov nodded his understanding. "Yes." He drew a breath. "After the revolution the Bolsheviks captured your father and several other Mensheviks in the neighborhood where we lived.''

Bolan could tell by the tone of Zhdanov's voice that he had rehearsed the speech many times in preparation for this day.

''They were temporarily under guard at our house. My brother was barely old enough to join, but he fought on the side of the Bolsheviks. He was one of three men watching the prisoners until they could be transported to a more permanent detainment center.'' He stopped speaking for a moment, then went on. ''Your father worked free of his restraints and pulled the revolver from the holster of one of the guards. He killed all three of the guards, including my brother, then he and the others escaped.'' The Russian paused, and when he spoke again it was with more of an animalistic snarl. ''Your father dropped the empty revolver as he ran out of the house. I still have it, and someday soon I will use it to kill you.''

''What my father did wasn't murder, Zhdanov,'' Katz said. ''He was a prisoner of war. He was escaping.''

''It was murder! The revolution was over!''

''The revolution might have been over,'' Katz countered, ''but the Communists were systematically exterminating the more moderate socialists like the Mensheviks. It was war—a new war.''

''It was murder!'' Zhdanov yelled again. ''Your father murdered my brother and my father's first wife. He killed her in her bed, while she was asleep.''

"I don't believe that," Katz said quietly.

"It is true! One of the rounds your father fired missed its target and went through the wall into the bedroom where my mother was asleep. It struck her in the head, and she never woke up.''

"That's not murder, either," Bolan argued. "That's an unfortunate accident. It's the kind of thing that happens during war.''

Katz didn't give Zhdanov time to respond. "So later, when they happened to bump into each other at Dachau," the Israeli said, "your father and mine recognized each other?''

"Yes.''

"And your father killed mine in revenge.''

"In a reckoning," Zhdanov corrected. "But before your father died, mine befriended him. The foolish man thought he had been forgiven, but my father only did so to learn more about your family. You see, one death was not enough. Your father had killed two.'' He paused, then cackled like a maniac. "An eye for an eye, a tooth for a tooth. You should be familiar with that philosophy.''

"So Gregor Zhdanov pretended to forgive my father, and acted as if they had become friends. So my father would open up with him," Katz said, nodding a new understanding. "My father told him about me. Then Gregor stabbed him and planned to come kill me after the war.''

"Precisely," Zhdanov confirmed.

"So why didn't he follow through with that plan?" Katz asked.

"Because he spent the rest of the war in a Nazi concentration camp," Zhdanov replied. "It ruined his health. After his release, he never regained enough strength to go searching for you."

"Things are beginning to take shape," Bolan said. "Gregor Zhdanov was too sick to go searching for Katz himself but not too sick to remarry and have another child."

"Very good, American," Zhdanov replied. "You are smart. It will be a shame to kill you in a few minutes."

"And you killed Cynthia Katzenelenbogen," Bolan said. "You planned to also kill Katz and his daughter but got arrested with your Baader-Meinhof buddies first."

"Correct."

"And Helmut Kaufman—calling himself Jurgen Schneider—had become a prison guard where you did your time?"

"Right again," Zhdanov said. "I told him of my plans one dark and lonely night when he had slipped in a bottle of vodka. I regretted it ever since, and went after him as soon as I was released, knowing he was the only man in the world who might tip you off. I got him, but not before he had told you part of the story."

"But why Cynthia?" Katz asked. "Why kill my

wife—why her? Why didn't you just kill me instead? That would have given you your two eyes for two eyes."

"Because things had not gone in the correct order," Zhdanov said. "My father suffered the loss of his child and wife. Your father did not—he died first. He did not suffer at all. So you had to pay for the sins of your father."

The whole plan suddenly dawned on Bolan, and it became clear why all the attacks Zhdanov had carried out on them so far seemed directed at him rather than Katz. He glanced out of the corner of his eye and saw that Katz understood, too.

"So what you're saying is that since my father didn't suffer the loss of a child and wife before he died, *I* have to," Katz said. "Is that right?"

"That is correct." The Russian's face rose slightly above the woman's shoulder as he spoke, and for a second Bolan had a shot between his eyes.

The Executioner's finger began to move back on the trigger.

Zhdanov either saw or sensed the movement. He ducked lower again.

"Cynthia had nothing to do with any of it!" Katz yelled, and for a moment Bolan was afraid his old friend might lose control and risk a shot. But he calmed down again immediately.

Zhdanov suddenly grew impatient. "Enough talk. I have plans that must be carried out." Suddenly and without warning, the Russian took a half step to the side of his hostage and swung the Tokarev away from her, aiming at Bolan.

The Executioner dived over the seats to one side a split second before Zhdanov pulled the trigger. The round blew through the back of his white coveralls, scorching the skin over his spine as he flew horizontally through the air. He fell between two rows of seats, hugging the floor as several more of the Tokarev's 7.62 mm rounds blasted through the backs of the chairs and sent slivers of plastic flying through the air.

Bolan felt something hot hit his arm. Although the 7.62 mm was hardly a high-velocity round, it had more than enough penetration to get through the plastic chairs. But in the back of his mind the Executioner suddenly remembered that because of the dense crowds at the St. Petersburg airport, the security personnel were issued frangible 7.62 mm bullets for their pistols. That meant that the bullets were breaking up on contact and that what had hit the Executioner had to be only a small part of a round.

Gripping the Beretta 93-R in both hands, Bolan took a deep breath, then rolled onto his side. He rose high enough to peer through the cracks between the chair backs, trying to get a fix on where Zhdanov stood. He saw men and women fleeing the area, but the Russian was nowhere to be seen.

Bolan rose higher, swinging the Beretta over the chair back in front of him and resting it on the back of the seats. He needn't have bothered.

The woman Zhdanov had held hostage lay in a weeping heap on the floor where the Russian had dropped her. Aside from the terror evident on her face, she appeared unharmed.

But Ulric Zhdanov was gone.

HE COULDN'T BE certain, but it looked as if the bullet from the Tokarev had struck the big man in the spine as he dived over the chairs bolted to the floor of the waiting area.

Zhdanov hoped so. The Tokarev pistol in his hand took 7.62 mm cartridges, little more than what the Americans had nicknamed "mouse guns." It would take a good hit like a spine shot to ensure the big man was down and out for the count.

The Russian squinted at the plastic chairs. Through the cracks between the seats, he could see flickers of the big man's white coveralls. They didn't move, which either meant he had killed him or the man was faking.

Just to make sure, the Russian raised the Tokarev and fired several more shots through the thin plastic chairs. Again he couldn't tell whether they had found their mark, but at that range he didn't see how he could have missed.

As he pulled the trigger, Zhdanov kept his other enemy under surveillance in his peripheral vision. Katzenelenbogen still moved back and forth on the opposite side of the waiting area, trying to get a shot around the woman in the Russian's arms. Each time the Israeli moved one way, the Russian shifted the other, continuing to use the woman as a shield.

Zhdanov fired a final round into the chairs, then turned his attention to the people in the waiting area. The initial shock that had driven them to the floor had worn off, and while most were still in a state of panic, they had decided that it was time to flee. Many were rising to their feet and sprinting past the Russian to the concourse outside.

Zhdanov knew it was time for him to do the same. The security officers at the metal detector had frozen impotently, but police in other parts of the airport would have heard the shots. Not being as near to the initial action, they wouldn't have been as shocked and would even now be on their way to find out what was going on. As the screaming men and women around him rushed down the concourse like stampeding cattle, Zhdanov thumbed on the Tokarev's safety and shoved the weapon into his belt under his jacket. Tripping the woman in his arms with a sweep kick, he dropped her to her back and left her sobbing on the floor.

The Russian turned on his heel, ripping the gray wig from his head as he joined the hysterical exodus from the waiting area. As he ran down the concourse past the security stand along with the others, he screamed in concert with them and pulled a handkerchief from his pocket to wipe away the makeup on his face. Ahead he saw a dozen or so uniformed men with drawn pistols coming toward the mob from the opposite direction. The officers in the front of the pack tried to stop the crowd, but most of the frantic passengers streamed by.

Zhdanov slowed as he reached the officers, then let one of them reach out and grab him by the sleeve. He stopped as the man said, "What is happening?"

"Two of them! Two terrorists! They have guns and are dressed as maintenance men!"

The officer dropped his arm and ran on.

Zhdanov rejoined the crowd headed down the concourse. They made their way to the terminal proper and toward the front doors that led to the parking areas. Most of the men and women were still screaming and sobbing as they pushed out of the terminal and raced down the sidewalks.

But by that time, Ulric Zhdanov's screams had turned to a smug smile.

THE EXECUTIONER vaulted the chairs and raced to the woman on the floor. Katz was already kneeling next to her.

"She's all right," the Israeli said. "Just shaken up." He turned to Bolan and shook his head in disgust. "I couldn't get a shot at him. This lady or someone else was always in the way."

"Where'd he go?" the Executioner asked.

"He mingled with the crowd," Katz replied, nodding down the concourse.

Both men rose to their feet. "Let's go," Bolan said.

Leading the way, the Executioner took off down the concourse at the rear of the running mob. He and Katz soon caught up to the slower-moving men, women and children, and began to zigzag in and out of the fleeing throng. They were almost to the main area and the ticket gates when a uniformed man stepped out from behind a large sign on a metal stand and shoved a Tokarev into Bolan's face.

"*Vy!*" the officer screamed in Russian. "Stop!"

Bolan froze as several other security officers appeared from places of hiding and aimed Tokarevs and Russian DPM submachine guns at him. At the same time other men in uniform appeared and surrounded Katz.

"You do not understand," Bolan shouted in Russian. "He is getting away!"

"No one is getting away," shouted the officer who had hidden behind the sign.

Without another word he stepped forward and brought his pistol down on the Executioner's skull.

ZHDANOV WALKED briskly down the sidewalk toward a row of parking meters. Just before he reached them, he came to a cab sitting in the zone marked off for taxis and limousines. Opening the back door, he slid onto the seat and gave the driver directions to the area of the airport designated for private aircraft.

The Russian settled in as the cab cruised away from the commercial terminal and began the half-mile drive toward several rows of small hangars. After obtaining intelligence from a Hezbollah cell working inside Israel that a certain German scientist would be flying to Tel Aviv, the Red Army Faction had kidnapped the man, killed him and procured his passport and plane ticket for Zhdanov's use. But the Russian had always believed in having a backup plan, and while most of the time they weren't necessary, this had proved to be one of the times they were.

The Lufthansa tickets were worthless now that the Israeli and his friend knew about them. But he could still use the passport, and Zhdanov thanked his lucky stars that he had arranged for the Learjet to stand by just in case.

Zhdanov's thoughts turned back to the incident at the airport. He didn't know how long the two men would be detained—if picked up by the security officers maybe overnight, maybe permanently. But he suspected the delay wouldn't be more than a few days at most. He hadn't been able to find out much about Yakov Katzenelenbogen's current employment status. But he knew that he—and his friend, too, Zhdanov suspected—worked for some top secret outfit based in the United States. No one seemed to know the name of the organization or exactly what it did. Some of the people Zhdanov had asked about the group claimed it didn't really exist.

Zhdanov knew better. He had seen too much evidence that led to some centrally organized core of intelligence upon which the Israeli and his friend were relying. And he knew that an organization that efficient would eventually see to it that Katzenelenbogen and his partner were released.

The cabdriver turned off the main road onto a gravel drive leading to the hangars. Zhdanov grinned. A few days of detainment were more than he needed. The fact of the matter was, a few hours' head start would get him to Tel Aviv and the Israeli's daughter well ahead of the other two. Then he would kill her and wait for Katzenelenbogen himself.

And then, it would be over.

"Stop here," Zhdanov ordered the driver as they neared a hangar. Just outside the large front entrance stood a Learjet 24F powered by a pair of 13.8 kN CJ610-8A engines.

Zhdanov paid the cabdriver and got out, glancing through the aircraft window into the flight deck. The man behind the controls, already warming up the engine, was of Mideastern descent—a Hezbollah man named Abdullah who had flown in to be on standby the day before. Once they reached Israel, Zhdanov would team up with Abdullah's men, who would provide him with assistance and backup.

The sound of another plane caused the Russian to look up. Not far down the row of hangars he saw what looked at first like another Learjet 24F turn off the runway and taxi toward him. Zhdanov studied the craft closer and saw that it was indeed a Learjet, but one of the newer 25 series. The aircraft was slightly longer than the 24F he was about to board, and the Russian wondered briefly to whom it belonged, then his attention returned to his own plane.

Zhdanov boarded and took a seat next to the pilot. The man had a long pointed nose and an evil grin as he worked the steering column, taxiing the Learjet forward. As they cruised past the Learjet 25 that had just arrived, Zhdanov looked out his window and into the other plane. Behind the controls of the other jet, he saw a man wearing a faded brown leather bomber jacket and a brown suede baseball cap.

The pilot looked back at him, frowning.

Zhdanov suddenly realized who the man in the other Learjet had to be and grinned. "Let's go," he said to his pilot, and the man turned the plane onto the runway. A few seconds later they were racing down the tarmac, and a few seconds after that they were in the air.

Ulric Zhdanov thought of the man he had just seen before takeoff and smiled. He looked American, and he had to be the pilot for his enemies. Zhdanov didn't know how he knew, but he did.

And as the Learjet raced through the sky Zhdanov was certain of one other thing, too. The man in the other plane had known who the Russian was, as well; Zhdanov had seen it on his face.

Not that it mattered. By the time his enemies had cleared up the mess with the security police in St.

Petersburg, and the pilot got them to Israel, he would have Sharon Katzenelenbogen and it would be too late.

THE STONY MAN FARM pilot heard the radio instruct him to proceed to hangar 47 and turned off the runway, taxiing toward the row of green-and-white-metal buildings in the distance. Each hangar had a large white sign out front, and he saw the number 47 roughly halfway from the end. His gaze moved on, and he was surprised to see another aircraft that looked identical to the one in which he now sat.

Grimaldi squinted through the window. No, not identical, just similar. The craft outside the hangar marked 54 was a Learjet 24. It was hard to tell from this distance, but it looked like the F model. As he crept his own plane along, the Stony Man pilot saw a cab pull up and stop next to the plane.

He had been a pilot all of his adult life. He had flown countless combat missions over the unfriendly skies of Vietnam, then had gone to work as a flyboy for the Mafia before Mack Bolan had caused him to have a change of heart. Since then he had been a devoted Bolan ally and the number-one flyer for Stony Man Farm since its inception. He was a pilot first and foremost.

But Jack Grimaldi was also a warrior, which meant that over the years he had developed the same warrior instincts that the other champions of Stony

Man Farm had cultivated. And now, something in his brain clicked, causing him to go on alert.

There was something about the other Learjet that made him uneasy.

A man got out of the cab and walked toward the other plane as Grimaldi turned off the runway and began to taxi along the asphalt in front of the hangars. Still too far away to make out details, the pilot watched the man board the 24F. The other Learjet began to taxi forward.

The wings of the two planes were less than thirty feet apart when they passed each other headed in opposite directions. Grimaldi squinted again. Inside the 24F he could see a man who looked Mideastern behind the controls. Next to him sat a Caucasian with a flat-top haircut.

Although he hadn't seen Ulric Zhdanov, Grimaldi had heard Bolan and Katz mention the haircut. That, combined with his instinct, told Grimaldi immediately who the man was.

As the planes passed, Zhdanov grinned at Jack Grimaldi.

Grimaldi pulled up in front of hangar 47 and stopped. He watched the other jet take off, then turned back to the hangar where it had been. The cab was still there, the driver looking down and engrossed in something Grimaldi could not see below the window.

The pilot thought a moment. His gut instinct told him that Bolan and Katz had to have been hot on

Zhdanov's trail. So why was the Russian leaving the airport so leisurely? Grimaldi didn't know, but he suspected Bolan and Katz had been detained, which meant they might well be under arrest in the airport right now.

Grimaldi reached under the seat and pressed a button. The button activated a toggle switch on the control panel, and he leaned forward, flipping it. The toggle switch, in turn, rerouted the electronic signal of the first button, and when Grimaldi tapped it again, the console at his side—which appeared to be of solid construction—flipped open.

The Stony Man pilot reached inside the cavity and pulled out a .357 Magnum Smith & Wesson Model 66 in an inside-the-pants clip holster. Along with the revolver, he retrieved four speed loaders filled with 125-grain semijacketed hollowpoint rounds. Grimaldi removed the .357 Magnum snubbie from the slow-draw clip holster, and shoved it into the hand-warmer pocket of his bomber jacket. The medium-sized K-frame S&W barely fit, and he was thankful that he'd had Stony Man Farm armorer John Kissinger trim the hammer spur off and round the sharp edges. The weapon could be fired through his pocket now if it had to be, and the chances of it snagging during a draw were minimized.

Yes, Grimaldi thought again as he shoved the speed loaders into the other hand warmer pocket, he had always been, and always would be, a flyboy. First and foremost. But he was also a warrior.

And it was time to put on that warrior's hat now and help his friends if they needed it.

BOLAN RETURNED to consciousness with his eyes still closed, and his first sensation was a dull, heavy pounding just over the bridge of his nose. Then he opened his eyelids, and the pain turned sharp as the bright light invaded his pupils.

"This one has come to," a voice said in Russian.

Bolan let his blurry vision clear as the hammers in his brain continued to pound. He looked down and saw that he was seated in a straight-backed metal chair. His hands lay in his lap, unbound. He shuffled his feet slightly and realized that they, too, were free.

The reason he hadn't been restrained became evident as the Executioner's vision continued to clear. Standing around him in a circle were at least a half-dozen security police. Two still had their Tokarevs aimed at his head and chest. Another officer trained his weapon on a target to Bolan's side, and the Executioner twisted his head painfully to see Katz seated next to him.

The former Phoenix Force leader had evidently been struck unconscious, too. His eyes were still closed.

One of the men, wearing sergeant's stripes on his uniform, stepped in and grasped Bolan by the collar. "Who are you?" he demanded. "Which terrorist group do you represent?"

Bolan looked up at the angry red face over him. The man had an almost perfectly square head and wore a huge Joseph Stalin mustache. When the Executioner didn't answer, he stepped back and pulled a pair of black leather gloves from the side pocket of his uniform tunic.

Bolan watched the smiles break out on the faces of the other security men. One of the three holding pistols holstered his weapon and folded his arms across his chest to await the show.

"I will ask you once more politely," the Joseph Stalin clone said as he tugged the gloves over his hands and wrists. "Then I will get the information I want however I have to." He paused, then repeated, "Who are you, and which terrorist group do you represent? And what is your mission?"

Bolan stared him in the eye. A quick call to Stony Man Farm would result in another call from the Farm directly to the Oval Office. There was every chance in the world that the U.S. President could then contact the Russian authorities and get Bolan and Katz on their way. On the other hand, there was no guarantee that the man in the White House would be willing to do that. For his own good, the President had to disavow any knowledge of the Farm, and unless he could help them without giving up that executive privilege, he would not do so. Nor was there any guarantee that Bolan could talk these security officers into letting him make the call in the first place. This wasn't the U.S.; even if they did grant him a call, the bureaucratic red tape that would have be waded through would take too long. By the time they were released, Ulric Zhdanov would have had time to reach Israel and kill Sharon Katzenelenbogen ten times over.

No, Bolan realized, he and Katz would have to rely on themselves for escape.

"We are not terrorists," he said, hoping to stall for time.

It didn't work.

The sergeant with the huge mustache clenched his gloved fist, drew it back behind his shoulder, then aimed at the Executioner's nose. Bolan felt the blood spurt from his nostrils as the pain already shooting through his head tripled.

"Wrong answer," the Russian cop said.

Bolan closed his eyes, feigning unconsciousness once more. As the sergeant had struck, he had seen the other two men still holding their Tokarevs reholster the pistols. Now no weapons were trained on them. The men were confident that not only did they have the two prisoners outnumbered, but that Bolan and Katz were beaten down to the point where covering them was no longer necessary.

His eyes still closed, the Executioner realized what a break that was. Even considering the pain that would slow him somewhat, he knew he could leap to his feet and overpower the sergeant, taking the man's weapon and holding him hostage, before the others could draw their guns. The problem with that plan was that then he'd have to make his way out of there with the man in tow.

That wouldn't be so hard if Katz were awake, but Bolan glanced at the Israeli and saw that wasn't the case. Katz's eyes remained closed. He couldn't carry his friend out of there and cover the sergeant at the same time.

The sergeant saw Bolan open his eyes and reached forward, grabbing his collar again. "I know you are awake," he said. With his other hand, he backhanded the Executioner across the face.

Bolan felt one of his lips split. The rusty taste of blood filled his mouth. "I'm telling you the truth," he said. "We aren't terrorists."

A series of punches and backhands followed. Bolan felt his head rock back and forth like a boxer's speed bag. His eyes began to swell, and when he opened them he could barely make out the sergeant. But he could see Katz out of the corner of his eye and knew that his friend was still unconscious. That meant he had no alternative but to take whatever beating was coming as he waited for the Israeli to awaken.

He would just have to hope when that happened he still had the strength to escape.

More blows rained over the Executioner's head and shoulders. Then the man with the Stalin mustache stepped back, breathing hard.

Bolan looked at him through his swollen eyes but said nothing. Then, through the tiny slits of vision,

he saw two things at the same time that gave him
hope. First he saw Katzenelenbogen's eyes flicker
open next to him. And second, in the doorway behind the sergeant and the other men, the Executioner
saw a man wearing a brown leather bomber jacket
and suede bush pilot's cap lean around the corner
and look through the doorway.

Jack Grimaldi held his .357 Magnum Smith &
Wesson Model 66 revolver in his right hand.

CHAPTER TEN

The cab Grimaldi had seen bring Ulric Zhdanov to hangar 54 still stood where it had parked as the pilot exited the Learjet. The Stony Man pilot walked quickly to the driver's side and knocked on the window. At the same time he looked through the glass to see that the cabbie had taken this opportunity to do some paperwork. A log of some kind rested in his lap.

The man rolled down the window and said hello in Russian.

"Hello," Grimaldi repeated. "Speak English?"

"Sure."

"Are you on the clock?"

The driver glanced down at the meter on the dashboard in front of him. "I can be," he said.

Grimaldi circled the cab and got into the passenger's seat in front. "Customs," he told the driver, and a moment later they were rolling down the asphalt in front of the hangars.

A few minutes later the driver pulled up in front

of the two-story wood-frame building that served as the customs office for private craft.

Grimaldi paid the man and added a generous tip. "Can you wait for me?" he asked. "I may be a half hour or so."

The driver looked at the money in his hand, and greed filled his eyes. "For double what you just gave me," he said, "I could sit right here and finish my paperwork, which will take me at least a half hour."

Grimaldi chuckled and passed more bills across the cab to the man. "You guys catch on to capitalism pretty fast." He got out and entered the customs building.

The private-craft customs office was overstaffed and underworked. Three men sat at a table against the far wall playing cards. Another sat on a high-backed stool just behind the counter reading a paperback book. He looked up disinterestedly as Grimaldi approached and laid his passport and flight plans down on the top of the stand.

"How long will you be in St. Petersburg?" the customs man asked in a practiced monotone.

"I'm just going into the terminal to look for some friends. They were supposed to be waiting for me." He forced a laugh. "Probably in the bar."

The other man chuckled. He glanced at the passport and other papers, then shoved them back to Grimaldi. "Go on," he said. "Your friends may have been delayed if they were in the part of the airport where the terrorists were."

Grimaldi's ears picked up. "Terrorists? What terrorists?"

The customs man shrugged, then shook his head. "It is not clear yet who they were or what they wanted to accomplish. But they are both in custody."

Grimaldi forced an expression of fear onto his face as a cover. "Is it safe to go inside?" he asked.

"Yes, yes," the customs man scoffed. "I told you, they are in custody. They are being questioned by security even as we speak."

Grimaldi continued to frown in concern as he gathered up his papers and shoved them into the inside pocket of his jacket. By the time he had left the wooden building and crossed the concrete parking lot to the main terminal, however, the frown had become a grim smile.

At least he knew where Bolan and Katz were.

The Stony Man pilot entered the terminal and saw a sign that read Security Police in several languages. He followed the arrows around two more corners and suddenly found himself in a short corridor outside a suite of offices with the same security sign over the entrance. The hallway ended at an exit door thirty feet farther on. The front door under the security sign was propped open.

Grimaldi took a deep breath. He stuck his right

hand into his jacket pocket, closed his fingers around the .357 and stepped inside.

The outer reception office was sparsely furnished. The walls were bare, and a gunmetal gray desk and two hard-backed wooden chairs were the only furniture. A lone door, closed, stood in the far wall.

But if the reception office itself was plain, the woman sitting in it was anything but. Seated behind the desk, filing her nails with an emery board, she was one of the most strikingly beautiful women Jack Grimaldi had even seen. She wore civilian clothes— a simple white blouse and a navy blue skirt—but on her they might as well have been a garter belt and fishnet hose. Long blond hair fell gracefully past her shoulders, and her skin looked as if she'd just stepped out of a television commercial for a moisturizing cream. She looked up at Grimaldi with sea blue eyes and smiled.

"Yes?" she said in Russian. "I am Luiza. What can I do for you?"

"I only speak a little Russian. I am looking for two friends of mine who have disappeared." He held his hand over his head, palm down. "One is tall...an American," he said. He lowered his hand to eye level. "The other is shorter, Israeli."

Grimaldi saw the woman's eyes flicker nervously over her shoulder, and he knew instinctively that Bolan and Katz had to be in one of the back security offices. When Luiza's eyes returned to his, she said, "One moment, please. Perhaps I can help you." She reached out and wrapped her fingers around the phone on her desk.

The Stony Man pilot slid in to the desk and placed his left hand over Luiza's, preventing her from lifting the receiver. With his right hand he drew the Model 66 out of his pocket just far enough to let her see what it was, then took his other hand off hers and held his index finger to his lips. "Keep quiet, Luiza," he said. "Just do as I tell you and you won't get hurt."

Fear clouded the deep blue eyes, and the woman nodded slowly.

"Stand up," Grimaldi ordered.

Luiza's lower lip quivered as she pushed her chair back and stood.

Grimaldi felt himself take in a deep breath as the woman's wasplike waist and shapely hips came into view.

"You are not going to…molest me, are you?" Luiza asked.

Grimaldi shook his head and chuckled. "That's not my style." Waving the barrel of the revolver toward the door, the Stony Man pilot said, "I'm guessing my friends are on the other side of door number one?"

"Door…number one?" Luiza asked, confused. "There is only one door."

"Sorry," Grimaldi said. "American joke, I guess." He paused. "They're back there?"

Luiza nodded.

"How many officers?"

Luiza shrugged. "Six. Maybe eight."

"Take me to them," Grimaldi ordered. He stepped in, taking the woman by the arm and turning her toward the door. "And when we see the officers, I suggest you advise them real fast to hold their fire." He pushed her gently forward. "Luiza?" he said just as she was about to open the door.

"Yes?"

"I was serious. Do this right and I promise you won't get hurt."

"What...what if I make a mistake?" the woman said.

"Then I'll kill you," Grimaldi replied. What the hell, he thought. She doesn't have to know I'm lying.

Luiza opened the door and let the pilot into a dimly lit hallway. The air smelled of sweat and spicy food, and at the end of the hall Grimaldi could hear voices. Luiza led him past six vacant offices with paperwork scattered across the desks, and it became obvious that the men who occupied the spaces had vacated them to take part in the interrogation at the end of the hall. The final open door they passed appeared to be a "nap" room for employees forced to work double shifts or other emergency situations in which they couldn't get home. Inside the opening, Grimaldi saw a row of six cots made up with sheets, blankets and pillows. Like the desks in the offices, all were empty.

When he reached the door at the end of the hall, Grimaldi moved in front of the woman and peered around the corner.

In the center of the room, the pilot saw six uniformed men circling two chairs. In one chair he saw Yakov Katzenelenbogen, who appeared to be unconscious. In the other chair he could see a pair of legs and torso he recognized as belonging to Mack Bolan. But a man wearing black leather gloves stood in front of the Executioner, blocking Grimaldi's view of Bolan's head.

As Grimaldi watched, the man shifted slightly and the pilot caught a glimpse of the Executioner's face. The man in the gloves had been using his friend for punching practice.

Grimaldi ducked back around the corner. Leaning in to Luiza's ear, he said, "Take a seat on the floor and don't move."

Luiza nodded her understanding and sat down. She leaned forward and covered her head with her hands.

Grimaldi drew the S&W from his jacket and looked back around the corner. He saw the man in the gloves hit Bolan again and step back. Katz moved slightly, and it appeared that the Israeli was returning to consciousness.

As he looked back to the Executioner, Grimaldi's eyes met the swollen slits on each side of Bolan's nose for a moment. When they did, he could see that the Executioner had seen him. Bolan even appeared to nod slightly.

Then Jack Grimaldi saw the Executioner go into action.

BOLAN TOOK a final glance at Katz and saw that his old friend had not only come fully awake, but he'd also had time to ascertain the situation. With Grimaldi in the hall, there would be no better time than the present to act.

As the sergeant wearing the black gloves stepped forward and raised his fist again, Bolan lashed out suddenly with a front kick to the man's left knee. The sergeant screamed in pain as he fell forward into Bolan's lap.

In one smooth movement the Executioner unfastened the flap on the man's belt holster and drew the Tokarev, thumbing the safety forward to the "fire" position. He jammed the weapon into the side of the man's head and stood, lifting the sergeant to his feet as he did so.

"Don't move," the Executioner ordered the rest of the security men stationed around the room. His words were unnecessary. The sudden and unexpected reversal of the balance of power in the room had frozen the uniformed men where they stood.

Katz stood and stepped forward. The former Phoenix Force leader reached down and unfastened the flap on the holster of the man nearest him. A moment later he held another Tokarev on the men.

A security man directly in front of the Executioner finally regained his composure. "There are six of us and only two of you," he said. "You can never get us all." His hand began moving slowly toward his holster,

Jack Grimaldi had remained motionless in the doorway so far, but now Bolan saw him slide in swiftly behind the man who had spoken. The Stony Man pilot stuck the snub-nosed barrel of his stainless-steel .357 into the man's kidney. The hammer made an audible click that echoed throughout the room as Grimaldi cocked the revolver. With a mere two pounds of trigger pull separating the security officer from death, the pilot said, "Better call that three. And even if we don't get you all, rest assured I'll get you."

The security man's hand froze halfway to his holster, then he dropped it back to his side and his entire body went rigid.

The sergeant wearing the black gloves was the next to speak. "All right," he said, his voice stripped of the cockiness it had held before. "What are your demands? What do you want?"

"Out of here," Bolan said.

"What else?"

"That's it," the Executioner said. "We leave, then it's business as usual for you guys."

"Then you may go," the sergeant said.

Bolan, Katz and Grimaldi all laughed. "Just like that?" Bolan asked.

"Certainly. You have my word."

The Executioner wrapped a forearm around the man's neck and transferred the Tokarev to the small of the sergeant's back. "I'm afraid we're going to need a little better insurance than that," he said.

He turned to Katz. "Pick out a shield. You too, Jack."

Katz and Grimaldi both grabbed the officers closest to them and twisted the men's arms behind their backs. Bolan pushed the sergeant ahead of him toward the table against the wall where he'd seen their weapons. The men hadn't bothered to remove his holsters, and he shoved the Beretta 93-R back into the shoulder rig and leathered the Desert Eagle back on his hip. He slid his Applegate-Fairbairn fighting knife into its Kydex sheath, then handed Katz the Israeli's own Beretta and knife.

The Executioner shoved the sergeant forward again, stopping just before they reached the door to the hall. Turning back to address the three security officers who remained in the room, he said, "You men stay put right where you are for the next thirty minutes. I see any of you after I leave this room, we'll kill these three. You understand me?"

The three heads bobbed up and down.

Bolan guided his hostage out of the room and into the hall. He was surprised to see an attractive young woman sitting on the floor in the hall. He turned toward Grimaldi, who was right behind him. The woman had to have been used as the pilot's ticket in.

Grimaldi shrugged. "She followed me home, Sarge," he said, deadpan. "Can I keep her?"

Bolan's sigh was audible as he shook his head.

The Executioner led the way past the other empty offices. He glanced over his shoulder twice, seeing Grimaldi and his hostage right behind. Katz brought up the rear, dragging the man in his arm backward and keeping an eye on the room where the other three security officers had been told to wait.

When they reached the reception area, Bolan pushed open the door. "What's the fastest route out of here to where you're parked, Jack?" he asked Grimaldi.

"I came in through the front," the pilot said. "Had to make several turns. If there's a side exit..." He let his voice trail off, and both he and Bolan turned to the man the Executioner was holding.

"There is an exit just to the left, down this hall," the man said, nodding his head as much as he could with Bolan's arm locked around his throat. "You can go out—"

"We can go out," Bolan corrected. "You'll be coming with us."

"All right, we," the sergeant replied, "can go out that way, cross a small employees' parking lot between here and the administration building and be at the private hangars."

The Executioner felt himself frowning. "How far from the door to the hangars?"

"From the door?" the sergeant said. "Twenty yards across the parking lot. Then perhaps another ten to the closest hangar."

"We going to be meeting up with any of your people on the way?" the Executioner demanded.

The sergeant hesitated, then said, "No."

The hesitation was enough to make Bolan suspicious. "Stay here," he told Grimaldi and Katz.

Then, shoving the sergeant ahead of him, he said, "Let's go."

Bolan pushed the sergeant out of the reception-room door. The short security hallway was deserted, with only a few people walking back and forth in the larger corridor that intersected the security wing. Bolan pushed his hostage to the left, hanging on to the man's neck as the sergeant led him to the exit door. Once at the door, the Executioner shifted the man slightly in his arm and, with the Tokarev still in his hand, used his forearm to push the safety bar.

The door opened slightly, and sunlight shot into the hallway. Bolan stuck his head partway out and saw the administration building thirty feet away. As he glanced to the roof, he saw a man wearing black fatigues and body armor holding a rifle.

The figure jumped back out of sight as the Executioner looked up.

Bolan pulled his head back into the hall and released the door. What had happened couldn't have been more clear if it were written down. The three security officers he had left in the back office had complied with his orders—they'd stayed put. But they'd picked up the phone and contacted another security office or substation somewhere in the airport.

The Executioner felt his eyebrows lower in concentration as the door swung back and snapped shut. He had seen one sniper, which meant there might well be a dozen others hidden on the roof and in other nooks and crannies. No matter how careful they were, there was no way he, Katz and Grimaldi could all make it across the open area without someone getting a shot at at least one of them. Unless...

Bolan tightened his grip on the sergeant's neck and pulled him back down the hall to the security office. As soon as they were inside again, he said, "Katz, leave your man here. I'll watch him. Go back to that sleeping area we passed and get three blankets off the cots."

Katz dropped his hostage and disappeared down the hall. Bolan kept one eye on Katz's man and the other on the sergeant until the Israeli returned a few seconds later carrying three heavy blankets and wearing a curious look on his face. Bolan took two of them and handed one to Grimaldi.

"They've got snipers set up outside," the Executioner explained. He turned toward the hallway and shouted toward the back room. "You men still where I told you to be?"

"Yes!" all three voices said in unison.

"Okay," Bolan continued. "Since you like using the phone, get back on it and tell your people we're coming out. Make sure they know we've got hostages, who they are, and tell them I said they can go ahead and take their best shot if they want. But tell them all we want is to get to our plane and get out of here. We'll release these men just before takeoff. Unless you people cause us trouble, in which case we'll kill them. You got it?"

"Yes!"

Bolan turned to his friends. "Ready?"

"Never been readier," Grimaldi said.

Katz nodded.

Bolan led the way back down the hallway to the exit. When they reached the door, he shoved the Tokarev into his belt long enough to spread the blanket over both the sergeant's and his heads and shoulders. Drawing the Tokarev once more, he used the tip of the barrel to raise the blanket slightly in front of his face, then turned to Katz, Grimaldi and their prisoners.

The Executioner couldn't suppress a smile. The thick wool blankets broke up the men's outlines perfectly. There was no way to know where one head started and the other stopped, no way to tell if the crosshairs of a rifle scope were centered on the heart of friend or foe. Any of the snipers who risked pulling the trigger stood a fifty-fifty chance of killing their own men rather than he or the other men from Stony Man Farm.

Turning back to the door, the Executioner pushed through.

Bolan heard a stifled gasp from the top of the building across from him as he stepped out into the parking lot. He pushed the sergeant in front of him, continuing to use the barrel of the Tokarev to raise the blanket just high enough to see. He led Grimaldi, Katz and their charges through a maze of parked automobiles toward a grassy area on the other side.

Muffled, whispering voices argued back and forth from various unseen hiding places as the men from Stony Man Farm moved on. Finally one of the voices called out in Russian, "Halt immediately or we'll shoot!"

"No!" the sergeant under the blanket with Bolan shouted. "Do not fire!"

Bolan stepped up off the parking lot onto the grass and started down the asphalt drive in front of the hangars, finally stopping at the Learjet still idling in front of number 47.

"Jack," the Executioner said, turning to Grimaldi and the Russian under the blanket with him, "get in, then let your man go."

Grimaldi edged his way to the door, slipped out from under the blanket and boarded the Learjet.

Bolan shoved the Tokarev straight out from his body into the belly of the man the pilot had just released. "I want you to run over there and tell them we'll let your friends go once we're about to take off."

The man nodded and started to walk away.

"I said run!" Bolan shouted, and the man broke into a sprint.

The Executioner turned to Katz. "Take your buddy and board," he ordered.

The blanket still over their heads, the Israeli pulled his man up into the jet.

Bolan followed, jerking the sergeant up after him, then pulling the door down behind them. Pushing the man to a sitting position, he threw off the blanket and moved up next to Grimaldi behind the steering column. "All ready?" he said.

The Stony Man pilot nodded.

Bolan turned to Katz. "Let your man go."

Katz unlatched the door, pushed it up far enough for his prisoner to crawl through onto the asphalt drive and helped him with a kick in the seat of the pants.

The sergeant started to follow, but Bolan swung the Tokarev around to him. "You wait." He turned back to Grimaldi. "Taxi over to the runway," he said. He moved back to the sergeant, catching a quick reflection of his swollen face in a piece of metal trim as he stepped.

"Stand up," the Executioner ordered as the plane began to roll toward the runway.

The sergeant obeyed, his eyes filled with terror. Mucus had dripped from his nose onto the bushy mustache, and it glistened under the bright lights inside the Learjet 25F. "You must understand," he said, his voice shaking, "I was only doing my job."

Bolan didn't answer. He continued to train the Tokarev on the man as they neared the runway.

Grimaldi made a sharp turn onto the tarmac, then tapped the brake, halting the craft. "Ready when you are," he called back into the cabin.

"Are you going to kill me?" the sergeant asked.

"No." Bolan stepped to the side of the plane and opened the door as high as it would go. "Get over in front of the door," he ordered. As the terrified sergeant complied, the Executioner turned toward the front of the plane. "Let's get her off the ground, Jack," he called out.

"No!" the sergeant roared. "You said you would let us all go!" His chest heaved in and out as he struggled for breath. "I was only doing my job!"

"And now I'm doing mine," Bolan said. As the wheels of the jet began to roll, he transferred the Tokarev to his left hand, drew back his right fist and sent a right cross drilling into the sergeant's jaw.

Bone crunched as the Executioner's knuckles made contact with the man's face. The sergeant was driven through the doorway and turned a complete back flip before bouncing on the tarmac.

As the airplane sped down the runway, then rose into the air, Bolan saw the sergeant rise unsteadily to his feet, his right hand holding his chin.

Hebron, Israel

"WE SHOULDN'T be doing this."

"Right."

"We should be working."

"Right."

"Then why are we doing this instead of working?" Sharon Katzenelenbogen asked.

"Because this is more fun," Yoni said. He rolled up onto one elbow, rested his head in his hand, and grinned at the woman next to him. "And because this is the first time Singer has been out of camp and we've been able to do it in a bed."

In spite of herself, Sharon grinned back. She had been delighted when Mayer had confessed his feelings for her. "It is kind of nice. I mean, making love in the desert at night under the stars is romantic. But it's also nice not to have to wash sand out of all of your body's orifices."

Mayer laughed and leaned forward, kissing her lightly on the lips. "Maybe we should take advantage of the opportunity and do it again," he whispered. "Who knows when we'll get another chance?"

Sharon rolled away from him under the light sheet and looked at her watch on the nightstand. It was almost evening. "We've got to get up," she said. "Singer could be getting back with Dr. Werner any time now."

"How do you figure that?"

"His flight was due in several hours ago. They've almost had time to—"

Mayer slapped his forehead and shook his head. "Damn," he said. "I forgot to tell you." He glanced to the field phone in the corner of the tent. "Singer called while you were taking your shower this morning. Werner had left a message at the airport that a friend of his was flying into Tel Aviv in a private plane and he'd decided to cash in his ticket and come that way. It threw him back a couple of hours but it made it a direct flight. And free." He paused. "I guess Werner's on as tight a budget as we are these days."

"So they won't be here for another few hours?" Sharon asked.

"Don't see how they could be," Yoni said. "Besides, we're in the desert. We'll be able to hear the Jeep miles before they get here." He leaned in again, this time kissing her neck. "We'll get dressed as soon as we hear them coming."

A short while later, the faint sound of a Jeep engine in the distance filtered across the desert and into the tent flap. Both she and Yoni jumped to their feet.

"I feel like a high-school girl whose parents were out of town but came home early," she said as she tugged on her shorts and blouse.

"I know what you mean."

As soon as they were dressed, Sharon pulled the tent flap back far enough to peek through. The vehicle was less than a quarter of a mile away on the road leading to the dig. She turned to Yoni. "Can you go out the back?" she said. "Circle around to your own tent?"

"I can, if that's what you want me to do. But I'll feel a little silly. We're not high-school kids, Sharon, and I don't think we're fooling Dr. Singer the least little bit."

"No, but there's no point flaunting our relationship in his face," Sharon said. "And we've never even met Dr. Werner. I don't want his first impression of me to be formed right after seeing me roll out of the sack with a co-worker."

"Okay." Mayer moved quickly to the back of the tent and dropped to his knees, then his belly. Lifting the hem of the canvas, he crawled under and disappeared.

Sharon checked herself in the mirror over her nightstand, quickly reapplying her lipstick, then stepped out of the tent as the Jeep pulled to a halt. She saw Dr. Singer get out of the driver's side, and her first impression of the older man was that he didn't look particularly happy.

A man of medium height and build got out of the Jeep's passenger seat and started to walk forward. Sharon was surprised to see that he was little older than she or Yoni. She had expected Dr. Werner to be closer to Herbert Singer's age.

And she certainly hadn't pictured him with a flat-top haircut.

Sharon Katzenelenbogen saw Mayer come out of

the other sleeping tent and yawn as if he'd just been taking a nap. Her American lover glanced her way, gave her a quick wink and walked forward to meet Dr. Werner.

It wasn't until then that Sharon heard the sound of the other Jeeps approaching across the desert.

CHAPTER ELEVEN

The wheels of the Learjet 25F touched down on the runway, and Jack Grimaldi slowed the craft to taxi speed across the tarmac. When they had come to a complete halt, Bolan and Katz waited as two Israeli customs officials walked out toward the plane.

Both men were dressed sharply, their crisp uniforms starched and creased. They smiled as they walked, leading Bolan to believe that the request to the U.S. President that he had relayed through Stony Man Farm had gotten through, and the President had in turn made the call to Israeli authorities.

They shouldn't be detained or checked for weapons.

Bolan felt the adrenaline coursing through his body as he waited for the men to arrive. His radio message to Barbara Price, Stony Man Farm's mission controller, had also contained another entreaty—that Price call Sharon Katzenelenbogen at either her office or apartment, advise her as to what was going down and have her immediately take a hotel room under the name Yental Wilenzik. She was then to contact David Weizmann, an old Mossad buddy of Katz's. Bolan had read Weizmann's personal number over the radio to Price from Katz's address book. He and Katz would contact Weizmann through the same number and learn Sharon's whereabouts as soon as they touched down.

There was only one problem. Sharon wasn't answering either her office or apartment phone. And the main switchboard operator at the State Antiquities Administration had informed Price that it was against policy to give out any information about employees to unknown voices over the phone.

That part didn't worry the Executioner. If something had happened to Sharon at work, there would have been an Israeli cop asking questions of Price before she'd hung up. But if Sharon had been attacked at home, the crime might not yet have been discovered. So Price had tried to reach Weizmann herself and have him check Sharon's apartment. But the retired Mossad man wasn't picking up the receiver, either.

The bottom line was, little things weren't going right, and that meant they knew absolutely nothing. Sharon Katzenelenbogen could be alive. Or she could be dead.

The two customs department men, one wearing captain's bars, arrived, and Katz flipped open the door. "Hello."

The other man in the well-pressed uniform smiled back. "Welcome to Israel," he said. "May we see your passports and Department of Justice IDs, please?''

Bolan and Grimaldi remained where they were as Katz handed all of their documents through the door. The captain glanced at each picture, then stuck his head through the door to compare them with the men inside. Satisfied, he handed them back to Katz. "You must be on a mission of some importance," he said. "Your President called the prime minister himself. They rerouted the call here, and I spoke to the President myself on a three-way conference call.'' His chest puffed out slightly with pride.

"We appreciate your getting us through quickly," Katz said.

"It is my pleasure," the captain replied. "But I must be honest. I do not do it because of your President—I help you men for two reasons. First because my prime minister instructed me to do so. But more importantly because you are like us.'' He tapped the badge on his chest and indicated the man at his side. "You enforce the laws."

The captain stuck his head inside the plane again and gave Grimaldi directions to a hangar that had been reserved for them. Then he saluted all three men, and he and the other customs officer started back across the tarmac.

Grimaldi followed the captain's directions, taxiing the jet toward a row of corrugated-tin buildings. "Want me to come with you?" he asked Bolan as they stopped again.

The Executioner shook his head. "No, Jack, stay here and keep this bird warmed up and ready to go. Sharon's not answering either phone, so we're likely to find out she's left town. If that's the case, I want to be ready to hit the air again as soon as possible."

"You got it, big guy," Grimaldi said. He pulled a paperback book from the inside map pocket of his bomber jacket and opened it to a page that had been dog-eared.

Bolan and Katz stepped down out of the plane. The Executioner led the way to the terminal, spotting a car-rental counter as soon as they'd pushed their way through one of the revolving glass doors. A few moments later they were driving away in a year-old black Toyota 4Runner.

It had been some time since the Executioner had been to Israel, and since Tel Aviv was Yakov Katzenelenbogen's old stomping grounds, he'd let the Israeli take the wheel. Katz drove quickly through the streets of the busy, cheerful metropolis. As they neared the Mediterranean, the smell of salt sea air drifted in through the windows of the vehicle.

Outdoor cafés lined the sides of the road, where men, women and children sat beneath umbrellas sipping tea. They passed Bar Ilan University and the Belinson Hospital, and then Katz turned into a large apartment complex. He parked in front of one of the buildings and pulled the keys from the ignition. He and Bolan were out of the 4Runner and inside the common hallway almost before the engine had died.

Katz's left hand fished through his pocket for another key as the knuckles of his right hand rapped a door with a metal numeral 7 nailed to the front. Getting no response, he inserted his key and led Bolan inside. Both men had their hands on the weapons beneath their jackets as they went in.

It proved unnecessary. The apartment was deserted.

It was small, consisting of a living-dining area, a kitchen, a bathroom and one bedroom. Systematically Bolan and Katz searched the living area, then the other rooms for any clues as to where Sharon might be. That, too, proved fruitless. The only thing Bolan learned was that Sharon Katzenelenbogen was an immaculate housekeeper.

"There's no sign of a fight or struggle or any kind of violence, Katz," the Executioner said. "At least we know nothing happened to her."

Katz snorted. "At least not here." It was clear he knew that Bolan's words were meant primarily to put his mind at ease. If Zhdanov had surprised Sharon with a gun, he might easily have gotten her out of the apartment without a struggle. Or he could already have found her at work, or shopping at the store, or at any number of other places.

Bolan moved in behind Katz as the man opened the closet door. He saw his friend's gaze shoot to an empty shelf above the clothes bar from which a variety of clothing hung on hangers. "She has left town," Katz said, his voice full of certainty. "That shelf—'' he pointed upward ''—when I was here last week held several suitcases.''

''Then let's get to her office,'' Bolan said. ''Find out where she's gone.''

he two men hurried back out of the apartment, locking the door behind them.

''The switchboard operator at State Antiquities refused to tell Barbara anything over the phone,'' Katz reminded the Executioner as they hurried back to the 4Runner. ''But I've got another old acquaintance—a lieutenant who served under me in the Israeli army—who's in charge of security at the State Antiquities Administration building.''

''He'll remember you, right?'' Bolan asked.

Katz nodded as they slipped back into the vehicle. ''I bumped into him when I went to see Sharon's office last week. We'll find out where she is.''

''And what if this friend is on vacation?'' Bolan asked.

Katz backed away from the apartment building and threw the 4Runner into gear. As the tires squealed off the parking lot and onto the street, he turned to face Bolan. ''We'll still find out,'' he said. ''One way or another, we'll still find out.''

The Executioner nodded. Someone at the antiquities office would know where Sharon had gone. And that someone would talk to them.

Whether they wanted to or not.

''THE BUILDING has more security than just these

cameras, doesn't it?'' Bolan asked as he watched the bracket-mounted video monitors outside the antiquities building swivel slowly back and forth.

Next to him, behind the wheel of the 4Runner, Katz nodded. ''Metal detectors just inside the doors,'' he said, ''and armed security guards, Israeli military, not minimum-wage rent-a-cops.''

Just then one of the glass doors in the front of the building opened, and a man wearing a navy blue blazer, gray slacks and hair almost the same shade as his pants stepped out onto the sidewalk. He held a walkie-talkie in his left hand and a leather-bound book in his right as his eyes scanned up and down the street.

''That's him,'' Katz said, opening the door. ''That's Abraham.''

Bolan got out on the other side. They had stopped at a phone booth between Sharon's apartment and the antiquities building long enough for Katz to call and determine that his old lieutenant, Abraham Mattathias, was indeed in his office. Katz had advised Mattathias that they were looking for Sharon but had been stonewalled by bureaucracy. Mattathias had agreed to come out to the sidewalk and walk them through the security checkpoints, then help Katz find out where his daughter was.

Bolan and Katz crossed the street. Introductions were short, with Katz introducing Bolan as Colonel Rance Pollock and giving Mattathias only the briefest of briefings as to what was going on. It was clear that it was enough for Mattathias, who obviously had the greatest respect and trust for his old commanding officer.

"Abe," Katz said. "Anyone odd been here today? Anyone else looking for Sharon?"

"Well," the security chief said, "there was the phone call I told you about when you called a few minutes ago. When the woman on the other end refused to leave a name, it was reported to me. Standard procedure."

Bolan knew who the woman on the other end had to have been—Barbara Price. "That was one of our people," he said.

"Let's go talk to Sharon's supervisor," Katz suggested. He started to step past Mattathias.

Mattathias reached out and gently took Katz's arm, stopping him. "I've saved you some time, Yakov," the security chief said. "I already checked with Sharon's supervisor. She and two other archaeologists—a Dr. Singer and Dr. Mayer—have gone on a dig at the Oaks of Mamre. You familiar with the area?"

"It's where Abraham—your namesake—camped. Has anyone had contact with them today?"

Mattathias shook his head. "They talked to Dr. Singer yesterday. He was getting ready to drive in to the airport and pick up a German archaeologist who is coming to help. But today, after the call from the unidentified woman earlier, Sharon's secretary tried to raise them on the field phone they have with them." He shrugged. "Nobody answered."

The Executioner frowned. "Is that unusual?"

Mattathias turned to face Bolan. "That's what I asked, of course, and they said 'not necessarily.' They could all be out at the dig site and maybe have left the phone back at the camp."

Bolan and Katz exchanged glances. Under other circumstances that would seem to be a reasonable explanation. Under these conditions it was impossible to know.

"Think hard, Abe," Katz said. "Did anyone else call or come by looking for Sharon today? Anything unusual at all that might relate to her?"

Mattathias opened the leather-covered book and began thumbing through the pages. Bolan could see that the pages were handwritten—a log book.

The security chief came to a page and stopped. "Two days ago a man wearing the uniform of our contract custodial firm was stopped just outside Sharon's office by one of my officers. My man didn't recognize his face and wanted to see some ID."

Katz leaned forward slightly. "And?"

"And the man patted down his coveralls, then said he must have left his billfold in the truck."

"Sounds like an underage kid trying to buy beer," Katz said.

Mattathias nodded. "Anyway, my officer sent him after it. He never came back."

Bolan had to admit it sounded suspicious. But two days ago Ulric Zhdanov had still been in St. Petersburg. "Did your officer give a description of the man?" he asked.

Mattathias nodded. "About five-ten, one-sixty," he said. "Brown eyes, medium dark complexion."

"Mideasterner, then?" Bolan asked.

The security chief glanced at the book and nodded. "Definitely," he said. "My officer suspected Iranian from his accent, although he spoke fluent Hebrew."

"Anything else?" Katz asked.

Mattathias turned the page and squinted. "My officer followed up with a call to the custodial service. They hadn't sent anyone new that day."

Bolan and Katz exchanged glances again. It was all too clear what had happened. Utilizing the international network between terrorist organizations the world over, Zhdanov had sent someone into the antiquities building to case the place, which meant he had known in advance that Sharon was at the dig, and would have gone straight there.

They were now more than an hour or two behind the Russian assassin. They were at least half a day.

"Is there a place to land a plane near the Oaks?" Bolan asked.

"Depends what kind," Mattathias said. "There are some flat areas nearby in the desert, but I wouldn't try it with a 747."

"Learjet," Katz said, "25F."

Mattathias rolled his eyes upward for a moment, thinking, then said, "Shouldn't be a problem for a decent pilot."

Bolan and Katz had turned to cross the street again when the glass door opened and a man wearing a security uniform hurried out. "Chief Mattathias!" he said, out of breath. "I think you had better come see this."

Mattathias turned back to Katz and Bolan. "Want to come?" he asked. "It might have something to do with what you're interested in."

Bolan and Katz followed Mattathias and the uniformed man into the building. The security chief hooked a thumb over his shoulder, okaying them through the security checkpoint. The beepers beeped as they walked through the metal detector, and then they followed the uniformed man up the steps to the second floor.

The man led them down a semilighted hallway that looked as if it served as a utility storage and janitor wing. Coming to the third door on the right, he reached forward and rested his hand on the knob.

The odor emanating through the door was enough to gag a person. But it was an odor familiar to Bolan, Katz and Abraham Mattathias.

The security officer twisted the knob and opened the door.

More of the nauseous stench shot out as the door swung wide. Bolan looked at the nude man on the floor. The corpse had been wedged between a ten-gallon barrel of cleaning solvent and a case of urinal deodorant disks, and the man's head shot out at an absurdly unnatural angle, the white bone of his neck poking through the skin.

The Executioner studied him for a second. He had been dead for at least a couple of days.

"Who is he?" Bolan asked, knowing the answer before he even asked.

"The regular janitor," Mattathias replied, shaking his head. He turned to face the Executioner. "The one the mysterious Iranian claimed to be replacing."

THIRTY MINUTES LATER Bolan and Katz pulled the 4Runner onto the asphalt approach to the hangars. Five minutes after that, they were leaving the runway in the Learjet again, the cabin depressurized this time.

"Jack," the Executioner had said before they rose into the air, "the guy back at the antiquities building said there were places nearby where you could land. But my guess is that Zhdanov—and probably a decent number of men from one of the local terrorist organizations—is already there. I don't want to alert them. Katz and I will jump. HALO."

Grimaldi and Bolan had worked together too long for the pilot not to know the next step. "The sun's setting now," he'd said. "I'll stay high enough that they don't notice me and spot a strip close by. As soon as it's dark enough, I'll touch down. Don't forget a walkie so I can give you my coordinates."

The jet rose as Bolan and Katz began to change clothes. Bolan pulled one of his blacksuits from a locker in the rear of the plane and slipped into it. The .44 Magnum Desert Eagle went into a black ballistic nylon hip holster attached to a belt of the same material. Also on the belt were extra magazine carriers for the big Magnum pistol, another Kydex sheath into which he transferred the Applegate-Fairbairn fighting knife and various other pouches.

The Beretta 93-R, with sound suppressor in place, went into a leather horizontal shoulder rig. Hanging opposite the select-fire pistol was a double 9 mm round magazine carrier. A battle harness consisting of suspenders—from which hung two concussion, two stun and two smoke grenades—completed the battle outfit. Bolan then stepped into a pair of black nylon combat boots and laced them tightly.

Katz had also chosen a blacksuit. The Israeli's Beretta 92 hung from a military flap holster on a web belt around his waist. Extra magazines, grenades and other paraphernalia also hung from the belt. Over his shoulder he slipped the strap of a canvas bag that contained six extra mags of 9 mm rounds.

A HALO—or High Altitude Low Opening—jump meant freezing temperatures, and Bolan and Katz's next step of preparation was to slip on insulated coveralls. Finally they stuck their arms through the straps of their parachutes and buckled the belts around their waists. Katz hung the sling of a 9 mm

Uzi submachine gun over his right shoulder. Bolan did the same with a Heckler & Koch MP-5 subgun in the same caliber.

Grimaldi took the craft higher. The HALO meant that Bolan and Katz would be mere specks in the sky for most of the jump. Combined with the dark blue canopies that they would finally open at the last possible second, they should be all but invisible in the sky over the Oaks of Mamre.

Slipping oxygen masks over their faces, both warriors began the prebreathing phase of the HALO jump.

Grimaldi reached an altitude of thirty thousand feet and leveled off, continuing to watch his instrument panel. A few minutes later, he swiveled slightly in his seat and called over his shoulder, "Five minutes, guys."

Bolan and Katz both nodded their understanding.

Three minutes later, Grimaldi held up two fingers. Both men activated their bailout bottles. As soon as the Executioner felt the pressure, he disconnected his unit from the aircraft oxygen system and watched Katz do the same. The Israeli gave him the thumbs-up sign.

Ninety seconds later Bolan and Katz pulled their masks over their faces. Grimaldi said, "Have a nice time, boys," as the Executioner opened the door and dived out.

Bolan spread his arms, falling through the air as if he'd just dived off a high diving board. Dusk had fallen, and below he could barely make out several spots he assumed to be tents at the dig camp where Sharon and the others were staying. As he dropped closer, they became more clear.

Every few seconds Bolan checked his altimeter. He could see no activity around the tents. Unless his eyes were deceiving him, there was only one vehicle parked there, but in the twilight it was impossible to be certain.

Bolan checked the altimeter a final time and pulled the rip cord, feeling his chute flower up and out, yanking him up momentarily before he began to float earthward once more. He looked up to see the dark blue nylon, barely visible against the sky, then pulled the oxygen mask from his face and let it hang around his neck. Another glance up told him Katz was a few hundred feet above and to the left.

The Executioner chose a landing site a few hundred yards from the tents, just beyond a large group of trees. It looked as if they would provide adequate cover for them to land and pull in the chutes without being seen from camp. Turning that way, he steered the canopy, "crabbing" toward the site at an angle with the wind.

A few minutes later Bolan's boots hit the sand, and he began hauling in his chute. Katz landed less than twenty yards away and did the same. The Executioner weighted his chute down with several large rocks and zipped down the insulated coveralls. Stepping out of the protective suit, he returned the sling of the MP-5 to his shoulder and waited for Katz to perform his own similar procedures.

When both men were ready, Bolan pulled the walkie-talkie from his belt and held it to his lips. "Stony Man One to Birdman," he said over the automatically scrambled airwaves. "Come in, Birdman."

"You've got the Birdman here," the voice came back.

"We're about to go in, Jack. If we find Sharon, we may have to move out fast. You find a landing site yet?"

"That's affirmative, Stony One," Grimaldi came back. "You remembered your compass, I assume?"

Bolan felt one of the pouches on his nylon belt. "Roger, Birdman."

"Then head due east from the camp about two klicks. You'll come to a large rock formation—only one of any size in sight—at the top of a ridge. I'm just the other side of the rocks, facing away and ready to hit the air again as soon as I see you."

"Affirmative. One out."

"Birdman out."

Bolan moved in closer to Katz. Night had fallen now, and the desert moonlight cast ghostly shadows over the chiseled features of the Israeli warrior's weathered face. It had become a mask of determination, a hallmark of man's pursuit of justice.

He also looked like a man who would kill, without hesitation, anyone who stood in the way of his rescuing his daughter.

"You ready?" Bolan asked.

"Let's do it."

They took off shoulder to shoulder, skirting the trees and across the dark sands of the desert. Keeping low to the ground, they ran as fast as they could without letting their feet slap the ground and announce their approach. Reaching the closest tent, the Executioner slowed, extending the collapsible stock of the MP-5 and bringing it up to his shoulder. He stopped to one side of the tent. A quick glance over his shoulder told him Katz was right behind him. A nod told the Israeli to get ready.

Bolan pulled a flashlight from a carrier on his belt, turned the corner of the tent and threw open the flap, the submachine gun and flashlight leading the way.

The Executioner cast the beam of the light back and forth, his eyes following it as he searched the large tent left to right, then right to left. He saw two beds, an old armchair, a straight-backed rocker and small card table. Men's clothes—a sock here, a shirt there—were scattered haphazardly around the furniture and sand floor. But the tent was unoccupied.

Bolan heard Katz breathing just to his rear. Turning, he shook his head, then followed the Israeli back outside. They made their way past a circle of stones that had evidently been used as a make-do grill, then entered another tent. A portable shower had been rigged up to a five-gallon water can. There was also a portable toilet in the corner.

Bolan and Katz moved on past a picnic table to the last of the three tents. This one contained one bed, a dresser with mirror and a chest of drawers. Little things—like the freshly cut desert flowers in the vase on the dresser, and the fact that whoever had stayed in this tent was a neat housekeeper—hinted to Bolan that this was where Sharon had been staying.

But something else confirmed it.

Taped to the mirror above the dresser was a page torn from a yellow legal pad. As Bolan directed the light that way, he saw the writing. Stepping in, he felt Katz at his side as he read the words: "Katzenelenbogen and friend: take a look under the bed."

Bolan dropped to all fours and threw the hem of the bedspread up over the mattress. Beneath the frame, reclining on his back, was the body of an elderly man with gray hair and beard. Bolan grabbed the man's arm as Katz grabbed a leg, and they dragged the body out from its hiding place.

The man's throat had been cut ear to ear. Pinned to the left breast of the corpse's shirt was an Israeli State Antiquities Administration identification card. The photograph on the card matched what the man would have looked like in life, and the name identified him as Dr. Herbert Singer.

The Executioner caught a glimpse of yellow on the other side of the man's chest and rolled the body slightly toward him and Katz. Another yellow page had been pinned to the man's right breast. Bolan trained the flashlight beam on the paper and read the words:

> Dr. Singer is dead. Sharon is still alive but will not remain so for long unless you follow my orders to the letter.
>
> Go back to Tel Aviv. Watch the Situations Wanted section of the want ads in the *Ha-aretz*.
>
> Cordially,
>
> U.Z.

Yakov Katzenelenbogen turned to face the Executioner. "My God," he said. "Zhdanov's got her, Striker. The bastard's got my daughter."

CHAPTER TWELVE

Caesarea

First built by Herod the Great, who made the city a significant harbor and center of government, Caesarea, Israel, was only a short picturesque drive along the Mediterranean from Tel Aviv. Long a location of historical importance for Christian and Jew alike, it was here that St. Peter preached to the Gentiles at the house of Cornelius. Here also St. Paul was imprisoned before being taken to Rome to stand trial.

Modern Caesarea includes remains of the ancient city's walls, a theater, a Crusader cathedral and a temple with marble columns. Along the path past an aged Roman aqueduct sits Crocodilopolis with its famous ancient tombs.

But like nearby Tel Aviv, Caesarea has become a twentieth-century city, as well. Modern stores, factories, houses and office buildings are scattered within the historical ruins. And it was in one of the recently developed residential areas that Hezbollah, using Iranian funds filtered through a British front company, had purchased the large one-story ranch-style safehouse.

Ulric Zhdanov awoke from his nap with a start and glanced at his watch. His eyes threatened to close again, but he forced them open and sat up, swinging his feet off the bed and onto the floor.

The Russian yawned as he slipped his feet into the house shoes next to the bed. He should check on the prisoners. He had left one of the Hezbollah men in charge of them, and they had been securely bound when he had retired to his room. Still, he knew there could be problems.

Zhdanov yawned again as he stood and headed wearily toward the next bedroom door. The international network that linked terrorist groups together often proved vital to a mission, like now. And he was taking advantage of the Hezbollah contacts he had made so many years ago when he had trained with the fanatics in Libya. But their objectives were different than his own—his current mission was personal—and the current regime in charge of Hezbollah was helping him only because they owed the Red Army Faction a favor.

Abdullah, the man heading up this particular cell of the terrorist group, had been lofty about the help he was giving Zhdanov. It was obvious the fanatic Muslim felt personal vendettas to be beneath him, and resented the time they were spending with the Russian. What that boiled down to was while he knew Hezbollah would continue to help him, Zhdanov doubted that they would have their hearts in it. Of course, it didn't hurt one bit that the man and woman currently tied up in the back bedroom were both Jews. But the Muslims had made it clear they had more-important things to do.

Zhdanov opened the door and walked quietly into the hall. He walked silently on the carpet as he passed Abdullah's bedroom. The house consisted of a large bedroom and bath on one side of the house and another bath and three smaller bedrooms on the other side of a large living room. In the master bedroom half a dozen Hezbollah zealots were camping out on the floor in sleeping bags. Several more men slept in the living room itself, with Zhdanov in the front bedroom opposite, and Abdullah in the middle.

The back bedroom was where Sharon Katzenelenbogen and Jonathan Mayer, the man who had been found with her and appeared to be her lover, were being held.

Zhdanov reached the rear door and opened it. He found Ali, one of Hezbollah's younger men, seated in a chair along a side wall, his AK-47 in his lap.

Ali looked up as the door opened and nodded. He closed the Koran he had been reading and held it with his right hand as he stood up with the AK in his left. "Praise God!" he said.

"Whatever floats your boat, Ali," Zhdanov said in Russian, knowing the young man didn't understand the language. He nodded good-naturedly, trying to keep the contempt he felt for the man—for all of the Muslim religious extremists—off his face. They were all the same. Foolishly dedicated to a God that Zhdanov knew didn't exist. But damn, they knew how to follow orders. As long as the command had the name God in it somewhere, they'd march into Hell and think it meant their death meant a rocket trip straight to Heaven.

Zhdanov turned his attention to the wall where the two prisoners sat on the floor, their feet bound with leather straps and their hands wrapped in gleaming stainless-steel handcuffs. Another strap ran from the cuffs to their feet, permanently fixing them in an awkward position. Even if they were able to stand, they would have to remain bent over. Hobbling away would be all but impossible.

The Russian studied the woman. Sharon Katzenelenbogen wore short canvas shorts with cargo pockets, heavy socks, running shoes and a T-shirt. She was attractive, Zhdanov realized for the first time. The helplessness brought on by her restraints was attractive, too, and for a second the Russian felt himself start to become aroused.

Perhaps there would be time for a little fun with the woman before he killed her. He had decided to use her as bait to bring her father and her father's friend to him, and he intended to kill the big man once and for all this time. But if he could capture Yakov Katzenelenbogen alive, Zhdanov could force the man to watch what he did to his daughter. When he was finished, he would let the Hezbollah men all have a turn with the "infidel bitch." That would be a nice touch—the old man having to watch his only remaining child so totally degraded before his very eyes. Then the man could also watch Zhdanov cut his daughter's throat ear to ear and let her bleed to death.

Zhdanov had turned to go back in the hall when he saw Harun, one of the men sleeping in the master bedroom, come walking down the hall. Harun was one of Hezbollah's experts at role camouflage and undercover work, and known as the best man for the job if you needed someone to impersonate a Jew. He wasn't dressed now as the other Hezbollah terrorists but instead wore a sport shirt, slacks and yarmulke skull cap.

"You placed the ad in the paper?" Zhdanov asked.

Harun nodded.

"Any problems?"

The man shook his head and smiled. "No, it will come out in the paper tomorrow morning."

"Good," Zhdanov said. Without further words he pushed past the other man and walked back down the hall to his bedroom.

Zhdanov sat on his bed for a moment. Things were going well. His enemies would have found the old doctor and the note at the dig site by now. They'd have no choice but to wait for the morning papers and respond to the advertisement Harun had placed for him.

The Russian smiled as he lay back on the bed and closed his eyes again. Yes, things were going well. He was just about to doze off when he heard what sounded like a board cracking in the back bedroom.

The crack was followed by a crash.

SHARON KATZENELENBOGEN felt Yoni twist against his restraints and glanced nervously up at the man in the chair. "Ali," the Russian and the others had called him. Ali sat with his legs crossed and a rifle across his lap. He had rested a copy of the Koran on top of the rifle and was reading. If she had learned one thing about him on her own, it was that he wasn't the brightest human being she had ever met. He was the ultimate follower, a perfect candidate for mindless Muslim terrorism. Sharon watched his lips move as he read. When she listened closely she could even hear him slowly whisper the words out loud. Every once in a while the mantra "Praise God!" would sound off in Arabic louder than the rest.

Sharon turned to face her companion. She knew what he was doing—he had been at it for over half an hour. Trussed the way they were, Yoni could just barely stretch the strap that connected his hand-cuffed hands to his bound feet far enough to get his right hand over his right thigh. He was trying to work something up out of the pocket of his cargo shorts, but every few seconds he had to stop and let the circulation back into his wrists.

Sharon glanced back to their guard and saw the man was still absorbed in his reading. She wondered what Yoni was trying to get out of his pocket, and what he intended to do with it. She had been a little surprised when neither of them had been searched, but then this mad Russian and his jihad pals probably considered them both archaeology dweebs who wouldn't even think of carrying weapons or putting up a fight.

If Sharon got a chance, she was going to change his mind on that subject. She had every intention in the world of showing them what it meant to grow up the daughter of a warrior like Yakov Katzenelenbogen.

Thinking of her father returned her mind to what the madman had said during the drive from the dig site. She hadn't been able to put it all together yet, but it had something to do with her grandfather killing the son of the Russian's father and his first wife. It was highly complex, and the revenge plot that her captor had come up with was remarkably multifarious. She had already learned that Zhdanov—as the others called him—was responsible for her mother's death, but his plan also involved killing all of her family in a complicated order to make her own father suffer.

Sharon had majored in archaeology but minored in psychology, and she recognized the intricate delusion as typical of certain forms of paranoia and schizophrenia. How Zhdanov had gotten the Hezbollah men to go along with his madness, and other details of the amazing story, she didn't know. But she *had* learned that her father, and one of his friends, was looking for them.

She would have to put her faith in the hope that the two would find her and Yoni without getting killed themselves.

Glancing back to Yoni, Sharon saw that he had worked whatever it was in his pocket higher. She watched the concentration on his face, the seriousness with which he went about his task, and felt the tenderness she had so recently developed for him flood through her very soul. Jonathan Mayer was a kind and sensitive man—very much like her own father in that respect. Of course he wasn't a warrior as her father was, but he was an adventurer. And if nothing else good came of what was happening to them, at least she had learned one thing from the experience: she loved Jonathan Mayer, and she was beginning to believe he was the man with whom she wanted to spend the rest of her life.

The lump in Mayer's pocket was near the top now, and he stopped, relaxing his hands and rubbing his wrists with his opposite hands as best he could within the confines of the handcuffs. Sharon looked down and saw that his wrists were cut and bleeding.

Mayer turned to face her and pressed his lips all the way into her ear. "When it gets to the top," he whispered so softly she could barely hear him, "you'll have to get it. I can't get my hand far enough up—" He ended his words quickly as they both heard a rustling of clothing.

Ali looked up from his Koran.

Mayer camouflaged his whispering with a soft kiss on Sharon's ear. Sharon felt a chill rush through her. Goose bumps broke out on her arms as her lover sat back against the wall, his expression one of total dejection.

Ali shook his head in disgust and went back to his reading.

Mayer went back to work. Sharon kept Ali under surveillance until the man next to her elbowed her lightly in the ribs. She turned toward him again to see a rounded piece of stainless steel sticking out of Mayer's pocket and suddenly realized what he had been digging for.

His pocketknife. Sharon remembered the unusual blade vividly. After seeing him use it for several small cutting chores back at camp, she had noticed that the handle bore colorful cartoonlike sketches on both sides. When she'd asked Yoni about it, he had handed it to her. On one side of the knife was a picture of the American movie cowboy, Roy Rogers. Dressed in a fancy fringed jacket, boots with eagles stitched into the leather and a white hat, he stood next to a cactus overlooking a canyon with his gun drawn and ready. On the other side Riders Of The Silver Screen was inscribed. Below the words were more sketches of other American cowboy and Indian actors and actresses. Mayer had smiled as he named them all off to her, but the only three Sharon could remember now were Dale Evans, the Lone Ranger and a small Indian boy named Little Beaver.

Mayer nodded at his pocket. Silently his lips formed the words, "Get it."

Sharon nodded. Stretching against her own restraints, she forced her hand over the tip of the knife and closed her fingers around it. She had to pull slowly, working more of the handle out before she had enough grip to keep from dropping it. But when she had done so she wrapped her fingers tightly around the knife and pulled it out.

She turned to face Mayer. The American frowned, nodding once at her hands, then at his own to indicate that she should cut the leather straps.

Sharon glanced once more at Ali to make sure he was preoccupied, then opened the larger of the two blades. Mayer had honed it to a razor's edge, and she quickly severed the strap that connected her hands to her feet. Another slice of the knife, and the strap binding her feet fell into two pieces.

The woman moved quickly to cut Mayer free, afraid that Ali would glance up and see what she was doing. She had no idea what her lover intended to do next. The fact was, she was somewhat surprised that he was even trying to escape. A whole new admiration for the man next to her swept over her.

As soon as Mayer's hands and feet were free, he reached out, gently taking the knife back from her. His gaze stayed locked on the man reading the Koran across the room. Sharon saw the fear in his shaking hands. But she also saw the determination on his face. Rolling quietly forward from his sitting position, Mayer got his feet under him, and Sharon saw he was planning to charge across the room and overpower Ali.

Once again, she prayed. Lord God Jehovah, be with him. Amen.

Mayer had crossed the room before Ali could even look up from his reading. His arm shot forward as he tried to drive the knife into Ali's throat. The thrust missed, and Sharon watched in horror as Ali looked up, the fires of Hell in his eyes.

Mayer pulled the blade back to his shoulder and jabbed forward once more. This time he aimed at a larger target—Ali's chest. The tip of the blade made contact with the vest Ali wore, then it folded back against his fingers and Mayer gasped.

In the back of her mind Sharon remembered the self-defense lessons her father had given her as a young girl. *Never try to thrust with a folding knife unless it has a lock blade,* she remembered him stressing. As the blood flowed from Mayer's fingers, she wished he had learned from her father, too.

Ali grunted, dropping the Koran from atop the rifle in his lap and grabbing for the weapon. But even with his fingers severely cut, Yoni was one step ahead of the terrorist. The American grabbed the rifle by the barrel and brought it back as Ali leaped to his feet. Then, swinging the rifle forward like a baseball bat, Mayer grand-slammed it across the young terrorist's face.

Ali's cheekbone cracked audibly as the rifle broke it nearly in two. The terrorist crashed back against the wall with enough force to shake the furniture around the room, then slumped to the carpet.

Sharon was on her feet and at Mayer's side. "Do you think the others heard?" she asked as she tore a large swath from Ali's shirt and wrapped her companion's bleeding fingers.

Mayer was staring down at the rifle in his hand. He winced slightly as the cloth made contact with his cuts. "I don't know how they could have missed it. Do you know how to use this thing?"

Sharon looked at the rifle. It was a Russian-made AK-47; she had learned that from her father. "It's been a long time, but I think this lever—on the side here—is the safety. Or, no—wait. My father always called it the selector. You decide whether you want it to shoot automatically, or single shot, or be on 'safe.'"

Mayer nodded and pressed down on the lever.

"What's it on?" Sharon asked as they turned to the door.

"I don't know. But it's showing red. I'm hoping that's good."

"Me, too."

He held the AK-47 in front of him and moved toward the door. He reached down, twisted the knob and swung it open.

Just in time to have Ulric Zhdanov step forward and hit him over the head with a pistol.

Sharon felt as if she were gagging as she watched new blood spurt suddenly from her lover's scalp. A moment later Zhdanov turned toward her, and a second after that everything went black.

Tel Aviv

IT WAS still dark when Bolan awoke in room 224 of the Hotel King Solomon in Tel Aviv. He glanced at his watch, then threw his legs over the side of the bed. He could hear Katz snoring softly in the bed on the other side of the room.

The Executioner stood and moved across the room. As usual during a mission, there had been little chance for rest. But the previous night, after what they had found at the dig site, there had been little else they could do but follow Zhdanov's orders and return to Tel Aviv to await the morning papers. At least it had afforded them an opportunity to catch up on much-needed sleep.

Quietly Bolan threw the latch and opened the glass door to the balcony. He stepped out, feeling the cool morning breeze brush over him as he looked down at the lights below. He took a seat next to the rail in an outdoor chair and looked down.

From where he sat, he could see a row of shops across the street. They were still closed in the early-morning hours, as was the white-painted plywood newsstand on the corner.

Bolan closed his eyes, letting his subconscious mind take over the problems he knew that he and Katz were about to face. He suspected he knew what Zhdanov was up to; the man had decided to use Sharon Katzenelenbogen as bait to draw him and Katz out into the open. As the Executioner looked back on things now, it was even more clear than ever that during each attack the Russian had made on the men from Stony Man Farm, he had ignored Katz and concentrated on killing Bolan.

There was a certain order in which Zhdanov wanted to wipe out the Katzenelenbogen family, and it ended with the former Mossad man himself. Bolan suspected that Zhdanov wanted the Israeli to suffer the death of all family members before finally dying.

A large engine purred on the street below. Bolan watched a white panel truck drive down the street. The sign painted on the side was in Hebrew, and he was unable to read it. He stared as the truck passed on.

The Executioner watched the sidewalk as he continued to contemplate the logistical difficulties Sharon's kidnapping presented. He watched a middle-aged man in a snap-brim hat, and a woman wearing a scarf, turn the corner next to the newsstand, then walk halfway down the block and stick a key into the door of a pharmacy. The lights inside went on as the couple prepared for the workday.

Gradually the city was coming awake.

Bolan rose and walked quietly back into the room, had a quick shower, then headed for the closet. Pulling a blue work shirt, faded blue jeans and a lightweight khaki safari jacket from the hangers, he quickly dressed, finally slipping his feet into heavy cotton socks and leather and nylon hiking boots. The Desert Eagle, Beretta, Applegate-Fairbairn fighting knife and extra magazines for both pistols came next. The jacket covered his weapons.

Returning to the bathroom, the Executioner shut the door behind him and turned on the light. Carefully he studied his reflection in the full-length mirror on the back of the door. He turned sideways and bent forward, touching his toes. Only the slightest hint of a lump appeared in the safari jacket where the Desert Eagle was holstered.

Flipping off the light, Bolan left the bathroom and crossed the room again. By the time he returned to the balcony, an elderly woman was unlocking the door on the side of the newsstand. He watched her disappear into the small structure. A few seconds later the window at the front of the building was sliding up.

Behind the old woman Bolan saw a stand filled with magazines and paperback books. To the sides of the stand were rows of candy, cigarettes, cigars and various other items. As the Executioner watched, a delivery truck pulled up. A man with gray hair and an olive green work uniform got out and began to stack newspapers on the counter.

Katz was still snoring when Bolan left the room, checked the lock behind him and hurried toward the elevators. A minute later he was exiting the front entrance of the Hotel King Solomon and crossing the street.

Bolan bought a copy of the *Ha-aretz*, tucked it under his arm and hurried back up to the room.

Katz had awakened, dressed and was brushing his teeth when the Executioner reentered the room. The Israeli came out of the bathroom with the toothbrush still in his mouth as Bolan dropped the newspaper on the table next to the balcony door. Katz was dressed casually like Bolan, wearing jeans, a khaki bush vest and short-sleeved shirt.

"Good morning," the Executioner said.

"Let's pray that it is," Katz replied, pulling the toothbrush from between his teeth.

Bolan could see the stress on the older man's face as Katz opened the paper to the classified section. He ran a thumb down one column, then said, "This has got to be it. Give me a second, then I'll translate."

Bolan waited.

Katz frowned, then began to read. "'Missing your Cats?'" he said. "And the bastard has spelled 'cats' with a capital *C*—it's in English."

"Twenty years is a long wait—for both of us. Meet me one-on-one. You win, you get your Cats back. I win, you don't. Simple, huh? If you agree, run ad in tomorrow's paper or contact me on public radio."

Katz shook his head. "It's signed 'U.Z.' I don't want to wait until tomorrow morning," he said as he reached for the phone on the table. "But the only way to get a spot on Israeli public radio at the last minute like this is to pull a few strings."

"Your old Mossad buddies?" Bolan asked.

Katz nodded as he punched in a number. A few seconds later he spoke in Hebrew. After a brief conversation, he hung up, moved to the nightstand next to his bed and shoved the Beretta 92 into his belt beneath his bush vest.

The Israeli turned to Bolan. "My friends will be waiting at the radio station when we arrive," he said. "Are you ready?"

Bolan nodded. "They can get you airtime?"

The grin on Katz's face was a mixture of humor and tension. "You have read the scripture that states that with God all things are possible?" he asked.

Bolan nodded his head again.

"Well, with Mossad, it is almost the same," Katz said. "No radio manager wants to wake up tomorrow morning with a .22 in his brain."

He turned and opened the door.

The Executioner followed his friend out of the room and into the hall.

BOLAN HAD ALWAYS been a little surprised at how small even large radio stations usually were. Their broadcasts might reach audiences hundreds of miles away, with megakilowatts left over, but it just didn't take much space to get that job done.

The Israeli public radio station was no exception. Bolan pulled the 4Runner into a parking space just in front of the small brick building and killed the ignition. He looked through the windshield to see two hard-looking men standing next to a life-size statue of Theodor Herzl, perhaps the most famous of the European Jews involved in the early Zionist movement at the turn of century. The stone arms were raised to chest level, the palms turned inward as if Herzl were speaking and using his hands to emphasize some point.

Bolan had seen a sketch of Herzl sometime in the past, standing in the exact same position. The statue appeared to have been sculpted using the sketch as a guide.

The man farthest from the statue wore a sport coat, slacks and tie. He was cue-ball bald on the top of his head but still had a thick mane around the sides. A bent briar pipe hung from a corner of his mouth, the wisps of smoke from the bowl drifting lazily up into the cool morning air. He looked like the word Mossad should have been tattooed across his forehead.

But it was the man standing between the pipe smoker and the statue who caught the Executioner's attention. Although he wore gray slacks and a black leather jacket, he had the same penetrating eyes and a beard similar to that of the stone figure of Herzl next to him. The fact was, he looked like the statue itself, if perhaps a little younger.

As Bolan watched, the man turned slightly and raised his hands into the same position as the statue. He frowned slightly and suddenly became Theodor Herzl. Then the frown faded and he grinned from ear to ear.

In spite of the strain he was under, Yakov Katzenelenbogen laughed.

"You know them?" Bolan asked.

"Just Bernard, the funny man," Katz said. "He is the son of Shimon Herzl, an old and dear Mossad friend who has since passed on. It was Bernard who I called. He is a Mossad operative now himself."

Bolan nodded in understanding. "Which would make him the grandson of Theodor Herzl."

Katz nodded. "And explain the fact that he looks identical to the statue."

Bolan and Katz got out of the car. Katz introduced the Executioner as Rance Pollock again, and Bernard Herzl introduced his Mossad supervisor, David Schwartz. Then Katz and Herzl embraced for a moment, and Herzl said, "It is good to see you, Uncle Yakov."

Although Herzl was taller that Katz, the former Phoenix Force leader reached up and ruffled the man's hair as one might do a little boy. "It is good to see *you* again, Bernie."

Schwartz led the way into the radio station, where it had already been arranged that Katz would speak at 0800 hours. Although he would say so in a way that no one but Zhdanov could understand what he meant, Katz would let the Russian know that he agreed to the terms Zhdanov had set down, and ask the man to call the radio station. Katz would repeat the message every hour, on the hour, until Zhdanov called in or it became apparent that the Russian had no intention of doing so.

The time was 0748 when the station manager greeted and ushered them into a private waiting area just off the sound room. As the four men all found seats, a young man wearing jeans and a Heckler & Koch USP .45-caliber pistol in a shoulder holster over his black T-shirt stuck his head out from a side office. The young man spoke quickly in Hebrew. He then handed Katz a sheet of paper with what appeared to be a phone number on it, and ducked back into the office.

Katz leaned toward the Executioner. "A Mossad electronics specialist," he said. "He installed a new phone line so the station's regular business wouldn't interfere. And he's all set up to trace Zhdanov's call as soon as it comes in. They assume Zhdanov will call from a phone booth, so they have operatives scattered in vehicles across the city, waiting."

Bolan nodded. Modern tracing equipment could zero in on a number almost as soon as the phone rang. But Zhdanov would know this as well as the Executioner did. And while they might trap the number immediately, that didn't mean Mossad could get agents to the site of the call before the Russian had hung up and left. The Executioner and Katz both knew that Zhdanov would be long gone before anyone arrived. Still, it was always worth a try.

The next twelve minutes seemed to take an eternity to pass. Finally the station manager stuck his head into the waiting area and waved them into the sound room.

Katz took a seat across from the announcer who had been reading the news. The Israeli wrapped a headset around his head. Bolan leaned against the wall as the former Phoenix Force leader began to speak.

"U.Z., I accept your terms," he said. "Call the station and we'll work out the details." He read off the new telephone number and then said, "I repeat, I accept your terms. Call the station." Unwrapping the headset, he stood up.

Bolan and Katz followed Schwartz and Herzl into the waiting area, then into the side office where the electronics man had set up his tracing equipment on a table against the wall. They all took seats around the room and stared silently at the phone on the desk.

Fifty-five minutes later they were still staring.

Herzl was the first to speak. "They could still be asleep."

Katzenelenbogen shook his head. "Not all of them," he said. "Zhdanov will have somebody awake and monitoring the radio." He closed his eyes briefly, then opened them again. "The bastard just wants me to sweat awhile." He glanced at Bolan.

The Executioner nodded his agreement.

At 0900 Katz repeated his announcement, then returned to the office. At 0902 the phone rang shrilly, causing Herzl and Schwartz to flinch in their seats.

Katz leaned forward and lifted the receiver from the cradle. "Yes?" he said in an even voice.

Bolan watched the Israeli's face grow grim. After a moment Katz said, "Please do not call again. You are tying up the line," and hung up. He turned to the Executioner, shrugging. "Some listener wanting to know what is going on."

Bolan nodded. "A cryptic message like that over the radio is bound to catch the attention of listeners with too much time on their hands," he said.

Between 0902 and 1000 hours two more meddlesome Israeli radio fans called the number Katz had broadcast over the air. Between 1000 and 1100 they got six more similar calls. For the 1100 broadcast,

Katz rewrote his speech, adding a request that people who were simply inquisitive please refrain from calling the number. That brought it back down to only three calls again between 1100 and 1200.

It wasn't until shortly after the 1200 broadcast that the phone rang and Bolan realized the voice on the other end of the line wasn't just another curious listener. Katz was listening intently. He leaned over and tapped the button to activate the speakerphone, then replaced the receiver and sat back in his chair.

"Ah, we are now on a speakerphone," Zhdanov said cheerfully. "So am I to understand that your big friend is with you, Jew?"

Katz hesitated.

"I'm here," Bolan said.

"Good. Very good." Zhdanov laughed slightly. "I am in a phone booth on the east edge of the city," he said. "But I have no doubt that you have already traced this call and know that. In any case, I will be brief. If you want to see your daughter alive again, you must meet me tonight. I will give you a chance, more of a chance than your father gave *my* family. We will meet in unarmed hand-to-hand combat. It will be a fight to the death. If I kill you, your daughter and her friend die also. If you win, my men have been instructed to let them go."

Right, Bolan thought, then felt his eyebrows lower in thought. This was the first they had heard about a "friend." Until now they had just assumed that Zhdanov had no other hostage besides Sharon.

The young man tracing the call looked up suddenly, then tore a page from a notepad next to his equipment and scribbled furiously. He rose from his seat and handed it to Schwartz.

The Mossad supervisor glanced at it, then handed it to Herzl and hurried out of the room.

Katz put Bolan's thought into words as Herzl read the note. "I was not aware that my daughter had a friend with her," he said. "Who is it?"

"A lover, is my guess. His name is Jonathan Mayer, another archaeologist. In any case he will die with her if I defeat you. If you win, they both go free."

"What assurance do I have of that?" Katz asked.

"None." Zhdanov laughed. "But then, it is I who am holding all the cards, is it not?"

Herzl crossed the room quietly and handed the note to Bolan. It had been written in English for his benefit and read, "Not east edge of Tel Aviv. Booth is in Caesarea." It went on to list a phone number and a street address.

"I want to talk to Sharon," Katz said.

"That will not be necessary," Zhdanov answered quickly. "She is fine."

"Oh, I'm sure I can trust you," Katz practically spit out. "Nevertheless, I want to speak to her."

"You are attempting to delay me here so police can arrive and arrest me," Zhdanov said. He was no longer laughing, and his voice held a new edge.

Bolan knew that was exactly what Katz was doing. The Israeli had seen the young electronics man hand the note to Schwartz, and seen the Mossad supervisor leave the room just like the Executioner had. He knew what it meant: Schwartz was broadcasting the location of the phone booth to the operatives in the field so they could close in on the booth. Still, Bolan knew they would never get there before Zhdanov had escaped. Especially since he was not even in Tel Aviv but in Caesarea.

"You cannot speak with your daughter," Zhdanov said. "She is not here."

"Then go get her," the former Phoenix Force leader demanded. "I'll agree to all your terms. But only if I speak to my daughter and find out she's still all right. That's my one requirement, and I won't bend."

There was a short pause on the other end. Then Zhdanov said, "I will go get her, then call you back." The line went dead.

Schwartz came hurrying back into the room with a walkie-talkie in his hand. "We have operatives on the way to Caesarea," he said.

Bolan and Katz sat where they were. Both of the men from Stony Man Farm knew how useless it was to even try. By now Zhdanov had disappeared.

A half hour later the radio buzzed, then a voice informed Schwartz that they had reached the phone booth in Caesarea but had found it empty.

"Any evidence at all?" Schwartz asked into the walkie-talkie.

Just then the phone rang again. Schwartz ended the radio transmission and turned off the walkie-talkie. Katz hit the speakerphone button and said, "Yes?"

"Hello, Daddy," Sharon Katzenelenbogen said.

"Hello, honey," Katz replied. "Are you all right?"

"Yes," Sharon said quickly. "Yoni is hurt a little. But not bad."

"Who is Yoni?" Katz asked.

"He's...my friend."

Bolan could tell by the tone of her voice that Zhdanov had been telling the truth—Sharon and this Yoni were more than just friends.

"Okay, darling," Katz said. "You just relax and don't worry. I intend to get you out of there." He paused and drew in a deep breath. "Put Zhdanov on, okay?"

Up until now, Sharon's voice had been strong and controlled. But as she spoke this time, it cracked slightly and Bolan heard a soft sob. "Okay, Daddy," she said, sounding like a frightened little girl.

Zhdanov came on the line. "Satisfied?" he said.

"Not until I've choked the last breath of air out of your worthless windpipe."

"Ah, how colorful you people do speak," Zhdanov replied.

Across the room the electronics man ripped another sheet of paper from the pad and wrote furiously again. He handed the paper to Schwartz, who took it and the walkie-talkie out of earshot once more.

The Russian laughed over the line. "Since I know you're tracing the call again, I'll be brief. Tonight, 2000 hours. Back at the dig site where I found your little beauty. Come alone and come unarmed. If I see anyone else, I'll kill this bitch. But not before I and all the other men I have with me have had a little fun with her." He paused to let it sink in. "Do you understand what I'm saying?"

Bolan watched Katz's face turn red with fury. A vein in the Israeli's temple began to pulse. He started to speak, but Bolan reached out and grabbed his friend's arm.

Katz turned to face the Executioner.

"Just say yes," Bolan advised.

"Yes," Katz said, turning back to the speaker-phone. "I understand."

The line went dead again.

Schwartz came back into the room as Bolan stood and pushed the button to kill the speakerphone. He turned to the young man against the wall. "Where was he this time?" he asked.

"Another phone booth. On the other side of Cae-sarea."

Schwartz opened his briefcase, pulled out a folded map and spread it across the desk. Bolan stepped in to see it was a city map of Caesarea.

The Mossad supervisor pulled a pen from his

pocket, clicked it with his thumb and leaned down, making an X on the map at the intersection of two streets on the southwest edge of Caesarea. "That's where he called from the first time," he said. Moving higher on the map, he made another X in the northwest corner of town. "And that's where he called from just now."

Bolan frowned. The area in between the two Xs appeared to be residential. "Then it's probably safe to assume that he's holed up in a safehouse somewhere roughly halfway in between."

Herzl stepped up and said, "Yes, but there are thousands of houses in between. There is no way to track him down, not before this evening." The young man turned to Katz. "I am sorry, Uncle Yakov."

Bolan followed the young man's gaze in time to see Katz nod in understanding. The Israeli stood. The Executioner could see the outrage still coursing through the former Phoenix Force leader's veins as they walked out of the room.

"I've got to go meet him, then," Katzenelenbogen said. "I've got to kill him, Mack. I've got to kill him for my father, for my wife and for my daughter." He turned and looked up at the taller man. "I don't care if I die. But we've got to save Sharon."

CHAPTER THIRTEEN

The sun was setting by the time the two vehicles pulled out of Tel Aviv. Katz was behind the wheel of the 4Runner with Bolan in the passenger's seat. Schwartz and Herzl followed in an unmarked Mossad Lumina APV as both vehicles made their way toward the campsite north of Hebron at the Oaks of Mamre.

The Executioner busied himself by breaking down and cleaning the Galil sniping rifle that Schwartz had checked out of the Mossad armory for him. With an effective range of 880 yards, a muzzle velocity of 2674 feet per second and a 20-round magazine filled with 7.62 mm NATO rounds, it should fit the bill for the plan of attack he and Katz had come up with.

Zhdanov had ordered Katz to go to the site alone or his daughter would be killed. But no one—not Bolan, Katz, Schwartz or Herzl—believed for a minute that the Russian would live up to his end of the bargain and let Sharon and Jonathan Mayer go free if Katz defeated him. Zhdanov planned to kill them no matter what. Then he'd kill Katz.

No, Bolan thought as he stared out of the window into the twilight, Katz would have to take Sharon back if he wanted her alive again. And for that, he'd need help.

Executioner-style help.

Bolan watched the sun finally fall over the horizon in a brilliant flash of red, yellow and orange as Katz drove on. The sniping rifle reassembled, he began loading soft-tip rounds into the four magazines that had accompanied the weapon. Four magazines—eighty rounds. If things went as planned, that should be more than enough ammunition to take out Zhdanov and his terrorist friends. Unless the Executioner missed his guess, the Russian wouldn't have more than a dozen or so men under his command. But it wasn't the amount of ammunition or the number of men that concerned Bolan.

The time element was the problem. The Executioner doubted that even at night he'd be able to work himself closer than two hundred yards or so without being spotted. He'd be shooting from a distance, at night, and that would require pinpoint accuracy. Sharon and Katz would be somewhere in the group, and Sharon would be kept close to Zhdanov himself and probably used as a shield. If there was a doubt in his mind, the Executioner had to err on the side of safety. That meant that in order to be certain he didn't hit Sharon, he had to aim wide enough that he might miss Zhdanov, too. So he would need pinpoint accuracy.

Pinpoint accuracy, however, required perfect sight alignment. Perfect sight alignment, in turn, dictated that sufficient time be taken, enough time that after the Executioner's first shot or two the rest of the terrorists would take cover.

Bolan knew he could easily end up with a drawn-out hostage situation in which Zhdanov now had three hostages instead of two.

The 4Runner and Lumina reached the turn off the highway, and Katz pulled onto the gravel road that led to the dig site. Bolan turned in his seat and saw the Mossad vehicle pull off the highway onto the shoulder behind them. As the 4Runner climbed a hill and began to make its way overland, Herzl got out of the APV with his shirtsleeves rolled up and opened the hood.

Bolan turned back to face the road, mentally reviewing the rest of the plan. Schwartz and Herzl would stay there on the highway, faking engine trouble, while Bolan and Katz continued toward the dig. A mile or so from the camp, Katz would slow just enough for the Executioner to roll out of the vehicle with the sniper's rifle. The Israeli would then drive on in to the camp while Bolan hoofed it on in as close as he dared, then set up to shoot.

Katz had been wired with a transmitter beneath his shirt. The Lumina had a built-in receiver hidden in the dash, and the Mossad men had provided Bolan with a portable monitor, which was clipped to his black nylon gun belt. The Executioner had headphones in his backpack that would silence the receiver for all but him once he plugged them into the unit. From their different locales, he and the Mossad men would be able to hear Katz and everyone else who spoke at the dig site. Schwartz and Herzl would jump back in their Lumina and come swooping in as soon as they heard Bolan's first shot.

The plan had some loose ends, the Executioner knew, but what plan didn't? In real life there were times when calculated risks had to be taken, and this was one of those times.

"We're getting fairly close," Katz finally said, breaking the silence that had fallen over the 4Runner as both men mentally went over their parts of the mission. Everyone knew the plan, was familiar with the individual assignments, and they were all professionals; there was no need for mindless chatter.

Bolan nodded. "Slow down when you reach that curve ahead." He pointed toward a twist in the road just before a thick underbrush of scrub trees. "I'll roll out into that thicket and wait a minute to make sure I wasn't spotted."

"Affirmative," Katz said.

Darkness had all but fallen now. The Executioner reached up, pulling the plastic cover off the dome light and unscrewing the bulb. No sense in letting the quick flash of light when he opened the door give them away in case Zhdanov had posted sentries along the road.

Katz took his foot off the accelerator and tapped the brake. Bolan swung the small pack that carried extra ammo and other gear over his back and gripped the Galil in his left hand, grasping the door handle with his right. He pulled on the handle, unlatching the clasp but holding the door shut as they neared the trees. Katz slowed to perhaps twenty miles per hour.

Ten yards before they drew abreast of the scrub trees, Bolan swung the door out and dived from the 4Runner. He hit the ground on his shoulder, rolled and popped back to his feet a foot in front of the thicket. Without further ado he dropped to all fours and crawled into cover.

As the 4Runner rolled on down the gravel road, Bolan checked the Galil. No mud or dirt in the barrel, and the action was clean. He pulled back on the bolt, then released it. A 7.62 mm NATO soft-point round chambered with a loud metallic clink. The Executioner engaged the safety, glad that he had thought to prime the rifle ahead of time. Given how noisy the steel was when it moved the first bullet from the magazine to the barrel, it could be heard for several hundred yards across the peaceful desert.

Bolan pulled out the headphones, plugged the attached cord into the receiver clipped to his belt and flipped the switch. A short burst of static met his ears, then he heard Katz whistling softly over the hum of the 4Runner's engine.

The Executioner took a fast inventory of his surroundings, then emerged from hiding with the Galil's muzzle carried low. Breaking into double time, he jogged across the rough terrain, staying twenty yards off the road where he could still follow it in the moonlight. The ground was craggy, and he silently prayed he wouldn't break an ankle on one of the bumps or depressions he encountered.

Katz's whistling stopped for a moment, and the Israeli said, "Well, I hope you can hear me, Striker, because I'm getting closer." The whistling started again.

Bolan picked up his pace, running faster now. He scouted ahead across the horizon. Three hundred yards in front of him he saw a steep rise. Unless his estimation was way off, he should be able to see the camp when he reached the top. He'd take a quick break when he got there and scan the area below. Depending on the terrain between him and the tents, he might or might not be able to work in closer.

Bolan was still breathing easily as he started up the steep incline. Halfway to the top, he dropped lower to the ground. Then, ten yards from the crest, he swung the Galil across his back on its sling and dropped to the ground. Scurrying on to the top of the rise on all fours, he fell forward onto his belly.

Below, at least three hundred yards away, the Executioner could barely make out the gray outlines of the tents. The 4Runner had almost reached the site, its headlights bouncing up and down over the rough gravel road. Bolan shrugged out of the backpack and unzipped the main pocket, digging through the contents until he came up with a binocular case. Unfastening the case's snap, he pulled out the instrument and removed the lens covers.

The Executioner pointed the infrared lenses down at the dig site camp. He gave his eyes a moment to focus, then frowned.

There was something down there besides the tents, picnic table and barbecue pit. In fact there were lots of somethings that looked like men moving in the shadows.

He looked closer and saw one of the men step just out of the darkness and into the moonlight, then disappear again. He began to count the movements around the camp.

One hundred and fifty men had to be down there. No way could he take out that many armed terrorists. He needed to warn Katz—the Israeli didn't have the benefit of infrared binoculars. But with the one-way connection Bolan couldn't reach the former Phoenix Force leader.

Yakov Katzenelenbogen would be walking into the mouth of the lion and not even know it until the teeth snapped shut. To make the situation even more frustrating, Katz's voice replaced the whistling over the receiver again. "I'm just about there, Striker. Wish me luck."

Bolan let out a deep breath, then swung the Galil around in front of him and pulled the lens caps off the scope. He checked the range finder: 325 feet. It was a joke. He had eighty rounds, and there looked to be twice that many terrorists below. Well, he would do what he could—get as many of them as he could before Katz went down. And who knew? Maybe his fire from afar would afford the Israeli a chance of escape. Stranger things had happened, and at this point he had no other choice.

Bolan saw the headlights round a curve below and come into view of the camp. Suddenly, just as he knew would happen when the lights appeared, all movement in the shadows halted.

The 4Runner arrived at the edge of camp and stopped. Bolan watched Katz step out of the vehicle through the binoculars. As the former Mossad operative walked forward, the Executioner set the binoculars down and shifted back to the rifle.

Katz had gone less than ten steps when the camp suddenly lit up. Hot white spotlights shot from every angle onto Katzenelenbogen. Across the still desert came the sound of what might have been two hundred rifle bolts closing at once. Bolan flipped the Galil's safety to the ''fire'' position as his finger tightened on the trigger.

A team of two dozen men armed with assault rifles converged on Katz, surrounding him. Bolan's finger moved farther back on the trigger as he centered the crosshairs on the chest of the lead man.

Then, suddenly, the Executioner recognized the man's uniform: rubber-soled boots with canvas uppers, OD combat kit and standard webbing ammo pouches. The rifle he carried was a Galil, similar to the one in Bolan's hands but in the full-auto version with a 35-round magazine rather than the Executioner's sniper model with twenty.

Bolan pulled his finger away from the trigger and squinted through the scope. What really gave the man away was the small marking he had printed on the band of his floppy hat—the man's blood type. The Executioner returned the binoculars to his eyes. These were not Hezbollah terrorists under Zhdanov's command that he saw below.

These men were from Israel's crack commando squad, the Golani Infantry Brigade.

Over the headset Bolan could hear one of the soldiers barking out orders in Hebrew. Then Katz's voice answered angrily in the same language. For several seconds a shouting match ensued, and then, as quickly as it had begun, it ended.

For a moment silence came from Katz's transmitter. Then finally the former Phoenix Force leader said, "Schwartz, I know you can hear me." After a short pause, he went on. "These men came out here to trap Zhdanov and his Hezbollah cohorts. That means somebody tipped them off. It had to be me, Pollock, you or Bernard. It wasn't me, and it wasn't Pollock. That leaves the two of you."

He paused for a moment to take a breath, and

when he spoke again his voice was even angrier than before. "These guys haven't seen anybody but me all night, but you can bet your ass Zhdanov has seen *them* because he didn't show. I'd give my daughter about a ten percent chance of being alive right now, boys," he finished. "But you better hope that long shot comes through. Because if she's dead, *your* chances of living are even slimmer than that."

THE LEARJET 24 had taken off from Caesarea, climbing to twenty-eight thousand feet long before it neared the Oaks of Mamre. Ulric Zhdanov watched through the glass, a little amazed in the knowledge that no one on the ground could see the plane. From where he sat the topography of the desert was clearly delineated. Even small details could be made out.

The Russian glanced to his side and watched Abdullah work the controls for a moment, then twisted in his seat, looking over his shoulder. Behind him the plane's four seats had been arranged so that the back two faced the front, the front pair faced the rear. Zhdanov could see the back of Harun's head, as well as the back of the head of a man named Zaid.

On the other side of the men, staring sullenly forward, ropes binding his hands and feet and more ropes wrapped around his chest to secure him to the seat, sat Jonathan Mayer. His lips were swollen like plump summer sausages, and a white gauze bandage was wrapped around his head. Another gauze bandage, attached with white adhesive tape, adorned the man's hand. It was there because the inexperienced fool had tried to stab Ali with a simple nonlocking pocketknife, never stopping to think that it would close on his own fingers if he struck bone.

Zhdanov reached into the pocket of his slacks, pulled the knife out and looked at it. It was decorated with pictures of American cowboys and Indians. Kind of unique, really—he had decided to keep it. But it was definitely not designed to be a weapon.

Zhdanov turned his attention to the woman seated next to Mayer. Sharon's hair had become matted with the sweat of both tension and exertion. But rather than detract from her appearance, the "used" look made her even more appealing. He could imagine that this might be just the way she looked after a long night of sex with the man next to her, and he decided then and there that regardless of what transpired later that night he would find out exactly what she looked like after sex.

Then he would kill her.

A few minutes later Abdullah said, "We are almost there. Do you want me to alter my speed?"

The Russian nodded. "Go as slow as you can," he said. "This may be the only chance we get to check things while there's still some daylight left."

Abdullah didn't respond verbally, but the plane slowed.

Zhdanov watched the ground, finally spotting the

tents. He could even see the tiny spot that had to be the picnic table. He wondered briefly what they had done with the old man's body he had left beneath the bed at the camp, then the thought flew out of his head as unimportant.

The plane glided over the camp, so high it was invisible to the naked eye. They might as well have been a ghost plane operating in another dimension.

Abdullah took the Learjet several miles on, then dipped a wing, banked and started back toward the camp. There was still a little light left when they slowed to fly over again. Nothing had changed; the campsite was clearly deserted.

As it should be. The Russian glanced at his watch. It was only 1938 hours. He had told Katzenelenbogen to come at 2000 sharp and warned him neither to be late nor early.

Two miles past the Oaks, Zhdanov twisted in his seat again. "Head south," he ordered Abdullah. "Let's come in from a different direction."

The Hezbollah leader nodded and dipped the wing of the plane.

A few seconds later they had made another U-turn in the air and started back toward the camp from the south. Darkness was almost complete now, and Zhdanov decided to take a chance. "Drop to twenty thousand feet," he commanded.

Abdullah glanced at him, then shrugged.

Zhdanov's ears popped as the Learjet dropped. He studied the camp through binoculars as they flew over again. Satisfied that no one occupied the camp, he was about to order Abdullah back to the landing strip where they would meet with the other Hezbollah men and transfer to land vehicles. But before the words could leave his mouth, a flicker of light on the ground farther north caught his eye.

With no change in directives, Abdullah continued to fly due north toward Jerusalem. Zhdanov grabbed the binoculars again and looked down as more lights appeared.

"What are they?" Abdullah asked.

Zhdanov didn't answer. He kept the binoculars pressed to his forehead and squinted through the lenses. He saw the lights bouncing slightly up and down, and counted close to twenty of them all in a row. "Fly lower," he finally told Abdullah.

"But we will be se—"

"Fly lower!" Zhdanov barked. "Do not make me tell you again! Drop another five thousand feet!"

The Hezbollah man shrugged once more and pushed the control forward. As they drew closer to the ground, Zhdanov saw each of the twenty or so lights split in two and suddenly realized what they were—headlights, moving along from Jerusalem toward the Oaks of Mamre dig site.

The Russian continued to watch through the binoculars as they flew over the convoy. He was even able to distinguish two of the vehicles as jeeps. Israeli army jeeps.

"Damn the man to hell!" Zhdanov roared. "Does

he think me a fool? Did he think I wouldn't learn of this? Or does he think me soft? Think that I will let his daughter live even after such treachery on his part?'' Unbuckling his seat belt, the Russian leaped from the flight deck into the passenger cabin and grabbed the woman by the hair. Sharon screamed in both pain and fear as Zhdanov pulled her lover's pocketknife from his pocket and opened it, then tore her from her seat.

"No!" Mayer screamed at the top of his lungs, struggling against his own restraints. "No! Please!"

Zhdanov ignored the man's pleas, his eyes lighting up with madness as he held the knife to Sharon Katzenelenbogen's throat. Sharon went limp in his hands. Then she spoke, sounding like a little girl.

"Please," she said softly, "there's nothing I can do to stop you. But please...don't kill me."

Zhdanov hesitated and looked at her. Her T-shirt had ridden up during the struggle and caught over her left breast. He stared at the firm-yet-soft flesh that threatened to spill over a lacy black bra, and remembered the fun he had planned to have with her before he killed her. Cutting her throat now would be dramatic, but it would also mean cutting the bait off his own hook for her father. And even when he cornered the man through other means, he couldn't force the man to watch his daughter degraded.

The Russian took a deep breath to regain control of himself, then grabbed Sharon with both hands and forced her back to her seat, slamming her down hard. For a moment he stared at her exposed breast and felt his groin tighten.

Then Ulric Zhdanov strode back to his own seat on the flight deck, sat down and rebuckled his seat belt.

THEY HADN'T TAKEN TIME to check out of the Hotel King Solomon, and so that was where Bolan and Katz returned. Katz looked distressed but continued to maintain the stoical bearing of the professional warrior who always kept a cool head regardless of what chaos might be going on around him.

Bolan lifted the phone and dialed room service, ordering a pair of T-bone steaks, baked potatoes, salad and small bottle of one of the local dry red wines. When he had hung up, he and Katz sat down on their beds to wait.

Finally Katz broke the silence. "Do you think he has killed her?"

Bolan stared his old friend in the face. "I wish I could say no, Katz," he said. "The truth is I don't know. But if I was a betting man, I'd say chances are better than ever that she's still alive."

The Israeli brightened slightly. "Why?" he asked. The tone of his voice reflected a clear need for encouragement. "What makes you say so?"

"Two things," Bolan said. "First Zhdanov's using Sharon as a lure to set you up, and if he kills her he has an empty trap." He took off the safari jacket and dropped it on the bed next to him. "Oh, I know he could always track you down some other way, later. The man's good. But my guess is that he's sick and tired of waiting. He had a twenty-year delay, and we haven't allowed things to go exactly his way since he killed Schneider. I get the feeling he's impatient for the payoff."

Katz nodded. "Could be," he said. "What's the second reason?"

"He's not through torturing you yet," the Executioner said bluntly. "He's already told you what he intends to do to Sharon. And he wants you to have to watch. He also wants you wondering if that's what he's doing to her right now. If you know she's dead, it won't work."

"We do not know where he is," Katz said, shrugging out of his vest. "Do you suppose he knows where we are? Will he call here?"

Bolan shrugged again. "He may know where we are, but I doubt it. My guess is he'll run another advertisement in the paper tomorrow."

Katz looked at his watch. "The *Ha-aretz* business office has been closed for hours," he said. "He can't possibly get an ad placed in tomorrow morning's paper. Tomorrow evening's edition would be the first it could come out in."

"Don't be so sure," Bolan said. "They'll be gearing up to run the presses soon. Somebody will be down there. A little money in the right hands could still sneak it in before the paper hits the printer.''

"Maybe," Katz said. He didn't sound particularly sold on the idea.

A knock sounded on the door. Bolan stood and started that way, then remembered that his weapons were showing. Shrugging back into the safari jacket, he moved to the peephole.

The man leaning against the stainless-steel cart wore a white jacket and dark slacks. Bolan opened the door and let him in.

Katz had turned sideways so the Beretta stuck in his belt didn't show. The Executioner let the room-service waiter push the cart to the middle of the room, signed the ticket after adding a tip and escorted the man back out.

Katz carried several covered dishes, silverware, one carafe of wine and another of ice water to the table by the balcony while Bolan closed and locked the door. The two warriors sat down to eat.

"This is rare," Katz said.

"What's that?" Bolan took the covers off his plates and picked up his fork.

"That we sit down to eat like civilized men."

The Executioner chuckled. Katz looked down at his food, then reached for the wine carafe and poured a glass for both of them.

Bolan set his knife and fork down and raised his glass. "To finding Sharon and Yoni," he said. He held the glass to his lips but didn't drink as he watched Katz down his own red liquid in two gulps.

The Executioner poured a glass of water, drinking it and ignoring his wine while he finished his salad and started in on the T-bone. He watched Katz pick at his food and pour more wine. Yakov Katzenelenbogen had always appeared to have an unlimited capacity when it came to alcohol. Bolan had seen the man drink enough to put ten other men under the table. But he had never seen the Israeli drunk, and Katz could stop after one or two when the situation required him to do so. Drinking was neither a problem nor a regular passtime for the man.

Well, tonight the Executioner had ordered the wine on purpose. Katz was a pro, but it was his daughter they were trying to save. That was enough to put stress on any man, no matter how battle hardened. The one bottle would be just enough to relax the former Phoenix Force leader, and Bolan hoped it would help his friend catch some more much needed sleep.

Katz picked at his food as Bolan continued to eat. He had finished two more glasses of wine, however, when the phone rang.

Bolan started to stand and go after it, but Katz beat him to the punch. The Israeli lifted the receiver and said, "Yes?"

No one who didn't know him as well as the Executioner did would have noted the anxiety in Yakov Katzenelenbogen's voice. There was a long pause during which Katz held the receiver tightly to the side of his face and frowned while he listened. As the silence went on, both his face and grip began to relax.

Bolan watched his old friend as he continued to eat. He didn't know who was on the other end, but considering the way Katz was acting, he didn't think it was Zhdanov.

Finally Katz spoke. "No," he said suddenly. "I will take care of it personally if it comes to that." Then, "Yes...yes...thank you." He hung up, returned to the table and sat down.

Katz glanced at Bolan's wineglass, saw that it was still full and poured the last of the bottle for himself. He downed half, then looked up again. "That was Bernard," he said. "He and Schwartz found the leak. One of the other Mossad officers, an operative who had been assigned the task of eliminating the Hezbollah faction operating within Israel, learned of what we were doing. He had a friend in the Golani Infantry. You can figure out the rest."

"You get the guy's name?" Bolan asked.

Katz shook his head. "No, I did not ask for it. Until we get Sharon back, I want no distractions."

Bolan nodded. Being the pro that he was, Katz had no intention of letting any petty desire for revenge divert his attention from their primary objective.

"It seems this operative has been remarkably unsuccessful, and decided this might be his chance."

Katz cut a small piece off the steak but left it on his plate. "A man named Abdullah is the leader of the Hezbollah cell here, and Mossad suspects it is he who is helping Zhdanov. Bernard is rounding up some of his informants hoping to learn the location of the safehouse in Caesarea."

Bolan nodded as he took the last bite of steak and looked down at what remained of his baked potato. "They giving this officer any disciplinary action?" he asked.

Katz shook his head. "I told them I would handle it. And if Sharon has been killed because of what this man has done, I will." He drained the rest of his wine.

Bolan nodded. He noted that the Israeli had eaten less than a third of his steak and none of his potato or salad.

Katz lifted the bottle, realized it was empty and set it back down. He glanced again at Bolan's glass then said, "Since it is obvious you ordered the wine simply to settle my nerves, and do not intend to drink any yourself, do you mind?"

The Executioner smiled. You never pulled one over on Katz. "Be my guest," he said.

The Israeli reached across the table and took Bolan's glass of wine. He lit his one-a-day unfiltered Camel, inhaled deeply and stood, taking a sip of the wine as he walked to his bed. The former Phoenix Force man sat down with the wine in one hand, the cigarette in the other and stared at the wall.

Bolan looked at the phone as he finished dinner, pulled the napkin from his lap and dropped it on the table. For Katz's sake he wished it would ring again. But he suspected that wasn't going to happen.

They were simply going to have to wait until tomorrow to find out if Sharon Katzenelenbogen was alive or dead.

BOLAN AWAKENED several times during the night. Each time he rolled over to see Katz's eyes still open. The Israeli had removed his prosthetic arm but lay on his back on top of the bedspread fully clothed, staring at the ceiling. The wine hadn't put the former Phoenix Force warrior to sleep as Bolan had hoped. But maybe it had at least relaxed him to the point where he was getting a little rest.

When the Executioner finally awakened for good in the early-morning darkness, Katz had finally drifted off and begun to snore. Bolan arose quietly to avoid waking his old friend.

From there on, the morning became an instant replay of the day before.

The Executioner yawned as he walked back out onto the balcony and dropped into the white chair again. He watched the same truck with Hebrew writing on the side come down the street, then saw the same little man in the hat and his wife open the pharmacy. He hurried inside and dressed, knowing that by the time he got down to the street the newsstand would be open and the newspapers would have arrived.

He wasn't disappointed.

Bolan paid the woman behind the counter and hurried back up to the room. Katz was waiting for him at the table when he arrived.

The Israeli opened the paper and frowned as he scanned the columns of the classified section. "You were right, Striker," he said suddenly. "Somehow, he got it in." He cleared his throat and began to read. "'Still want your Cats back? Be at the phone booth on the corner of Akka and Peres at 0700.'"

"That's all?" Bolan asked.

"That's all," Katz said.

"You know the place?"

Katz nodded his head. "Café area. Breakfast places—that sort. It'll be crowded at that time of day."

"That's probably what he's counting on," Bolan said. "He may have somebody watching us when we get there." He paused. "It could even be a setup. An ambush."

Katz shook his head. "I don't think so."

"Neither do I," Bolan agreed. "He still wants to do things right and kill you last." The Executioner turned and looked out the window, over the balcony, as the new day dawned. "But it could be a setup to kidnap you. Grab you off the street at gunpoint and take you somewhere where he *could* do things in order."

Katz frowned at the ceiling for a moment, then said, "We'll keep that in mind." He looked back down. "What time is it?"

"Time to take a shower, get dressed, check out and go," Bolan said.

Katz squinted at him, the lines in his face deepening into crevices. "So," he said, "do we want Herzl and Schwartz or any of the Mossad in on this?" he asked.

"That's your call."

The Israeli nodded his understanding. "Yes, but I want your opinion."

"My opinion is that Sharon is your daughter. Therefore, like I said, it's your call."

Katz stood, and for a brief second the strain of the past few days in which his daughter—the only family he had left—had been in danger, took its toll and he looked his age. Then he turned to the Executioner. Suddenly the vitality returned, and Katzenelenbogen became the age of his heart again rather than the age of his body. "It's been a long time since I worked with them."

"I know."

"Very few of the ones I knew are still around."

Bolan didn't reply.

"The fact is, I didn't call an old friend when I needed help. I felt closer to, and called, the son of an old friend. Bernard Herzl."

Bolan nodded. "That's not good. It's too far removed for work like this."

"I know," Katz agreed. "But Bernard and Schwartz will think they should be in on it. They're the Mossad, and this is their country, after all."

Bolan nodded. "Then give them something to do where they feel useful. Some kind of busy work that will keep them out of our way."

Katz's eyebrows lowered in concentration, then his face lightened and he picked up the phone. A moment later he had dialed the Mossad number and was speaking to Herzl. "Yes…uh-huh…okay."

Bolan heard the Israeli give Herzl one of Stony Man Farm's "Hello" numbers. Like most police and intelligence agencies that ran clandestine ops, Stony Man had several phone lines that were answered simply with "Hello?" The difference in the Farm's undercover numbers, however, was that the computer genius Aaron Kurtzman had rigged them to bounce all over the world and be untraceable.

Even if the Mossad man tried to trace the call, he'd run into a dead end.

Katz hung up and looked at the Executioner. "They've already got their own angle going, Mack, and it might not be bad. One of Bernie's snitches got a lead on what they think is a Hezbollah safehouse in Caesarea. It might even be the one Zhdanov was using. They're on their way there to check it out now." He paused to take a breath. "I gave them one of the Hello numbers just in case something came of it."

"I heard," Bolan said. "At the very least they should stay occupied and not leak any more info."

"Yes," Katz agreed. "So are you ready for the showdown?"

"Let's do it, Katz. Just like old times."

"Thee and me," Katz said, nodding. "So. You want the first shower or should I take it?"

THE PHONE WAS ringing when they pulled up in the 4Runner. Katz jumped out of the passenger's side, watching a fat man in a plaid windbreaker pick up the receiver as he raced toward the booth.

"Hello?" the fat man said as Katz reached the doorway.

He ripped the phone from the man's hand and said, "It's for me."

The man was at least six inches taller than Katz and outweighed the Israeli by a good 150 pounds. He started to get nasty, then he heard a voice behind him on the sidewalk say, "Hey, friend."

The fat man turned.

Bolan had gotten out from behind the wheel and stood looking at him.

The man in the plaid windbreaker looked the Executioner up and down from head to foot, then said, "Sorry. Just a little misunderstanding."

Bolan nodded and hooked a thumb down the street. "Take off."

The fat man lumbered off in the direction the Executioner's thumb pointed.

Bolan moved up next to the phone booth where

he could hear Katz speak. The Israeli held the receiver slightly away from his ear, letting Bolan slide up next to him so they could both hear.

"I thought about throwing her out of the plane," the voice on the other end said, "and believe me, I wanted to." There was a pause during which Bolan heard a heavy breath. "But I wanted to play with your mind a little longer."

The Executioner glanced down at his friend's face and saw it suddenly turn purple. It was clear Katz had had all the "playing with" he wanted. Things had come to a head. The Israeli wanted it over, one way or the other.

"You want to play with me, do you?" Katz shouted into the phone. "You want drama? You want to be melodramatic about all this? Okay, let's do it, then. We'll meet where it all started twenty years ago. We'll meet south of Paris, along the road where you killed my wife. You like that?"

The voice on the other end was silent. For a moment Bolan thought Zhdanov might even have hung up. Then, reverently and almost so quietly as not to be heard, the Russian said, "I like it."

"What?" Katz demanded. Bolan could see he was a little taken aback. His words had been blurted out in anger with no thought that the suggestion might be taken seriously, let alone accepted.

"I said I like it," Zhdanov said. "We will meet at the bridge. Tomorrow at 1900 Paris time." He laughed. "Do not mistake the situation though. Sharon will be somewhere else. You cannot show up with the police or military and hope to take her away from me.''

''The deal is the same, though,'' Katz said into the receiver. ''You win, you kill my daughter, too. I win, she and her friend go free.''

The laughter on the other end of the line reminded both Bolan and Katz that it made no difference what the Russian said—his word was no good.

''Why, of course,'' Zhdanov said. ''Tomorrow night, then. France. The bridge between Paris and Versailles.'' There was a click on the other end of the line, and the phone went dead.

Katz slammed the receiver back onto the hook and stepped out of the phone booth. ''Is Grimaldi still waiting for us?'' he asked as he strode back toward the 4Runner.

Bolan nodded.

''Good,'' the Israeli said. ''We've got a flight to France to catch.''

CHAPTER FOURTEEN

France

Jack Grimaldi had just set the Learjet's wheels on the Orly Airport runway when the crisp static came over the radio. "Stony Man Base, Stony Man One," Barbara Price's voice said clearly. "Come in, Stony One."

Bolan reached forward, jerking the microphone from the clip in front of him. "Stony Man One," he said. "Go ahead, Barb."

"Be advised, One. We just received a call from a Bernard Herzl. He was looking for Katz."

"Affirmative," Bolan said. "Katz is with me now."

"Roger," Price said. "Herzl left a number for you to call." The Stony Man mission controller read off the number, then ended the transmission.

Bolan turned in his seat and watched Katz open one of the lockers mounted along the wall of the jet. Inside he saw a tangle of electronic devices such as walkie-talkies, recorders, transmitters and receivers.

Katz pulled a cellular phone out and plugged it into a portable speaker as Grimaldi taxied them down the runway toward French customs.

A few seconds later the phone was ringing, and a few seconds after that, a voice said, "Hello?"

"It is Katz," the Israeli said.

There was a short pause, then Bernard Herzl chuckled. "Uncle Yakov, sometime you really must tell me who you work for these days. We tried to trace the call to that Hello number and came up with nothing. All we know is it was not the CIA like we'd suspected."

"Someday I will tell you, Bernie," Katz said, laughing lightly himself. "But as the tired old joke goes—"

"I know," Herzl interrupted. "Then you'll have to kill me." He paused a moment, then went on. "But don't kill me until you've heard this. It may be useful."

The jet pulled to a stop near customs. Grimaldi opened a panel in the console and pulled out three passports. "We were supposed to have been cleared ahead of time," he whispered. "I'll go double-check."

Bolan nodded as the pilot opened the door and got out.

Herzl cleared his throat and went on. "We busted the Hezbollah safehouse in Caesarea," he said. "Only one guy there. Recovering from an injury. It looks like somebody used his face for batting practice. We've IDed him as one Ali al-Sadr. He's Hezbollah, all right, and he's with Abdullah's bunch.''

"Does he know where they'll be holding Sharon when I meet Zhdanov?" Katz asked.

"He hasn't talked...yet."

"You paused before 'yet,', Bernie. Does that mean you think he will talk?"

"Uncle Yakov, do you remember Mort Berstein?" Herzl asked.

"Yes. *He's* conducting the interrogation?"

"He is," Herzl affirmed. "Will you have a cellular phone with you?"

"Yes," Katz told him.

"Good. We should have more news for you soon."

"Just tell Morty to leave some of this Ali for me," Katz said.

"I'll try," Herzl said. "But you know how he is."

Grimaldi returned and got back in the plane. "I'll take care of everything here," he offered. "You guys get going." He glanced at his wrist. "You're running out of time." He pointed between two planes at a glass door leading into the terminal. "Go through there and pick up your passports. They've already been stamped." He turned and extended his hand over the seat to Katz. "And good luck, buddy."

Katz shook the pilot's hand and nodded.

A few minutes later Bolan and Katz had rented a

Mercedes 450 SLC and were headed into the heart of the city on the freeway. Bolan glanced at the gas gauge and saw they had less than a quarter of a tank. They were passing the Hotel Novotel when the phone rang.

"Hello?" Katz said.

"Morty's working fast," Herzl stated. "You got something to write with?"

Katz pulled a pen and a small notepad from the pocket of his safari vest and said, "Yeah. Go ahead."

"Try 11637 Rue LeSalle," Herzl said. "You know the area?"

"Doesn't ring a bell," Katz said. "But we'll find it." He cleared his throat. "Ali thinks Sharon will be there?"

"He doesn't know. But that's the only current Hezbollah safehouse he's aware of in the Paris area."

"You think he's telling the truth?"

"I told you who was doing the interrogation, didn't I?" Herzl paused. "Morty's still working on him. Keep the phone with you just in case."

"Affirmative," Katz said. "Talk to you soon." He punched the Off button.

Bolan saw an exit ramp and pulled off. A service station stood just off the freeway, and he pulled the Mercedes up to a pump. Katz hurried inside while the Executioner pumped the tank full of gasoline. The Israeli came back out holding a folded map.

Katz had the map spread across his lap by the time Bolan returned from paying for the gas. "We must backtrack," the former Phoenix Force leader said. "Rue LeSalle is not far from the Hotel Novotel we just passed."

Bolan got behind the wheel, fired up the engine and pulled across an overpass to the other side of the freeway. A few moments later they were on the thoroughfare again, heading back in the direction from which they'd come.

The Novotel sat in a gloomy, high-rise neighborhood that completely lacked the charm of most of Paris's other areas. Bolan took the exit and drove past the hotel, then several office buildings that exhibited all the romance of sheet metal. About a mile past the office buildings, they turned into a medium-income residential area and found Rue LeSalle.

Bolan turned onto the street, seeing they were in the 9900 block. He drove past several blocks of tract homes, then came to an older section of wood-frame houses.

The building that was 11637 was small and stood in the center of the block. The yellow paint that had once covered it was chipped and flaked, and the grass looked as if it hadn't been mowed during the past decade. The front yard dipped sharply halfway from the house, descending to the cracked curb next to the mailbox. Broken concrete steps led up from the street to the short sidewalk just off the porch. Two windows faced the street, and the curtains were closed on both. There was no driveway, and no vehicles were parked outside along the street.

Bolan drove past the house, wishing he had rented something other than the 450 SLC. The Mercedes stood out in this neighborhood. At the corner he turned right, noting that an alley ran between the houses on both sides of the block. He glanced at his wrist.

The bridge where Cynthia Katzenelenbogen had died twenty years before was at least an hour's ride from where they were. That gave them a little over two hours to hit the house and rescue Sharon and Jonathan Mayer.

If the two hostages were even there.

Deciding to take a chance, Bolan turned down the alley and cruised past the garbage containers, old furniture and other rubble that lined the sides. The rear of 11637 was as shabby as the front. A single wooden door led into the house, and the upper window in the storm door was shattered. Again there was no sign of a vehicle.

The Executioner drove onto the street. "It doesn't look like there's anybody there to me," he told Katz.

"To me, either," the Israeli said.

They turned onto the street and circled the block again. Bolan took a deep breath. He knew what he had to do; at least what had to *try* to do. He didn't like trying to deceive a friend but felt that at this point in time it was necessary. He hoped Katz wouldn't snap to what he was up to but was afraid the shrewd Israeli would see through his words. He was right.

"Why don't I let you out and you go in and check?" Bolan said.

Katz turned to look at him, his face a mask of shock. The shock quickly disappeared as understanding took its place. "No," he said simply.

"But there's nobody there," Bolan said. "I'll call Herzl again while I wait for you. They might have gotten some more informa—"

"No," Katz said again, more firmly this time. "I know what you have in mind. As soon as I'm out of the car, you'll be on your way to Versailles. I thank you for it, Mack. As the Bible says, 'Greater love hath no man but he lay down his life for a brother.' But I can't let you do it."

Bolan turned the corner and drove two more blocks before speaking again. "Katz," he said, "it's a trap. I know it's a trap. You know it's a trap. Zhdanov has no intention of letting your daughter go free."

"Of course he doesn't. But if you show up in my place, he'll have her killed immediately."

"Give me your vest and shirt," Bolan said, knowing his argument was futile. "It'll be dark. I'll—"

Katz laughed. "Give me a break. You going to cut six inches off your ankles and gain twenty-five pounds in the next hour? Maybe hit a cosmetic surgeon on the way and have him make you look Jewish? No, the only chance we have is to locate Sharon before I go meet Zhdanov. If we don't, you keep trying and I go on alone. But there's another reason I have to be the one who goes.''

"What?" Bolan asked, knowing the answer without asking.

"Cynthia," Katz said simply. "The bastard killed my wife, and it's my right.''

The Executioner couldn't argue.

Pulling past the house once more, Bolan circled the block and parked on the other side. "Then we'll both go check,'' he said, and they got out.

Bolan and Katz cut between two ramshackle houses and crossed the alley to the back door of 11637 LeSalle. The Executioner drew the Desert Eagle and took up position on the right side of the door. Katz pulled his Beretta, looked up at his old friend, then pulled open the storm door and kicked in the wooden door.

They went in low and fast, their weapons sweeping left to right and back again. They found themselves in a small kitchen with two doors leading off it. Katz took the door to the left, and Bolan watched him disappear into what looked like a bedroom. The Executioner entered an empty dining room, then he and Katz met again in the living room.

The house was empty. What's more, it didn't look like anyone had been there for some time.

Bolan walked into the bedroom and opened the top drawer of a chest of drawers. Empty. So were the rest of the drawers in the chest and those in a rotting wooden desk. Returning to the kitchen, he saw that Katz had opened the refrigerator. Not only was it empty of food, but also it had been unplugged. The shelves and drawers in the kitchen were as empty as the rest of the house.

"I don't think Ali's quite telling us the truth," Katz said. He pulled out the cellular phone, dialed Herzl and held the instrument where Bolan could hear, too.

The young Mossad man answered on the first ring. "I was just getting ready to call you," he said. "Morty wants to apologize. Ali was lying. He finally said that they hadn't been in that safehouse for over a year."

"Did he say anything else?" Katz asked.

"Uh, no. I don't think he really knew anything else, Uncle Yakov."

"Is Morty still with him?"

There was a long pause, then Bernard Herzl said, "No. I'm sorry. I guess he had a weak heart for somebody that young. Is there anything else we can be doing?"

Katz looked down at his watch, then up at Bolan, for the second time that day looking every bit his age. "No," he replied, and pushed the button to end the call. He dropped the phone back into his vest. "It's over, Mack. There's no way of finding out where she is before time runs out. I'll go meet Zhdanov at the bridge, and I'll do my best to kill the bastard. But it won't save my daughter or her boyfriend."

"We're still breathing, Katz," the Executioner said. "And as long as we're doing that, it's *never* over."

Katz looked up at him. "What do you mean?"

"I mean I've got an idea."

IT WAS COLD and dark. That was all she knew.

Sharon Katzenelenbogen awakened with a headache, wondering what kind of drug she had been given. She remembered the plane landing after Zhdanov had spotted the soldiers at the dig site below. She also remembered returning to the safehouse where she and Yoni had been kept. But then Zhdanov had ordered Abdullah to administer an injection to both of them, and after that everything—at least most everything—was blank. She had awakened for a few groggy seconds earlier and gotten the feeling they were in the air again. But before she could get her bearings, she had felt another needle pierce the skin on her upper arm.

Sharon shifted slightly and realized she was lying on her back. Whatever surface she was on was hard and bumpy, making her hurt from neck to calves. She opened her eyelids but still saw darkness, then felt the cloth wrapped tightly around her eyes. She was blindfolded, and tied up again; she could move neither hands nor legs.

But she wasn't alone. Next to her she could hear breathing, and the sound comforted her. It was Yoni.

"Are you awake?" Sharon whispered.

"Yes."

"Are we alone?"

"I think so. I haven't heard anybody. And no one's telling us to shut up now."

"Where are we?"

"I don't know," he replied quietly. "In the back of a pickup, I think."

Sharon lay still for a moment. She could hear crickets chirping and somewhere, not so very far in the distance, the sound of automobiles. "It feels like we're inside," she said.

Mayer shifted next to her. "I think it's a camper shell," he said. "Can you feel the floor?"

Sharon moved slightly, again noticing the bumpy surface beneath her. It could be a pickup. The bumps were narrow and long and ran the length of her body and beyond. They could be the corrugated-steel bed of a pickup. "But where are we?" she asked again.

"Your guess is as good as mine. But I don't think it's Israel anymore." Mayer shifted again as he spoke, and Sharon could feel his warm breath on her neck. It was the most wonderful, reassuring sensation she had ever experienced. She might not know where she was. She might be a prisoner and at the mercy of this mad Russian with some vendetta against her family, and she might be about to die.

But she had finally found true love. And if she

died, she would die with the man who had given it to her.

"Sharon," Mayer whispered, "I love you."

"I love you, too," Sharon said without hesitation.

"Sharon, I have something—"

The sound of metal against metal—a pickup's tailgate opening?—sounded, stopping him in mid-sentence. Cool air blew in over them, and Sharon heard voices speaking. She lay as still as death itself, hoping they would think she was still asleep. Next to her, Mayer did the same.

A moment later the tailgate closed again.

Neither Sharon, or her companion spoke again for several minutes. Then, even softer than before, Mayer said, "Sharon?"

"Yes?"

"I have something I want to ask you."

Sharon waited silently.

"If we make it through this," he said, his breath again tickling her neck and throat, "I want you to be my wife."

Sharon Katzenelenbogen felt the chill run through her. Beneath the blindfold she felt the wetness in her eyes. She had dated many men over the years. A few had seemed like they were the right ones. But they never had been, and each and every relationship had eventually run its course and ended.

Finally she had found true love. Yoni was the one she had waited for all of her life. And now that the moment had come, there was a good chance neither of them would live to see the fruits of their love.

"Sharon?" he whispered again.

Sharon realized she hadn't answered him. "Yes," she said as softly as she could. "I would love to be your wife, Jonathan Mayer."

"Then just in case we can't find a rabbi—"

"Yoni, don't talk like that. We'll get out of this. I know we will." She paused. "My father is coming. He will find us."

"Sharon," he said, "I hope you are right. But in case you are not, we will marry as the Hebrews of old once did. Simply. But meaningfully, and for as long as God gives us." He pushed in closer to Sharon. "Sharon Katzenelenbogen, I take you as my wife in the eyes of the Lord."

"Jonathan Mayer, I take you as my husband."

The tailgate grated open, and Zhdanov snickered. "What a beautiful ceremony," he said. "You spoke louder than you intended, and I was privileged to be in the congregation. I heard it all from just outside. Would you like me to sign the marriage certificate as a witness?" His laugh grew louder. "You have followed the custom of your ancient people. But did you know that in many early societies, when a man wanted to marry a woman, the king always had her first? I think we should follow that custom, too, and I'm the closest to a king you have, woman."

Sharon felt Mayer struggling against his restraints. Then she heard a thud—either a kick or a punch—and he relaxed again. She smelled Abdullah and sensed him moving over her in the pickup.

She started to scream, then felt the Hezbollah terrorist move on to Mayer. She heard a zipper unzip and tensed, then remembered the small leather case in which Abdullah had carried the syringe and whatever drug he had given them. She felt the rustle of clothing and knew the terrorist was injecting Mayer.

A moment later it was her turn. As she felt the needle prick her arm, Zhdanov said, "It is only a light dose. The time for your wedding consummation is nearing." He cackled once more. "I want you to be fully awake to enjoy me and the others when your father gets here."

Sharon felt the needle penetrate her arm. The familiar wooziness begin to sweep over her again. She thought of what might soon happen, and suddenly the thought didn't scare her like it had.

She had found love in Yoni. A love that went deeper than anything sexual, physical or earthly. And while the thought of being ravaged and murdered by these barbarians was still frightening, she knew that nothing Zhdanov or the others could do to her would ever change that.

Besides, her father was coming. He loved her and would save them.

Sharon drifted back to unconsciousness with love in her mind having replaced the terror.

THE MAN in the formfitting blacksuit had also covered his face and hands with black makeup. He was all but invisible, the whites of his eyes being the only part of him that reflected what little light shone down from the quarter moon. He kept to the shadows along the edge of the creek bed as he ran, following it toward the bridge where Cynthia Katzenelenbogen had been murdered more than twenty years earlier.

Bolan moved swiftly but silently, walking that perilous path between noise and the fastest possible speed. He carried the Beretta 93-R in a black nylon horizontal shoulder rig that tied the gun down to the nylon utility belt around his waist. The Desert Eagle rode on the belt on his right hip in a black Helweg holster. The custom-made Applegate-Fairbairn fighting knife was opposite the big .44 Magnum pistol in a Kydex speed sheath.

The Executioner's feet were protected by black nylon and leather assault boots. The pockets of his blacksuit, and the black nylon pack he wore on his back, were filled with extra magazines for his pistols and various other items of equipment that he might, or might not, need during the life-or-death ordeal he knew he was about to encounter.

With no further leads to follow in finding Sharon and her friend, the Executioner had been forced to follow a hunch. Twice Zhdanov had tried to mentally torture Katz by telling the Israeli that he intended to sexually abuse Sharon before Katz's very eyes. But during the last telephone conversation, the

Russian had stressed that his hostages wouldn't be present at the bridge tonight.

As he jogged along under the moon, Bolan knew that both of those statements couldn't be true. Simple logic dictated that Zhdanov couldn't hurt Sharon if she wasn't there. And Bolan's guess was that telling Katz that his daughter would be elsewhere was simply a ruse to keep the Israeli from bringing along reinforcements.

Bolan was guessing that the Russian's demented urge to abuse Sharon in front of her father was strong enough that he would bring her along. He might not have Katz's daughter where she could be seen, but she would be close enough that he could bring her out for his perversions once he had captured Katz.

At least the Executioner hoped she would be. If she wasn't, she and Jonathan Mayer were both as good as dead already.

Bolan's boot hit a dry twig, and the noise echoed like a gunshot in the quiet night between Paris and Versailles. He stopped, darted into the tall reeds higher up the bank and dropped to a squat. The sound-suppressed Beretta leaped into his right hand as the Applegate-Fairbairn came out of its sheath in his left. His eyes scanned the area ahead of him for any sign that he had been heard. Then, satisfied, he returned both weapons to their carriers and moved on.

The Executioner's mind raced as he ran. With so

little time left before Katz's appointed showdown with Zhdanov, they had been forced to keep their plan of attack simple. The former Phoenix Force leader had driven the Mercedes off the main road onto an asphalt drive that paralleled the creek. He had dropped the Executioner off three miles from the bridge, then raced back to the highway and gone on. If their timing was correct, Katz should reach the top of the bridge on the highway roughly at the same time the Executioner arrived below.

Bolan's foot hit the ground too close to a frog and the amphibian croaked as loudly as the twig had snapped a few minutes before. The noise set off all the other frogs in the immediate area and forced the Executioner back to the cover of the reeds. He waited until the cacophony of sound died down again, rose and moved on.

Perhaps a mile ahead Bolan could see the headlights of cars and trucks passing over the bridge. Would Zhdanov and his Hezbollah henchmen be waiting up top or below? He didn't know, but his guess was that there would be sentries stationed both places. He might be many things, but Ulric Zhdanov was definitely not stupid. He would know that even though he had demanded Katz come alone, the "big friend"—as he had been calling the Executioner— would be somewhere in the area.

In fact Bolan knew he might encounter the first of a series of guards along the creek anytime now.

He slowed to a walk, bending his knees and dropping lower.

He saw the first terrorist less than ten yards later.

Bolan dropped to his belly on the damp earth next to the creek and looked up. Less than a hundred yards away, standing directly in his path, he saw what looked like the silhouette of a man in front of the car lights passing in the distance. He crept slowly forward, his gaze glued to the motionless form. It was impossible to be sure that what he was seeing was actually a man. It could just as easily be an illusion created by the lights and shadows. But there was no sense in taking chances. Not this late in the game.

Bolan rose to all fours and crept through the reeds and up the creek bank. When he reached the top, he dropped back to his face, wriggling silently along the dryer packed earth above the shadowy form. As he drew closer, he saw the shadow moved slightly, and another shape appeared in the man's arms.

This shadow was more distinct in front of the soft moonlight reflecting off the water in the creek. Bolan saw the barrel, the stock and most of all the banana-shaped magazine fastened to the sling. It was perhaps the most easily identifiable of all rifles the world over—an AK-47. The favorite weapon of terrorists the world over who had once been supplied by the Soviet Union.

Still on his stomach, Bolan swiveled on the ground, turning his body to face the bank. He could see the man with the rifle a little better now, too. Wearing a waist-length jacket, the terrorist kept glancing in the direction from which the Executioner had come, then twisting his head back to the creek. Back and forth. Back and forth. In perfect time, never changing the rhythm. His head looked like some bizarre horizontal pendulum as he scanned the area.

Looking down, Bolan saw that the bank sloped at roughly a forty-five-degree angle to where the Hezbollah terrorist stood, twenty feet below. With the drop, it shouldn't be a hard jump, but to ensure silence he would have to move when the man faced the creek, away from him.

The Executioner watched the terrorist turn to look down the creek, then back to the water. Bolan counted off two seconds with each movement of the man's head. Slowly, so as to keep the Kydex sheath from giving him away as the blade slid out, Bolan drew the Applegate-Fairbairn. The next time the Hezbollah man turned to scan the shore, Bolan waited for one second, then leaped to his feet.

As Zhdanov's sentry turned back to face the water, Bolan's feet left the ground. He dived headfirst down the bank, the fighting knife held over his head in an ice-pick grip. As he fell over the man with the AK-47, he brought the knife down at the back of the man's neck with all the force in his arm and shoulder.

Perhaps the terrorist heard the Executioner rise to

his feet in the reeds. Perhaps some sixth sense warned him. Whatever it was, the Hezbollah man started to turn toward the threat as Bolan descended. He made it only halfway, turning his profile to the Executioner. The movement also moved his head an inch or two closer to the bank.

The tip of the knife came down, not on the spinal cord in the back of the man's neck as Bolan had hoped, but through the top of the terrorist's skull. The sickening sound of splintering bone echoed along the creek bank as the six-inch blade penetrated the terrorist's cranium and sank into his brain.

The effect, however, was the same. The Hezbollah terrorist was dead before he hit the ground.

Bolan rode the man's body to the soft creek bank, his fingers still wrapped around the fighting knife's grip. He tried to withdraw the blade, but it was wedged tightly in the skull. Placing a boot on the side of the man's face to steady his head, the Executioner pried the blade back and forth with both hands. More pops and crackles sounded as the skull continued to chip. The blade finally came out covered with blood and gray matter.

The Executioner wiped the knife on the dead man's jacket, then dragged the body back into the reeds. He sheathed the blade and moved on.

Perhaps half a mile from the bridge now, the Executioner paid even more attention to his pace. He stepped slowly but surely, his eyes down to warn him of twigs that might snap, broken glass that could crunch.

The next guard he encountered had a partner, and both men were fools. They stood at the top of the bank vividly silhouetted against the indigo sky. The outlines of more AK-47s carelessly slung over their backs were almost as clear. As Bolan froze below them, squatting behind the reeds on the incline, the man on the Executioner's left reached into his coat pocket and pulled something out. Bolan frowned, wondering what it might be. A grenade? Had they spotted him? Nothing in their body language indicated that they had.

The answer to the Executioner's question came a moment later when he saw a flicker of flame in front of a face. In the light he could see that the terrorist who had reached into his pocket was lighting a cigarette for his partner. Another cigarette extended from the first man's mouth. The strong scent of tobacco drifted down to the creek from the bank above.

Bolan watched the man bring the match in front of his own face. Without further ado he drew the Beretta and thumbed the selector to semiauto. He raised the gun and lined up the sights on the flame still in front of the terrorist's face. He squeezed the trigger, and the 93-R coughed quietly in the darkness.

The flame went out, then the man fell forward, rolling down the hill to the creek.

"Salim?" the man still standing whispered. "What—?"

They were his last words. Bolan's second sound-suppressed 9 mm hollowpoint round struck him squarely in the chest. He followed his partner down the hill, making a soft splash in the water.

Bolan dropped to a combat stance, scanning farther down the bank toward the bridge to see if the sounds had drawn anyone's attention. He saw nothing and dragged both bodies back into the tall weeds and out of sight.

The Executioner pulled back the black nylon flap that covered the luminous hands of his wristwatch. He had less than five minutes to cover the last half mile to the bridge. Plenty of time unless he encountered more of Zhdanov's men. If he did, there could be delays of indeterminate length. He moved faster now, knowing that he might be heard but also aware that he could not afford to be late.

As he drew nearer to the bridge, the Executioner dropped to his knees and pulled the infrared binoculars from his backpack. Focusing them on the creek bed beneath the bridge, he saw a blocky-looking shadow parked along the bank on the other side. He twisted the rings, bringing the lenses into better focus and saw that it was a pickup with a camper shell. At the same time, a car passed on the highway overhead. Its headlights cast a quick beam of light onto a short dirt road that wound down from the highway to the creek.

Bolan raised the binoculars to the top of the bridge. There he saw another vehicle—from where he knelt it looked like a Chevy Nova—parked on the wide shoulder next to the rail that ran the length of the bridge.

Two men stood outside of the vehicle, leaning against the Nova, the vehicle between them and the cars passing by only ten feet away. To anyone who crossed the bridge, it would look no more interesting than two men who had felt the "call of nature" and stopped to relieve themselves, not an uncommon sight in France.

Bolan studied the men closer. One had dark features and a bushy beard. He wore a faded blue denim jacket and jeans that hadn't seen the washer in quite a while. The man standing next to him had on a navy blue sport coat, gray slacks and a blue pullover shirt. He held a walkie-talkie in one hand.

He also wore his hair in a closely clipped flattop.

Bolan studied the men. This could be the perfect opportunity to take Zhdanov out, before Katz even arrived. He didn't know where Sharon and her boyfriend were, but if they were here at the bridge they had to be in the Nova or the pickup parked below. His guess would be the pickup, and that the walkie-talkie was Zhdanov's link to whomever he had guarding them. All of this meant that he would have to sneak past Zhdanov and the other man before he got to Sharon and Jonathan. That meant going under the bridge, directly under Zhdanov's nose, both literally and figuratively. The Russian would have at least one other guard beneath the bridge—of that the Executioner was certain—and this man wasn't likely to be as careless as the two he'd just left behind with their half-smoked cigarettes.

The odds were that he'd be spotted. If he was, Zhdanov would have plenty of time to contact whoever was guarding Sharon and Jonathan over the walkie-talkie. The two hostages would be dead long before the Executioner could reach them.

No, he had to kill Zhdanov first, and he had to do it in a way that the Russian had no time to use his radio.

Bolan pulled the range finder out of his pack and zeroed in on the men atop the bridge: eighty-seven yards. Bolan blew air between his clenched teeth. Too far for a night shot with either of his pistols. He might take them both in a larger target, like the chest, but unless he wanted to chance the Russian putting out the order to kill the hostages, he needed a brain-stem shot on both men. Within one or two seconds, at that.

The Executioner silently cursed himself for not picking up one of the AK-47s he had left with the corpses in his wake. Too late to worry about that now. Besides, he would have no way of knowing if the weapons had been properly sighted in for such distance.

Dropping the binoculars back in his pocket, Bolan began making his way closer. If he could just get within fifty yards or so, he was sure he could put two fast rounds where they needed to go, then sprint to the pickup and take out whoever was guarding the hostages before the guard realized what had happened. The odds weren't particularly in his favor, but he had made even longer odds come through in the past. Besides, it was a last-ditch effort and the only chance he had. He would just have to find out.

He never got the chance.

Bolan was still seventy-five yards away when the Mercedes pulled up behind the Nova on top of the bridge. Katz got out, closed the door and walked toward the two men with his hands over his head.

The Executioner froze in his tracks as Zhdanov and the other man pulled pistols from under their jackets. Looking closely, Bolan could see that Zhdanov's weapon was a Nagant revolver, undoubtedly the heirloom that had killed his older half brother and his father's first wife, and with which he had sworn to kill Katz.

With the Nova still shielding what transpired from passing vehicles, the man with the dark features—Bolan was guessing at this point that it was the Abdullah that Mossad was after—stepped forward and frisked the Israeli. He would be looking for weapons, but he would also be checking to see if Katz was wearing a transmitter. Finding a bug would be an immediate death sentence to both the former Phoenix Force leader and his daughter, which was why Bolan and Katz had decided against using one.

Besides, considering the terrain where all this was going down, they knew they had other options.

The Executioner moved into the reeds once more and squatted. Setting the binoculars on the ground next to him, he reached back into his pack and produced a microphone, headset and an object that looked like a small steel dish. The unit, known as a Bionic Ear, enabled the user to pick up whispers up to fifty yards away. The steel dish—a booster—increased the instrument's listening surface thirty-seven times, and all but eliminated background noise.

Wrapping the headset around his ears, Bolan plugged the booster into the mike with a patch cord, adjusted the volume control and aimed the mike at the men on the bridge.

"He is clean," the Executioner heard Abdullah say as clearly as if he'd been standing right next to the man. The terrorist stepped back from Katz again.

Zhdanov's chuckle came over the Bionic Ear. "You are such a fool," he said. "But then, you are from a race of fools."

"We had a deal, Zhdanov," Katz said. "We fight—unarmed—you and me. Winner takes all."

"Yes, yes, winner takes all," the Russian said. He paused then added, "Where is your big friend?"

"He didn't come," Katz said. "You told me to come alone. I did. I kept up my end of the bargain. Are you going to keep up yours?"

Zhdanov laughed again. "Why, of course." He

stuck the Nagant under the Israeli's throat and opened the back door of the Nova with the other hand. "Get in."

Bolan transferred the mike to his left hand and raised the Beretta. But by the time he had the sights on Zhdanov, Katz was in the back seat and Abdullah had moved around to the other side of the car. If he shot the Russian now, Abdullah would finish off Katz and give the orders to kill Sharon and her boyfriend.

The Executioner watched helplessly as the Hezbollah leader started the Nova's engine, then guided the vehicle toward the dirt road just to the side of the bridge. Bolan kept the Bionic Ear pointed toward them as the car descended the slope and parked next to the pickup, angling the vehicle so the headlights illuminated the area directly beneath the bridge. He saw the three men get out of the car and watched as Abdullah moved quickly to the pickup, opening the tailgate.

Another dark-complected man got out of the camper shell, then reached in and jerked a blindfolded man out after him. Bolan could see that the man's legs were tied together and his hands bound in front of him. The terrorist dragged him several feet from the pickup and dropped him in a sitting position before removing the blindfold.

The Nagant at the back of Katz's head, Zhdanov pushed the Israeli under the bridge and into the glow of the Nova's headlight, turned him around and shoved the gun beneath the former Phoenix Force leader's chin again. A fourth man—the terrorist Bolan had known would be hiding somewhere in the area there—emerged from the shadows of the overpass.

Abdullah returned to the pickup and reached inside. A second later a woman came sliding out feetfirst. The terrorist jerked her off the end of the tailgate and let her fall to her back on the ground.

"You bastard!" Katz growled, and stepped in toward Zhdanov.

The Russian thrust his revolver harder into Katz's throat, stopping him.

Abdullah dropped Sharon in a sitting position next to Mayer and used a knife to cut off her blindfold.

"Daddy?" Sharon said, her voice sounding like that of a little girl.

"I'm here, honey," Katz said. "Don't worry."

Bolan began to move in slowly. He was still too far away to hear without the Bionic Ear, and although they were all out in the open now, and he had a clear shot at Zhdanov and the three Hezbollah men, they were too spread out to shoot quickly. Abdullah and the man who had been in the pickup stood behind the hostages, their pistols aimed down at the top of the prisoners' heads. The man who had emerged from under the bridge had moved off to the side to cover Katz from another angle.

No matter whom Bolan shot from this distance,

he would never get his gun on the other terrorists before Katz, Sharon or Jonathan Mayer took a bullet.

Zhdanov turned suddenly, tossing the Nagant to the man who had hidden beneath the bridge. He turned back to Katz. "I am going to have fun with your daughter," he said in a voice clearly filled with eagerness. "But first, before I let you watch, a little foreplay." Without warning he lashed out, striking the Israeli across the jaw.

Katz went down but was back on his feet in a heartbeat. Zhdanov charged forward like a raging bull, but the Israeli shuffled to the side and let him pass as if he were the matador. The former Phoenix Force leader had taken the full force of the Russian's blow on the jaw, and Bolan could see his old friend was still woozy. But Katz got his hands up in front of him as Zhdanov pivoted back. The Israeli blocked an overhand blow from the Russian, and his right foot shot out, catching Zhdanov in the knee. But the Russian had seen the kick coming and twisted. Katz's boot hit the side of the joint and slid off without doing any damage.

As Bolan increased his pace, moving closer now, he could hear both men's breathing through the Bionic Ear. He moved up into the reeds where the shadows were darker as he neared, knowing he would have to begin to fire immediately if any of the men spotted him.

Zhdanov and Katz continued to exchange blows,

sometimes blocking, sometimes dodging, bobbing and weaving. A snap kick from the Russian caught the Israeli in the chest, driving him back. But it appeared to have done little damage as Katz moved quickly back in to send an uppercut up into Zhdanov's chin.

The headlights of the cars passing on the bridge overhead flashed by as the Executioner closed in. But the sounds of their engines were muffled by the Bionic Ear's booster.

"Daddy! Oh, Daddy!" Sharon cried.

Abdullah brought his pistol down on top of her scalp and growled, "Shut up!"

Ten yards away, Bolan dropped to one knee. He hadn't been spotted, but if he tried to get any closer he knew that he would be. He surveyed the scene quickly. Abdullah and the other man holding their guns on the hostages presented the most immediate threat. The other terrorist, standing off to one side, came next. Bolan would leave Zhdanov, who was distracted and apparently unarmed, for last.

Placing the Bionic Ear microphone and booster unit in the grass in front of him, Bolan moved his left hand over to support his right and dropped the Beretta's sights on Abdullah.

It was then he heard the movement behind him, then he felt the cold hard steel of a gun barrel jam into the back of his neck.

What had happened flashed through the Executioner's mind in a microsecond. Somewhere along the creek, he had missed one of the sentries. Perhaps the man had hidden and let him pass by. More likely he had been stationed farther down the creek from where Katz had let Bolan out, and began making his way toward the bridge when the time for the meeting drew near. The Bionic Ear hadn't only focused the Executioner's hearing forward rather than rearward, but the booster unit had also muffled the man's approach as it had done the passing cars and all other background noises.

"Drop your weapon!" a heavily accented voice shouted behind Bolan. "Raise your hands over your head!"

Ahead of him the Executioner saw the fight grind to a halt. Zhdanov and Katz turned to face him. Abdullah and the other two men all strained to see through the night.

Bolan set the Beretta in front of him and raised his arms. He felt the Desert Eagle come out of its holster, then the knife was pulled from his sheath.

"Stand up!" the same voice ordered.

Bolan rose and was pushed roughly forward. He saw Zhdanov grinning as he stepped under the bridge.

"Well," the Russian said, "it appears that you lied to me."

"How thoughtless of me," Katz said. "And after all the kindness you have shown me."

Bolan felt a foot in the back of one knee, then his legs buckled. He fell to a kneeling position.

"Put your hands behind your head!" the voice behind him ordered. As the Executioner complied, the man walked around to his side.

Bolan saw that the new Hezbollah man wore a wispy mustache and a little triangle of hair directly under his lower lip. The Executioner's Desert Eagle had been shoved down the front of the terrorist's pants, and the man held the Applegate-Fairbairn knife in his left hand. His right hand gripped a Russian Tokarev pistol, which was aimed at the Executioner's head.

"Well," Zhdanov said, still smiling as he turned back to Katz, "shall we begin again?"

Jonathan Mayer hadn't moved a muscle since he'd been jerked from the back of the pickup, but he chose to at that moment.

As fast as lightning, Mayer whirled and tried to strike the terrorist behind him with his bound hands. The blow struck the pistol in the Hezbollah man's hand, but the terrorist held on to it. With a low grunting noise the man raised his gun to his attacker's face and pulled the trigger.

Sharon Katzenelenbogen screamed as blood blew out of her boyfriend's head and he fell to the ground.

Zhdanov cackled. "You Jews," he said. "Is it any wonder the world hates you? Can you not understand why you are persecuted? You are fools!"

He turned suddenly to Katz and caught the Israeli with a backhand blow that reeled the Israeli in a full circle. A short jab to the older man's midsection doubled him over, then Zhdanov knocked Katz's feet from under him with a sweep of his own foot.

Katz fell to his back, and Zhdanov fell over him, drawing a knife from under his jacket. Holding it to the Israeli's throat, he said, "I am so inclined to kill you now. But I do want you to see what I do to your daughter first."

Bolan started to move, but the man at his side jammed the Tokarev into his ear.

When Katz spoke, his voice was filled with pain. "You are going to rape her," he said, "and you are going to kill her. Then you are going to kill me and my friend. I have accepted that."

"Good," Zhdanov said, "because you are correct. Although it has been a long time coming, justice is about to be brought down upon you."

"I ask only one last request," Katz breathed, still choking for air from the punch to his stomach.

Zhdanov laughed. "What is that?"

"Before you kill us, before you hurt my daughter in any way, allow me to pray. Allow me to get on my knees and make peace with my God."

The idea had to have struck Zhdanov as hilarious. He threw back his head and laughed at the sky. Then, looking back down at the man beneath him, he said, "All right. It should be amusing to watch. Speak to this God of yours. He does not exist, but speak to him anyway. In fact I give you permission to go ahead and ask him to save you." He roared with laughter again. "Perhaps he will send a legion of angels down to destroy me.'' Turning to the man who had his revolver, Zhdanov held out his hand.

The terrorist returned the Nagant to the Russian. Zhdanov pulled the knife away from Katz's throat and stood.

Slowly Katzenelenbogen rose to his knees in front of the Russian. Zhdanov stood over him, the revolver that had killed his half brother and his father's first wife aimed at the top of the Israeli's head. A smile that held no mirth covered the Russian's face as he prepared to listen to Katzenelenbogen's last prayer.

The motion looking like the tired, painful movement of an old man, Katz raised his hands under his chin and pressed his palms together. He closed his eyes, then spoke. ''Lord God, deliver us, your children, from our enemies. Amen.''

Then, opening his eyes again, the former Phoenix Force leader moved his hands slightly so that the tips of his steepled fingers pointed directly up at Ulric Zhdanov.

A split second later an explosion sounded. Flame shot from the index finger of Katz's right hand—the prosthetic limb that hid the tiny single-shot .22 Magnum pistol. Blood, brains and bone blew up into the air as the hollowpoint bullet blew the back of Zhdanov's head off.

From there, what happened became a blur.

Bolan dropped his hands and drove an elbow into the knee of the man standing at his side. He heard the bone crunch as the joint snapped. The man began to topple and the Tokarev fell out of his hand. Bolan caught it by the barrel, twirling it in his hand and jamming it into the man's chest a second before the terrorist hit the ground. He pulled the trigger twice, then turned, raising the weapon to shoulder height and point-shooting another shot over Sharon's head into Abdullah's face.

Katz had grabbed Zhdanov's Nagant as soon as the Russian went down and tapped two rounds into the terrorist who had killed Jonathan Mayer.

The Executioner turned the Tokarev toward the final man, who stood beneath the other side of the bridge. The man's mouth had fallen open in shock at the unexpected turn of events as Bolan lined up the sights on his chest. The Executioner pulled the trigger and heard the tiny blast of the primer. But the gunpowder in the cartridge failed to ignite, causing a "hangfire."

The terrorist had recovered from his shock and now raised his own weapon to fire.

Knowing the bullet had lodged in the barrel and that the Tokarev would explode if he fired again, the Executioner brought the Tokarev back and hurled it forward. The gun sailed a foot from the Hezbollah gunmen's head. But it was enough to ruin the man's aim, and the round sailed harmlessly past the Executioner.

Bolan dived forward, prying the Applegate-Fairbairn knife from the fingers of the corpse on the ground in front of him. The Executioner brought the knife back over his shoulder. This time his aim was true, and the custom-made fighting knife flipped end over end through the air to embed itself to the hilt in the final terrorist's chest.

Suddenly all was quiet beneath the bridge where Cynthia Katzenelenbogen had been murdered so long ago.

Bolan rose to his feet, crossed to the man with the knife in his chest and pulled it free. He wiped the blood on the man's sleeve, then went to where Sharon Katzenelenbogen was sobbing softly next to her dead lover. The Executioner cut her restraints, and she hurried to where her father still sat next to what had once been Ulric Zhdanov.

For a moment they embraced, Sharon's sobs coming harder now as her father held her. Then the former Phoenix Force leader got wearily to his feet and helped his daughter up.

"We'd better go," Bolan said. "There'll be cops."

Katz nodded. "Just one more thing."

Leaning down over Zhdanov's body, he spoke to the corpse. "My prayer worked, you soulless bastard," the Israeli said. "The Lord helps those who help themselves."

Then, arm in arm, Yakov Katzenelenbogen and his daughter followed the Executioner up the dirt road to the top of the bridge.

ground in front of him. The cemetery had brought back

EPILOGUE

Yakov Katzenelenbogen knelt and placed the bouquet of flowers in front of the granite marker. He closed his eyes, said a silent prayer, then stood and put his arm around his daughter. He stared at the letters sandblasted into the stone: Cynthia Armstrong Katzenelenbogen.

Cynthia Armstrong Katzenelenbogen, the Israeli thought. His daughter's and son's mother. His wife.

And the only woman he had ever truly loved.

Next to him, Katz heard a sniffle. He turned to Sharon and for a moment felt startled. Sometimes he forgot just how much she looked like Cynthia. Sharon's skin was a shade darker than her mother's—she had inherited that from him—but their features were almost identical.

Sharon wore a black dress, which she had rent in mourning as was their custom. "You loved her, didn't you, Daddy," she said softly. It was a statement rather than a question.

"With all my heart," Katz answered.

For a few minutes father and daughter remained

silent, both staring at the memorial. Then Katz looked back at the last surviving member of his family. He knew Sharon's grief was twofold: Her mother's death had been brought back to the forefront of her mind by all that had transpired. But Sharon had also lost the man she loved, the man who would have become her husband, and in a sense already had when he was murdered by the Hezbollah terrorists working with Ulric Zhdanov.

"I loved her, too, Daddy," Sharon said softly, "and I loved him."

Katz didn't answer. He knew there was nothing he could say to ease her pain.

"Does it ever stop hurting?" Sharon asked. "Does the pain ever go away?"

Katz shook his head. "No," he whispered, still staring at Cynthia's name, "but you learn to live with it."

He hugged his daughter, looking beyond the trees to the Mercedes in the parking lot.

A big man wearing a black suit, white shirt and black tie stood next to the car.

Katz found a grim smile working itself over his face as he looked at the man. Life wasn't always easy and not always fun, he thought. A series of ups and downs, peaks and valleys, joys and sorrows. Some of the people you loved died too young, and you never forgot them. Other people came along and you learned to love them. They didn't take the place of the ones you had lost, but they helped fill the void a little.

Katz knew that the big man in the black suit standing next to the Mercedes understood that. In his younger days Bolan had lost his own family tragically. Then, years after that, again like Katz, the only woman the big man had ever loved had been murdered. Although he never showed it outwardly, Katz knew his friend well enough to know that Bolan would never completely get over the losses he had experienced, either.

"What will you do now, Daddy?" Sharon asked.

"Go back to America," he said. "I still have work to do." He turned his eyes back to his daughter. "What will *you* do?"

"Go back to Israel," she said without hesitation. "Bury myself in work like you plan to do."

Katz nodded. "I will visit more often."

Sharon laughed softly. "Sure, you will."

Katz chuckled himself. "I will *try*," he amended. "Shall we go?"

Sharon nodded.

They dropped their arms from around each other's waist but held hands as they walked toward the parking lot. Katz's eyes returned to his friend. He had asked Bolan to come down to the grave site with them but his friend had shaken his head, saying he felt it was a family matter.

Well, as far as Katz was concerned, Mack Bolan *was* family. The two of them had lived the lives of warriors together, fought side by side over the years and formed a bond closer than brothers. Without hesitation the man had risked his own life to help Katz find his daughter and end the threat to the Katzenelenbogens that Zhdanov's perverse quest had presented.

But that was just Bolan's way. He had made a career of doing the same for innocent people, most of whom were neither family nor friend—they just needed his help.

Bolan hugged Sharon as they reached the car, then opened the door for her. "You all right?" he asked.

Sharon nodded, tears in her eyes.

Bolan walked around the Mercedes and slid behind the wheel. Then they drove away from the cemetery without a backward glance.

In the badlands, there is only survival....

JAMES AXLER

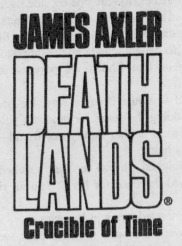

DEATH LANDS®

Crucible of Time

A connection to his past awaits Ryan Cawdor as the group takes a mat-trans jump to the remnants of California. Brother Joshua Wolfe is the leader of the Children of the Rock—a cult that has left a trail of barbarism and hate across the ravaged California countryside. Far from welcoming the group with open arms, the cult forces them into a deadly battle-ritual— which is only their first taste of combat....

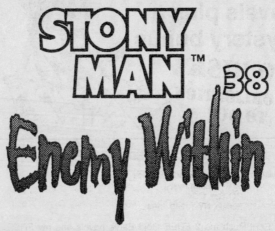

James Axler

OUTLANDERS™

ICEBLOOD

Kane and his companions race to find a piece of the Chintamanti Stone, which they believe to have power over the collective mind of the evil Archons. Their journey sees them foiled by a Russian mystic named Zakat in Manhattan, and there is another dangerous encounter waiting for them in the Kun Lun mountains of China.

One man's quest for power unleashes a cataclysm in America's wastelands.

Available in December 1998 at your favorite retail outlet. Or order your copy now by sending your name, address, zip or postal code, along with a check or money order (please do not send cash) for $5.99 for each book ordered ($6.99 in Canada), plus 75¢ postage and handling ($1.00 in Canada), payable to Gold Eagle Books, to: